25 CANDLES

IRIS BAXTER

Important Note To The Readers

Dear Reader,

This story was built like an Advent calendar, twenty-five chapters, twenty-five small doors to open, one for each day leading up to Christmas.

Each chapter is a candle, a spark of light against the winter dark, meant to be read slowly, one day at a time, as December unfolds.

So, I invite you to make it a ritual.

Light a candle. Wrap yourself in a soft blanket. Let a cup of hot chocolate warm your hands and maybe set out a plate of gingerbread cookies beside you. Read by the glow of the tree or beneath the hush of snow at your window. Let the story breathe with the rhythm of the season.

This is more than a tale of mystery. It is a journey through faith tested, love lost, and grace rediscovered.

It is about the quiet endurance of the human spirit, the unity that can rise from ruin, and the light that refuses to die even when everything around it turns to ash.

You will walk through darkness in these pages, but you will also find warmth.

You will see how faith bends but does not break, how forgiveness can burn brighter than revenge, and how the smallest flame can guide even the most lost heart home.

When you reach the final chapter, the twenty-fifth candle, I hope you feel that same warmth that Christmas brings.

Not the glitter of perfection, but the deeper peace that comes from survival, from compassion, from believing that goodness still exists in us all.

So, take your time. One chapter each night. One candle. One heartbeat of hope.

And when the last page closes, may your heart be steady, your home be filled with light, and your faith, whatever shape it takes, burn bright and true.

Merry Christmas, dear reader.

May you find comfort, warmth, and grace in every flame.

— Iris Baxter

CHAPTER 1

Coming Home

The frost made the highway glitter like ground glass, the kind of pretty that could kill you if you blinked at the wrong curve. I loosened my grip on the wheel and breathed out, counting to four the way the therapist said. In for four, hold for four, out for six. She'd also suggested warm baths and gratitude journaling. Cute. My gratitude right now was that the tires hadn't skated me into a ditch and the heater worked well enough to keep my fingers attached.

The sign rose out of the dark like a punchline: WELCOME TO GREENRIDGE - WHERE CHRISTMAS LIVES ALL YEAR.

Of course it does. Why stop at one month of performative joy when you can franchise it?

They'd repainted it, fresh red script, twined with holly I could see even at night. Someone in town cared enough to keep the illusion spotless. I almost admired the commitment. Almost.

I'd sworn I wouldn't come back. Ten years of night shifts had shown me what December really was: drunk driving, space heaters and extension cords doing their worst, sad people trying to out-bake their grief. The last case wouldn't leave me, the little boy with a fever that hid something worse until the monitors screamed and my hands did everything right and it still wasn't enough. The nightmares came on a loop after that. Code blue. Tiny ribs under my palms. A mother sound that could split bone. My supervisor called it compassion fatigue and ordered me to take leave. I called it running out of places to hide.

So, home. Or whatever this was.

My mother's street unfurled the way it always had. Victorians with porches meant for lemonade in July, every gable now hooked with lights that trembled in the wind. Inflatable reindeer bobbed on a neighbor's lawn like they were trying to lift the house and fly it someplace warmer. Greenridge never did subtle.

I pulled into the driveway and sat with the engine ticking, hands still at ten and two like a rookie. The porch had the same lean on the left, the same handrail you had to watch, or it would kiss your hipbone in the dark. Through the window, I caught the glint of a star on top of a tree. Of course she'd put it up already. She was constitutionally incapable of waiting until Advent actually started. Why follow a calendar when you can steamroll it with cheer?

I cut the engine, opened the door, and the cold hit my face like a rinsing. Crisp, clean, thin. I stood there just long enough to call it bravery, then hauled my bag out of the backseat.

The front door opened before I reached the porch. My mother was there in a red cardigan I remembered from college, her hair more silver than white now, mouth already soft with the kind of smile that forgives you before you do anything.

"Hannah." It came out on a breath. She stepped forward and folded me in. Cinnamon and laundry detergent. Home and not-home. I let her, stiff for a beat, then pressed my cheek to her shoulder because I couldn't make myself punish her for being herself.

"You made it," she said into my hair.

"Roads were clear." I pulled back. "You redecorated again?"

"I only put up what we already had." She moved to let me in. "And a few new candles. It felt…necessary."

Necessary. That was a word we both knew how to stretch.

Inside, the house was warm enough to melt bone. Garlands looped across archways like it was contractually obligated. The tree was all white lights and old ornaments, school crafts with peeling glitter, porcelain angels with hands pressed like they were afraid to touch anything. The nativity scene had been upgraded since I left; the manger glowed softly as if it had its own private sunrise.

And on the hallway wall, in the place it had always hung, was his photograph. Father Mark, clerical collar, that politician's smile. People used to say his eyes were kind. They didn't have to take his eyes home with them after the homily. They didn't have to live inside them.

I looked away fast enough to give myself a neck twinge.

"Let me take your bag," Mom said. "I changed the sheets this morning. Thought you'd want the blue ones."

Blue for calm. Or penance.

"I can take it up." I hooked the strap over my shoulder and followed her down the hall, past the picture I wasn't looking at, past the table with the thick Bible he used to thump with two fingers when he wanted you to know God had an opinion that matched his.

My old room had shrunk. The bed looked smaller, the desk tinier. My teenage handwriting was still carved into the underside, probably: H + ? scratched out with a key so many times the wood wore a groove. The window faced the maple in the yard where I'd used to sit and pretend the leaves moving were an ocean. The bookshelf held exactly what I'd left, paperbacks, a shoebox of folded notes, a music box my mother loved more than I did.

"Do you want tea?" she asked, hands already twisting in front of her. "Or cocoa. I got that peppermint one you liked."

"Tea's fine." I didn't want peppermint. I wanted something that burned. "Chamomile?"

"I have lemon ginger."

"Sure." I set the bag at the foot of the bed and sat, springs complaining. "How are you, Mom?"

"I'm…all right." She tilted her head in that way she had when she was deciding whether honesty would help. "Holidays make it noisy in here." She tapped her chest lightly. "But you being home quiets it."

My mouth tried to be cruel. It wanted to say I wasn't here to be a sedative. Instead I nodded. "We'll get through it."

Her eyes warmed, then slid toward the hall, toward the portrait, the Bible, the whole shrine to a man who had built a life on Sunday light and weekday shadows.

"People still ask about you," she said carefully. "The McKennas. Mrs. Doyle. Sheriff Collins said if you ever wanted—"

"The sheriff can keep his thoughts." I heard the flatness in my voice and let it sit. "I'm here to rest."

"Of course." She smoothed the bedspread, a ritual of helplessness. "Dinner at seven? I made stew."

Stew. Safe, neutral, fills the house with a smell that says no, we're not falling apart.

"Stew is good." I stood. "I'll wash up."

In the bathroom, I stared at my reflection and saw the sleep debt etched in the delicate skin beneath my eyes, the windburn on my cheeks, the little vertical line between my eyebrows that had deepened this past year into something permanent. I pulled the rubber band from my hair and shook it loose. The house hummed softly around me, furnace, fridge, some old heating duct that always rattled when the temperature dropped below thirty. Familiar. Suffocating. The way a too-tight sweater is familiar.

When I came back down, Mom had tea waiting in a mug with a snowman wearing a scarf so aggressive it seemed like a dare.

"Tomorrow's the first," she said, as if I didn't know what month we were in. "You'll go with me?"

To the square. To the wreath. To the candles. Twenty-five of them in a circle, lit night after night until Christmas Day, as if light added up to absolution. Where Christmas Lives All Year wasn't just a sign; it was town policy.

"I'll go," I said. It came out as a sigh wearing a sentence's clothes.

She smiled with relief. "It means a lot."

It meant she didn't have to stand there alone. It meant we'd pretend a little longer that this town hadn't been built on a story we did not tell.

We ate stew at the old kitchen table, elbows not quite touching, radio low with carols that made the corners of my mouth itch. When "O Come, All Ye Faithful" came on, I pictured my father at the pulpit, head tipped back, baritone filling the sanctuary like steam. Faithful. He'd loved that word. He'd wielded it like a yardstick and measured us until we came up wanting.

8

"Did you ever think he—" I stopped.

Mom's spoon hovered. "Think he what?"

"Nothing." The stew had too much thyme; or I did. "I'm tired."

She let me go. That was another of her gifts: knowing when to save the question for later, when the answer might land softer.

Upstairs, I lay on the bed with my boots still on and stared at the ceiling where I'd once taped glow-in-the-dark stars. One or two still clung on like stubborn barnacles. I closed my eyes and saw the boy from the ER, the way his lashes trembled as if he were dreaming. I heard the monitor go from chatter to scream. I felt bone under my hands. I reminded myself that other people were sleeping tonight. That I could, too. That if I couldn't, at least tomorrow I'd be standing in a crowd pretending light fixed things.

Sleep was kind enough to come, eventually, like a cat that takes your lap only when you stop looking at it.

The First Candle

December arrived with bells. Greenridge liked to ring them wide and loud, as if sheer decibels could corral joy.

Mom and I stood at the back of the square while the crowd pressed forward in their good coats. Kids hopped from foot to foot, sugar already making their eyes too bright. A brass band oompah-ed through "Joy to the World," and somewhere behind us a vendor sold kettle corn that smelled like my childhood and the paper cut of it. The air bit at my cheeks. Snow wasn't falling yet, but it thought it might.

The advent wreath rose from the center like a crown laid on a pillow, twenty-five tall candles in a perfect circle, evergreen woven thick at the base. Fresh pine, clean and resinous. The town had rebuilt the wreath many years ago after some teens knocked it over trying to take a selfie at two a.m. We'd had a special offering that

9

Sunday to pay for it. I remembered because my father had locked his jaw while he preached about stewardship. Stewardship of what, exactly, he'd never said.

Mayor Evelyn Hargrove took the stage in a coat the color of cranberry sauce, her hair sprayed into the kind of helmet older women wear when they intend to outlast weather and truth. "Welcome, Greenridge!" she called, the microphone crackling. "Another blessed season. Another chance to lift our hearts. Tonight we light the first candle, hope, because hope is what brought us here and what will carry us through."

Hope had poor shoulders for all this weight, but sure.

Sheriff Collins stood at her side, gaze doing that slow sweep that said I could find your secret under all this tinsel if I felt like it. He'd aged into his uniform the way some men age into a favorite armchair, comfortably, smugly. He saw me, gave the nod you give to the priest's daughter because she is permanent in the town ledger whether you like it or not. I nodded back with exactly the warmth I felt, somewhere between freezer-burn and Arctic drift.

Mom squeezed my mitten. "It's good you're here."

"It's freezing I'm here," I muttered, breath fogging the air. She smiled anyway, because she insisted on translating me into something kinder.

The choir of grade-schoolers shuffled forward in knitted hats and sang a verse of an old local carol that town historians swore had been written "in the founding days." I'd always found it eerie. Minor key. Words about flame and ash and keeping watch. It wasn't the merry kind of Christmas song. It was a warning disguised as tradition. People hummed along without thinking, the way you hum along to things that predate your thinking.

"Ready?" the mayor said, turning on the smile that belonged in brochures. "Three, two, one…"

A chorus of oohs rose as the wick caught, and the first candle blazed. The flame made the air around it ripple. For a second, I felt something I didn't want, my chest lifting, a stitch loosening. Stupid body. Pavlovian. Someone lights a big candle, and you think maybe, maybe.

Applause broke out, mittened hands banging together like muffled fireworks. The brass band surged. A kid on my left dropped his hot chocolate and burst into tears. The world kept doing what it always did, moving forward as if it had a plan.

The ceremony dissolved into milling. People hugged and promised coffee soon; we should really catch up; how is your mother; are you staying long; we miss your father's homilies; he had a gift. My mouth said thank you automatically. My brain said other things and kept them to itself.

By the time we made it back to the car, my toes were numb, and my patience had a hairline crack. Mom drove; she still preferred the familiar rattle of the Subaru over anything newer. "See?" she said gently. "That wasn't so bad."

"I didn't burst into flames," I said. "Gold star."

She chuckled, the sound lightly shocked out of her. The kind of laugh she hadn't let herself have in a while. Okay. There was that.

We were two streets from home when the sirens opened like a zipper down the night. One truck. Two. A third. Red and white strobed off the snowbanks, making the houses glow like they'd swallowed emergency. Mom's hands tightened on the wheel until the knuckles showed. The sirens were headed toward the far end of town, where the road fell away to the river and the old orphanage ruins sat like a scab the town pretended was a freckle.

"What is it?" I asked, though the sirens were already answering with the worst possibilities.

"Fire," she said, as if a declaration could make it smaller. "It sounds like the far lots."

"Pull over," I told her, and when she didn't, I added, "Mom."

She nodded once, turned at the next intersection, and followed the trucks' echo to the dirt access road that skirted the ruins. By the time we crested the rise, a knot of neighbors had gathered in parkas and slippers, drawn by sound the way deer lift their heads all at once. The storage shed that crouched beside the collapsed stone foundation of the orphanage was lit up like a furnace door. Flames gnawed at the roofline, punched black smoke into the sky, spat amber into the cold.

The heat hit my face from twenty yards. I could taste it, tar and old wood and something oddly sweet. Pine sap. The fire crew was already running lines from the hydrant, voices clipped, movements choreography that said they'd done this often enough to know each other's rhythms.

"Back up!" one firefighter shouted. "Everyone back."

We did, for once obedient. The ground under my boots was frozen hard; the water jetting from the hose turned the dirt at the edges to slick glass.

"What was even in there?" a man near us asked no one in particular.

"Maintenance junk," someone else answered. "Old ladders. Paint thinner, probably. Could've been anything."

Paint thinner. Perfect. Accelerant with a Christmas bow.

"It's the wiring," a woman said with the certainty of a person who couldn't bear the math of intent. "Those sheds are ancient."

I stepped closer to the police tape as an officer unrolled it, my breath a steady engine I could control if nothing else obeyed. I looked where the fire began: at the left corner, low. The way the roof was going told a story. Fires like to climb; they tell on their starting point if you watch.

"Hannah, don't," Mom said softly behind me. "You don't need to see this."

I'd seen worse. I'd seen small bodies and the way heat takes color out of hair. But my stomach still did that elevator drop as the roof sighed inward and a fountain of sparks kicked up bright enough to make the crowd gasp like an audience. One of the firefighters swore, adjusted his stance, and carved the flame down with water until it screamed and guttered and tried again.

"Faulty wiring," the woman insisted to anyone who'd listen. "They said for years that place needed work. They never did it. Typical town."

I stared and felt the tick of something in my head line up with the candle in the square. One flame birthed another. Ceremony, then consequence. If I'd believed in signs, I would have called it one. I didn't believe in signs. I believed in people who made choices and other people who'd rather believe in faulty wires.

Sheriff Collins appeared at my elbow like an old habit. "Evening, Miss Mark." He'd called me that since I was five, as if my last name were my father's profession. He lifted his chin toward the shed. "Shame. Real shame."

"Lucky no one was inside," I said. My eyes were on the seam of roof that still glowed like a cigar tip.

"Luck's better than the alternative." He slid his gaze to me. "Saw you at the lighting."

"Greenridge attendance list would be incomplete without me." I kept my voice dry enough to crack.

He didn't rise to it. He never did. "You staying long?"

"I'm here to rest." I forced a smile that showed the correct number of teeth.

"Then rest." He looked past me to my mother, softened his mouth. "Ma'am."

She nodded, eyes on the fire like it might turn and speak.

Across the line, a firefighter shouted "Knockdown!" and the word lifted the shoulders of the crowd. The flames skulked into themselves, orange shrinking to sullen red, smoke muscling up and laying itself over everything like a damp blanket. Someone coughed. Someone else cried quietly into a scarf. Disaster at a digestible distance.

The shed sagged, a jaw without a hinge. In the watery light, the orphanage ruins seemed to lean forward, one black window like a socket. I remembered a field trip to the place when I was young, before the last collapse. Our teacher had made us draw the old stone in charcoal and told us to imagine the past. I'd drawn fire by mistake. Or not by mistake. He'd said imagine; I'd done it too well.

"Let's go home," Mom said, as if home were a verb we could still do.

We walked back to the car, our boots making the crisp little squeaks that only happen on the coldest nights. When she started the engine, the heater gusted and smelled faintly like dust that

13

remembered summer. We didn't talk until we were halfway down the hill.

"It's probably nothing," she said.

"It's something." I didn't sugar it. "Even if it's an accident, it's something."

"The first night is always big." She nodded toward town, where the square still threw up light like a promise. "Everyone's excited."

"Everyone's excited," I repeated, and wanted the words to mean what she meant. The seatbelt cut across my chest like a hand holding me in place.

At the house, I stood for a second on the porch, breath ghosting, and looked up. Stars pricked the sky hard and cold. Behind me, the town buzzed faintly under the sound of its own joy. Ahead of me, the entryway smelled like evergreen and lemon polish and history trying to sweeten itself.

Inside, Mom hung up her coat and looked like she might say something and then didn't. That was the problem with us: too many words warehouses, too few delivery trucks.

"I'm going to make tea," she said finally, moving toward the kitchen.

"I'm going to stand here and pretend that helped," I said to nobody, and the nobody answered me back with quiet.

I toed off my boots, walked to the hallway table, and laid my hand on the Bible like a person checking a pulse. The leather was cool. The ribbon marker lay parenthetically in the Old Testament like a joke I didn't get. My father's handwriting filled the margins in small careful script, theology and to-do lists married without irony. Christmas Eve homily: LIGHT CONQUERS. Committee call Evelyn about fundraiser. Visit Mrs. Doyle.

He'd visited everyone. He'd missed the people he lived with.

From the living room, a carol lifted, the choir on the radio harmonizing about tender and mild. I pictured the shed, the way the fire had sprinted up the corner like it had been waiting its whole life to be asked.

One candle lit, two flames burning. Tradition and accident holding hands. I wasn't superstitious, but I was not in the mood for coincidence.

In the hallway mirror, my face looked like someone else's: older, yes, but also sharpened. I touched the place between my brows and smoothed it the way my mother used to do when I was little and worried about tests. Relax your face, Hannah. It doesn't need to work this hard.

I left the Bible where it was and went to help with the tea before it became a peace offering we didn't know how to accept.

When I finally crawled into bed, the house had tucked itself in. The furnace breathed. Somewhere in the walls, pipes clicked like distant hoofbeats. I lay on my side and told myself a story I did not believe: Tomorrow would be normal. The town would do its rituals. Nothing else would catch fire.

We would move day by day toward an uncomplicated Christmas, and I would be better by then, soothed by garlands and cookies and the precise number of candles required to light grief into surrender.

I closed my eyes. Behind them, the shed roof sank again in a little whoof of light. My last thought before sleep slid in was simple and rude and honest: Hope is just a candle. And anything can blow it out.

Chapter 2

Ghosts In The House

I woke to the smell of cinnamon and the faintest hiss of the furnace pushing heat through old vents. For a luxurious six seconds, I forgot whose house I was in. Then the ceiling came into focus, and the memories trooped in like carolers who refused to leave until you sang back.

Cinnamon rolls. Of course. My mother had always believed butter and sugar could bargain with December.

I pulled on yesterday's sweater and padded to the kitchen. The counters were already dusted with flour like early snow. A cooling rack held spirals so perfect they could've posed for the town newsletter. My mother stood at the stove in her cardigan armor, hair twisted into a clip, humming a carol that had no business being that cheerful before coffee.

"Good morning," she said without turning, the way mothers do when they can feel you arrive.

"It's morning." I opened the cupboard and stared at the mugs until the snowman's grin annoyed me into grabbing a plain one. "Jury's still out on good."

She slid a plate toward me. The roll shone. I wanted to want it. Instead, my stomach sent up a warning flare. Trauma by association, how festive.

"You used to eat two," she said, smiling like we could just step back into a softer decade.

"I used to believe Santa wrapped gifts at two a.m. in the garage," I said. "People change."

Her smile went brittle at the edges. She cut it back into neutral and rinsed a bowl with surgical precision. Retreat was her specialty. I hated that it was also her survival skill.

I tore off a corner of roll and set it back down like a kid pretending to try broccoli. "I'm going to walk," I said. "Get the map of town back in my bones."

"Bundle. It's colder today." Her eyes flicked to my face like she was checking for frostbite the way other mothers check for attitude.

"It's Greenridge. I'm surprised the cold doesn't have a committee."

She huffed a laugh she didn't mean to let out. "Coffee first," she added, because she was still my mother, and coffee could fix the part of me that sarcasm didn't reach.

I drank standing at the sink, because sitting felt like commitment. The backyard maple was black against the sky, its branches fingered with ice. The bird feeder knocked lightly in the wind—empty. Of course it was. December had demands.

My mother dried her hands and leaned on the counter. Not casual, exactly poised, like a gymnast before a beam. "People will be glad to see you," she said, too carefully. "It matters that you're here."

"Does it?" I set the mug down and watched a coffee ring bloom like an eclipse. "Or does it matter that the priest's daughter can be accounted for at all major seasonal events?"

"You're not a checkbox," she said softly.

"Then why do I feel like one?" Because my father taught me to be a symbol before I was a person. I didn't say it. It hung there anyway, steam no one could wipe from the glass.

She touched the edge of the plate. "I know you think I…stood by too often."

"Think?" The word came out more bark than laugh. I swallowed it. "Forget it."

Her mouth thinned. "Hannah."

"What?" I set my palms on the cool counter and forced air into my lungs. "I'm trying not to fight before nine a.m. I'm new at this. Be patient."

Another ghost of a smile. "All right. Walk. I'll be here when you're back."

Of course she would. She was always here when it was too late to change anything.

17

***

The streets were bare this morning, a scattering of tire tracks etched in last night's frost. The decorations looked more garish without a crowd to hide behind them. A blow-up Santa across the street sagged to one side, drunk on the job.

I ducked into the bakery for warmth. The bell jingled like it had twenty years ago. Mrs. Doyle, hair pewter now, blinked at me from behind the counter.

"Well, if it isn't Hannah Mark. You're a sight."

"I can be less of one." I managed a real smile for her. "How's your hip?"

"Predictable." She winked at me and bagged a brioche with the efficiency of someone who knew what everyone in town wanted before they did. "On the house," she added when I reached for my wallet. "Your father—"

"Would have lectured you about generosity and then written it off on a tax deduction." The joke slipped out, and we both looked at it, surprised.

She slid the bag across anyway. "He could be a stiff wind," she allowed. "He did love this town. We all do; Lord help us."

I stepped back onto the sidewalk with the bag warm in my hand and a pinprick of guilt at the base of my throat. He had loved this town. He just loved it more in public than he loved us in private. Some men are fountains in the square and dry wells at home. Ask any pastor's kid.

The square looked stripped without last night's crowd—just a wreath on its stand and the wind worrying the ribbon. A maintenance truck idled while a man in a neon vest adjusted a cord. He glanced at me with the reflex of someone expecting to be scolded by volunteers. I lifted a hand. "Just looking."

"Check back at six," he said. "We'll make it pretty again."

"It wasn't ugly," I said. "Just…loud."

He grinned, a crack of white in a red face. "It's the point."

I kept walking, letting old routes do what muscle memory does best. By the time I crested the hill toward the river, my breath came in clouds. The road to the orphanage dipped and then broke into packed dirt where plows didn't bother to pretend. The shed from last night sat black-mouthed and humped, roof caved like a ribcage. The ruin of the orphanage itself watched from ten yards away, stone teeth jutting where walls had given up.

A firefighter in a navy jacket was coiling hose with the slowness of someone who had already done the hard part. He looked up as I approached. "We're closed to spectators," he said, not unkindly.

"I'm not a spectator." It was defensive and unhelpful, so I tacked on, "Nurse."

He tipped his head. "Then you know it smells like somebody used accelerant." He said it low, like he was telling me something he shouldn't say out loud where tape flapped.

"It smelled…sweet," I admitted. "Pine sap?"

"And other things." His mouth went sideways. "Official line will be an electrical issue until we know more. You didn't hear anything from me."

"I didn't hear anything from you," I repeated, and tried to file the conversation somewhere sensible. It didn't want to sit. It wanted to pace.

On the walk back, wind found the seam at my collar and slid a knife in. I pulled my hat lower and thought about the way the flame had climbed—hungry, fast. About the old carol the kids sang with their careful vowels. Keep the watch, keep the flame. About how much a small town can forget on purpose.

At the grocery, Mayor Evelyn Hargrove intercepted me as efficiently as a well-mannered linebacker.

"Hannah," she said warmly, as if last night's fire had been nothing more than a hiccup in the program. "You're settling back in?"

Translation: Are you planning on stirring things up, or will you play along like a good priest's daughter until Christmas is over?

"Trying," I said, grabbing coffee. "Though the cinnamon roll assault nearly did me in."

Her lipstick Cranberry Resolve, or something equally determined didn't crack. "We all want this season to feel steady, especially after… that incident."

Incident. Right. Three fire trucks worth of an incident.

"We're steady," I said. "Nothing says stability like calling the fire department on the first day of Advent."

She touched my arm with that politician's blend of warmth and pressure. "Your father gave this town hope. We need that remembered now more than ever."

I gave her the nurse smile the one that says I hear you, but we're moving on now. "Yeah. He gave plenty."

Her gaze lingered, sharp under the sugar. Then she wheeled off to another aisle, her cart rattling like applause.

Back home, my mother was taking down a box from the hall closet that had no business being on the top shelf. I grabbed it from her before it toppled her into Advent in traction.

"I had it," she protested.

"You had disaster flirting with your kneecaps." I set the box on the table. It was labeled ORPHANAGE DRIVE PROGRAMS in my father's handwriting. The O was a perfect loop like he was showing the O what a good O should be.

Mom looked at it like it had wandered in under its own power. "Oh, that. I was going to sort—"

"I'll do it." I lifted the lid. Programs curled at the edges lay in neat stacks, yellowed with the particular dignity of paper that refused to admit it was old. Christmas Benefaction Gala, St. Cecilia's Home for Children. Advent Carol Service Benefiting St. Cecilia's. Names of donors in italic fonts and too much ink.

I thumbed through until I found a flier with a photograph— children in winter coats lined up, a nun's hand on a small shoulder. The kids' smiles weren't Christmas morning. They were Christmas pageant: told, not felt.

"You kept all this?" I asked.

"He kept it," she said. "I didn't have the heart to throw it away."

"Because he touched it?"

"Because it's ours," she said, too fast. Then, softer, "Because it's what we did."

We. Not he. We are the family pronouns you use when you're drafting history.

I slipped the flier back. "What do you remember about the fire?" I asked, as if the question were casual. As if fire belonged in a conversational bowl beside the oranges.

Her throat moved. "I remember the sirens. And the smoke from the river side. Your father leaving before the second verse of 'Hark! The Herald Angels Sing' because the phone rang in the sacristy and he said he had to go where he was called."

"Did he tell you anything when he came back?"

"He said it was...contained." She watched my face as if my expression could grade the past. "He said it was better to soothe than to inflame. Those were his words. I wrote them down because I thought they were wise."

"They were convenient," I said. It came out flat as an EKG at zero. "How many times did he soothe the town so it didn't have to know itself?"

She raised her chin a fraction. "Hannah."

"I'm asking." I am asking now because I did not ask then because I wasn't allowed to ask ever.

She pressed her hands together until the knuckles blanched, then released them one finger at a time. "He told me not to worry. And I let him tell me that." She swallowed. "I let a lot of things stand."

Honesty. It didn't come here in big pieces. When it did, it knocked furniture.

I closed the box and slid it aside. "Thank you," I said, which wasn't for the box.

She nodded once, grateful and hurt at the same time. Welcome to our love language.

We made dinner without choreography her chopping, me stirring like two people who had practiced peace enough times to be competent if not gifted. After, we stood in the doorway and assessed

21

the sky. The cold had deepened into a thing with edges. Across town, bells warmed up like throats.

"Ready?" Mom asked.

"As I'll ever be. Which is not, but here we are."

She tucked her arm through mine like we were ladies in an old movie and not two women trying not to be haunted.

The Second Candle

The square glittered like it had found another gear of bright. I stood with my weight in my left hip and tried not to count the number of times the brass section missed the same note. People around us shimmered with layers wool, down, hope. Children pinwheeled in boots that weren't broken in yet. Someone's dog wore antlers with the mortified patience of a saint.

Mayor Evelyn took the mic and purred the same pieties with fresh adjectives. Sheriff Collins did his slow lawman scan like he could lasso trouble with his eyes. The grade-school choir gathered, and their teacher held up two fingers for verse two of the old carol, the one that made my skin think about crawling off.

I mouthed along, because I was a glutton for honesty tonight: Keep the watch, keep the flame; ashes tell the secret's name. Who exactly had written this and decided it was festive? Somewhere, a founding mother with a sharp pen was laughing.

"Three, two, one…" the mayor counted, and the second candle caught as if it had been waiting its whole life for the match.

Applause blew out across the square. My mother's mitten found mine for exactly three squeezes ritual, not romance. I let her. Sometimes mercy is not pointing out the obvious.

We lasted thirty minutes. Hot cocoa was admired. Kettle corn was declined because my teeth hurt just thinking about it. I talked to two people who told me my father had saved their marriages by telling them to be kinder and one who told me he had saved the town by being stern when sternness was needed. I was polite. My inner monologue put on a show with knives.

When the band finally packed and the clusters thinned, we cut along the church to take the side street home. That's when I saw it.

At first, my brain made it shadows. Then the streetlight shrugged, and the black paint stood out on the stone like a confession:

THE SECOND FLAME REVEALS WHAT'S HIDDEN.

All caps. Block letters with confidence. The paint was fresh enough to glisten. Whoever had done it had waited for the crowd to thin and the air to sharpen.

Behind me, my mother made a small sound the kind you let out when you drop a glass and know it'll shatter before it hits.

"Teenagers," someone said too loudly behind us, trying to set the narrative like jelly. "Damned kids."

Sheriff Collins materialized as if the word teenagers were his Bat Signal. "Step back," he told the little knot of spectators. He didn't look at me, which meant he definitely saw me.

"This is a message," I said, because tact has never been my cardio.

"Everything's a message if you want it to be." He motioned to an officer for tape. "We'll get it off by morning."

"Like it never happened," I said, sweet as a candy cane dipped in arsenic.

He finally glanced at me. "You got something to say, Miss Mark?"

The old name snapped into place like a collar. I smiled as nicely as I could stand. "I'm just admiring the penmanship."

Mom touched my sleeve, a tug with history. "Hannah."

But my eyes were taking inventory. The letters were even, straight, no hesitation in the curves. Whoever did this wasn't rushed. They stood here and wrote while the town hummed two blocks away, and they didn't shake. That confidence had weight.

A gust of wind shivered the trees. The paint winked, wet and sure.

"Go on home," Collins told the crowd. "Nothing to see." Which, coming from him, meant a lot to see.

"Oh, we see," Mrs. Doyle said from somewhere over my shoulder, voice small but carrying. "We always see."

Collins shot her a look that said he respected her enough not to scold her in public. Then he turned to his officer. "Photos. Then get a pressure washer up first thing." He added, to no one, "Kids think December is for jokes."

Kids. Or someone who had waited a very long time to talk to a town that refused to listen.

We moved on because standing there would stain you, too. Mom kept hold of my sleeve as if I were a kite and she had learned what happened when she let go. Halfway down the block, she stopped and faced me.

"Don't," she said, meaning don't chase this.

"It's chasing us," I said, and the words put a chill under my coat that the wind hadn't managed.

She swallowed. The porch light from a nearby house gilded the fine lines at the corners of her mouth the map of years you earn by keeping quiet. "Maybe it will pass."

"Sure," I said. "Like a kidney stone."

She snorted, startled and unwilling to like the image, which only made it funnier. Laughter did a neat job of letting air back into the world after it had gone thin.

We walked the rest of the way in a silence that had learned its manners. At home, she headed for the kitchen like cupboards could cure messages spray-painted on churches. I stood in the hall and looked at my father's photograph. In the low light, his eyes seemed to do their old trick watchful, assessing, patient in the way men are patient when they're sure patience will be mistaken for virtue.

"The second flame reveals what's hidden," I said to the frame, because talking to dead men is free. "Do you hear that? Somebody's tired of covering us with garland."

My reflection ghosted over his face on the glass. I made a face at my ghost and my father both.

Upstairs, I sat on the edge of the bed and felt the day on my skin like grit. The town had its ritual. The town had its accident. Now the town had its sentence in black paint. I thought about the firefighter's quiet accelerant and the way the carol's minor key skated under the major one like a rumor. I thought about my mother's hands, how they had shaken for exactly one second under the streetlight and then remembered themselves.

I lay down and stared at the dark, which stared back. Somewhere in the distance, bells rang the hour. My brain floated one last sharp thought before sleep finally came for me like a tide I didn't fight:

Candles are supposed to light the way.

So why does each one make the shadows longer?

CHAPTER 3

Faith In Silence

The morning started with the kind of cold that turns air into knives. I pulled my coat tighter and told myself a brisk walk into town would keep me from brooding. Brooding is my cardio, but I tried anyway.

The streets had that December hush that sounds like peace until you listen closer. Wreaths hung from every porch. Red bows flared on railings. The whole block looked like it had been staged by a committee with clipboards and strong opinions about joy. Ten years away and it all looked the same, like the town had been vacuum sealed. I had only come back for the funeral, and I told myself I would leave right after. Then the house rearranged itself around me, and the town put on its costume, and somehow, I was back here.

I passed the elementary school and felt the small shock of recognition that childhood gives you when it is still standing. Same brick, same faded mural of smiling children holding hands around a globe. I remembered the nurse's office cot with the plastic pillow that stuck to sweaty cheeks, the peppermint the secretary would hand out like a cure, the way my father used to pop in during lunch and make the second graders call him Pastor Mark. He would pat my head like I was a well-trained pet and tell the class that service was the highest calling. He did not specify who would be serving whom.

By the time I reached Main Street, the shop windows wore frost like lace. The pharmacy smelled like rubbing alcohol and vanilla candles pretending to be cookies. I grabbed toothpaste and ibuprofen I did not need because this is what you do in small towns. You buy something so the clerk does not add you to the gossip rotation.

Two women near the cough drops lowered their voices when they saw me. The move was synchronized, like they had rehearsed it between greeting cards and hand cream.

"Terrible, simply terrible," one whispered, eyes round.

"Could have been worse," the other said, which in Greenridge passes for comfort.

Their glances slid over me and snapped back like rubber bands. They smiled as if the priest's daughter could not possibly mind being the topic, as if I had been born for this job and should be grateful the town kept me employed.

I paid for my unnecessary purchase and stepped back into the cold. Across the street the hardware store window displayed snow shovels arranged like soldiers. My father used to bless this place every December. He would stand just inside the door with a thermos and his picture smile, telling customers that a prepared home is a godly home. He never salted our own steps. My mother did, quietly, before dawn.

I ducked into the bakery for heat. Mrs. Doyle looked smaller than I remembered and twice as sharp. Her hair had gone from steel to pewter. Her eyes missed nothing.

"You are thin as a match," she said. "Eat."

"I am fine." I was not fine, but I did not need a pastry to confirm it.

She leaned across the counter anyway, voice low. "You would think they would call it what it is. Fire does not start that hot without help."

Her assistant shot her a look like a stage cue. Eyes to me, then to the floor. Lower the volume. Be careful. I wanted to say, it is a little late for careful, but I swallowed it and took a coffee outside.

Sheriff Collins had parked crooked by the curb, as if urgency excused geometry. He leaned against the cruiser, arms folded, jaw tight. Steam drifted from his cup. His breath made little ghosts in the air.

"Morning, Miss Mark," he said. The tone suggested morning was a concept the day was failing to achieve.

"Morning, Sheriff. Quiet?" I asked, as if quiet is something you can measure with a ruler.

"Quiet enough." His eyes swept the square without landing on me. "You should not let the talk get to you. Fires happen. Graffiti happens. Kids, most likely."

"Accelerant smells like kids to you?" I asked, light as icing. The coffee tasted like scorched beans and stubbornness.

He shifted his weight by half an inch. I counted it as a win. "We are handling it."

Translation: stop poking the bear. Or maybe, the bear bites people who poke.

"Of course," I said, saccharine on purpose. "Everything under control. That is what everyone keeps saying."

His gaze met mine. Steady. Defensive. "It is under control."

I let silence do the work. Hospitals taught me that distance between questions is where truth slips out. Collins had more practice than my average parent at three in the morning. He tipped his hat and walked off, and I was left with a coffee that had gone suddenly bitter. Behind him the mayor strode across the square in a coat that could block weather and shame. I turned away before she could decide I was in need of civic comfort.

On the way home I felt it again, that prickle between the shoulder blades that is older than language. I turned once, then again. The street was empty except for a kid dragging a red sled with no snow under it. He waved. I waved back, and the prickle did not stop. Some feelings do not care about evidence.

I cut down Maple to avoid the church. My boots found every squeaky patch of frozen snow, the sound like little gasps. Passing the parsonage made my throat tighten anyway. I could still see the line of mourners from the funeral, the casseroles lined up like bricks. People had told me I was brave. I had nodded like a good child and accepted their compliments for standing next to a casket that did not deserve my grief. After the reception I had washed the punch cups in my mother's sink until my knuckles went white. The house felt bigger without him and smaller in every other way.

When I reached the porch, my mother was folding laundry with military precision. Towels in perfect thirds. Sheets squared like maps. She looked up and read my face the way mothers read thermometers.

"Something wrong?" she asked.

"Besides the part where half the town pretends fires light themselves?" I hung my coat and tried to leave the wind outside.

She stacked the towels. "People talk less when they are afraid."

"And you?" I asked. "Are you afraid?"

Her hands smoothed a sheet, folded it, placed it on the pile. She did not look up. "Some things are better left alone."

There it was. The family motto. Etched on a headstone I had not agreed to buy. Her eyes did not meet mine, which told me more than shouting could have.

I stood in the doorway and watched her retreat into chores. I knew the choreography. When I was ten, she polished silver for three hours after a parishioner accused my father of misusing a fund. When I was sixteen, she alphabetized every pantry item while a rumor about a church elder was making the rounds. This was how she kept the flood back. Plates, towels, sugar in straight lines. The house would gleam, and, for a while, she could pretend the world was behaving.

The whole town had learned the same trick. Sweep, stage, sing louder. Maybe that is what faith was here. Pretend hard enough, and the truth loses interest.

I went upstairs before I said something sharp enough to cut both of us. The hallway held the smell of lemon oil and old carpet. Halfway up, the old board complained the way it had my whole childhood. My father had promised to fix it every Advent. He never did. People loved his sermons about diligence. I loved proof, and there was none.

His photo caught me mid step like it always did. The frame sat where it had always sat, as if the wall itself had formed around it. Clerical collar. Politician's smile. The kind of eyes people call kind when they only see them for forty minutes a week. We had taken that picture the year the town voted to add three more candles to the wreath. He had been giddy for a month. He said Greenridge had vision. I stood in the back pew and watched him work the room like a violin.

"What did you bury?" I asked the glass now. My voice sounded too loud in the narrow hall. "And how many people helped you shovel?"

The photo did not answer. Of course it did not. The dead do not argue. They just hang there and let you practice your lines.

I kept walking, past the guest room that used to smell like peppermint lotion and now smelled like dust, past the closet where my mother kept the keepsakes he did not know she kept. In my room I sat on the bed and watched the maple branches drag dark lines across the ceiling. I could almost hear the bells already, the third night warming up its throat. When we first moved here, I loved those bells. I used to count them, then make wishes. Later I learned you cannot wish a fire out once it decides to take.

I opened the top drawer of the desk and found a stack of Polaroids I had left behind like a time capsule. School plays. Choir robes. A winter carnival where I am smiling with my mouth and not my eyes. In one, the orphanage roof is a jagged line behind a snowman built by kids who did not live to be teenagers. Someone had written Joy in the snow with a boot heel. The ink had bled, which felt appropriate.

Downstairs, a pot lid clinked. My mother humming drifted up the stairwell. Not a hymn. Something older, the tune her hands reached for when they needed permission to keep moving. I set the photos back and closed the drawer with care I did not feel.

Back in the hall I paused at the photo again. His eyes followed me because that is what eyes in frames do. The air felt thick, like the house had taken a long breath and was waiting to see if I would exhale too.

"The third tonight," I told him. "You always liked the middle. You said it holds the story."

I waited, as if he might roll his eyes from the other side and tell me not to be dramatic. Nothing. Only the furnace knocking like a polite ghost.

I went to the bathroom and splashed water on my face that was colder than the air. The mirror gave me a version of myself I did not recognize. Older, yes. Sharper, definitely. A woman who had pressed her hands to too many small rib cages and told too many mothers to sit down because the floor was going to drop out from under them.

The bells started then. A single peal, then another, then the slow count that means the town will gather whether it wants to or not. I dried my hands and listened until the vibrations faded into the walls.

Faith in silence. That is what Greenridge does best. Smile for the ceremony. Fold the towels. Pretend the wind is only wind and not a voice. I stood there until the last tremor left the glass and then headed for the stairs.

The photo kept its secrets. The town kept its script. And somewhere across the river, the ruins held their breath for one more night.

The Third Candle

By the time we reached the square that evening, the air had sharpened to ice. People gathered anyway, scarves pulled high, boots crunching on salted sidewalks. Nothing would stop Greenridge from its rituals, not even the nagging fear painted on the church wall.

Mayor Evelyn looked radiant under the lights, which was her job. She held the microphone like she was hosting a gala instead of praying away scandal. "We come together again," she purred, "to celebrate the hope of this season."

Hope. If repetition made it true, Greenridge would be the happiest town in America.

The choir filed in, little voices braving the cold, and launched into the third verse of that eerie carol. Keep the watch, keep the flame; ashes tell the secret's name. The third light shows the way, though shadows beg to stay.

I mouthed the words with them, half in defiance, half to taste the shape of the threat. My mother gave me a sideways look but didn't speak.

Evelyn raised her hand. "Three, two, one…"

The third candle caught flame, tall and sure. Applause rose, though thinner this time, as if the crowd's hands weren't entirely convinced. Sheriff Collins stood at the edge, eyes scanning like a storm dog waiting for lightning.

We stayed through cocoa and carols, the chatter brittle around us. I spoke to people who told me how much my father had meant to them, how his sermons had saved them, how he'd kept the town steady. I smiled. My thoughts sharpened knives behind my teeth.

Later, we cut across the side street near the orphanage ruins. That's when the noise hit—a screech, a desperate crunch, the splintering snap of wood.

We ran. A sedan had plowed through the fence by the old foundation, nose buried in a tree. Steam hissed from under the hood. The driver's door sagged open, and inside, retired deputy Frank Miller clutched the wheel with blood streaking down his temple.

"Brakes," he gasped when Collins and another man pulled him out. "The pedal went to the floor. Nothing. Nothing."

Collins barked orders for an ambulance and crowd control, but I caught the flicker in his eyes—the one that said he didn't believe in coincidence either.

Frank was loaded onto a stretcher, still mumbling about the brakes. The crowd whispered around us: black ice, bad luck, old cars. Anything but intent.

On the walk home, my mother finally spoke. Her voice was low, more to herself than to me. "Maybe… maybe there are signs. Maybe they're not accidents."

I stopped. "What do you mean?"

She shook her head quickly, too quickly. "Forget it. Just a thought."

"No," I pressed. "You know something."

Her face tightened. "I know nothing."

We walked the rest of the way in silence, her hand gripping her coat tighter than the cold required.

Halfway up the porch steps, I said quietly, "Wasn't Frank a deputy when the orphanage burned?"

She froze. Just for a second, but it was enough. Her knuckles went white on the railing. "It was a long time ago," she said. "Don't start connecting things that don't need connecting."

I stared at her profile, the hard line of her mouth against the dark. "And if they already are?"

She didn't answer. Just went inside, shutting the door with the kind of finality that sounded practiced.

Back in the hall, I looked again at my father's portrait. "The third flame shows the way," I whispered. "But to what? And who's leaving the trail?"

His eyes, smug behind glass, didn't move. But I could feel the shadows lengthening.

CHAPTER 4

The Market

The Christmas market in Greenridge had always been more ritual than celebration. People called it festive, but it was really about obedience. You showed up because everyone else did, and if you didn't, someone noticed. Tradition wasn't joy here; it was surveillance dressed in lights.

My mother insisted we go. Of course she did. She believed in public appearances the way other people believed in salvation. So, I trudged beside her down Main Street, pretending the cold wasn't biting through my gloves and pretending the bells above weren't pounding straight through my skull.

The market stretched along the street like a theater set; every booth painted in cheerful colors that looked one snowstorm away from peeling. Evergreen garlands drooped beneath cheap lights that blinked like they were on life support. The air was thick with cinnamon, roasting chestnuts, and cider, but beneath it lingered the sharp, sour smell of woodsmoke and fear. It clung to everything. Even the laughter felt artificial, too loud, too quick, the kind people use to keep the dark from listening.

"Doesn't it look lovely?" my mother asked. Her scarf was tied too tightly beneath her chin, her tote bag pressed close to her side like it contained something fragile.

"Lovely," I said. The wreaths were plastic. The gingerbread in the bakery window looked staged, all perfect smiles and no soul.

I recognized every face because that's what happens in small towns; you grow up memorizing people whether you want to or not. The butcher's wife gave me a smile that faltered halfway through. Old Mr. Keegan tipped his hat, then immediately pretended to look for someone else. Pastor Lewis, a young man, my father's replacement, moved through the crowd like a well-trained actor, all warm smiles and measured pauses. His collar gleamed under the lights, though he wore it like it itched.

Children darted between legs, chasing the smell of sugar and cocoa. Parents yanked them back with voices tight from more than cold. A brass band stumbled through "Hark! The Herald Angels Sing," the trumpets too bright, the harmony wobbling at the edges.

"Brooding again," my mother said softly, her voice just light enough to count as teasing.

"Cardio," I muttered.

We reached the cider stall, where Mrs. Caldwell sat slumped in a folding chair. Once, she had been the director of the orphanage. Once, she had been the woman everyone in town went to for advice. Now she looked like a shadow wearing a wool blanket. Her hair stuck out in pale, uneven tufts, and her hands trembled as she held a paper cup. People stopped to greet her but never stayed long. Grief, in Greenridge, was treated like contagion.

We were only a few feet away when her voice cut through the noise.

"The children," she said.

At first, I thought she was talking to someone beside her. Then her voice rose, cracked, desperate. "The children, the children! Where are they?"

The brass band faltered to silence. My mother's hand clamped down on my arm, hard enough to leave marks. The whole square froze.

A few women rushed over, their smiles bright with panic. "Now, now, Mrs. Caldwell," one said gently. "It's all right. You're safe."

Caldwell's head turned sharply toward her. "Safe?" she echoed, her voice breaking on the word. "None of them were safe. You think I don't remember?"

The crowd stiffened. Someone coughed. Someone else muttered a prayer.

She was crying now, her breath coming out in short gasps. "We left them there. The fire, the screaming. No one came. No one."

35

A collective murmur rippled through the market. People looked anywhere but at her. I watched her closely, heart beating harder than I wanted to admit. There was something in her eyes that didn't look like confusion. It looked like memory.

"She's old," my mother whispered. "She gets confused."

Mrs. Caldwell's hands clutched at her blanket. "You think it's over, but it's not," she said, her voice suddenly low and steady, almost lucid. "It comes back. Always does. The truth burns until someone lets it out."

No one moved. The only sound was the faint hiss of the cider kettle.

Then her niece appeared, red-faced and embarrassed, and wrapped the blanket around her shoulders. "I'm sorry, she's not been well," she said quickly, steering the wheelchair toward the edge of the crowd.

The silence held until they turned the corner. Then someone laughed—too loudly, too bright. The band started up again. The moment folded itself neatly out of sight, tucked under the town's favorite rug of denial.

My mother exhaled sharply. "Poor woman. She doesn't know what she's saying."

"Doesn't she?" I asked. My voice came out quieter than I meant it to. "She ran the place. She was there when it burned."

"She's confused, Hannah," my mother said, faster now, like speed could make it true. "You saw how she was trembling."

"I saw a woman remembering," I said.

Her jaw clenched, the line of her mouth flattening into silence. She walked faster, and I let her.

We passed the bookstall next. Emily Hill was there, arranging paperbacks in tidy rows. She was new—thirty, maybe—pleasant face, soft voice, the kind of person who still believed in happy endings. My mother brightened like someone had turned on a light.

"Hannah, this is Emily Hill," she said quickly.

Emily smiled. "Your mother tells me you're a nurse. That must take a lot of heart."

"Mostly caffeine," I said.

She laughed. "I teach at the orphanage. Well, the new one. Three years now."

"You like it?"

"I do. The children are wonderful. Resilient." Her smile faltered slightly. "They've been through enough."

"You worked with Mrs. Caldwell?" I asked.

"Oh, no," she said quickly. "She retired before I came. I just teach math and literature. Stability matters most, don't you think?" Her gaze flicked in the direction Mrs. Caldwell had gone. "Some people can't move forward."

My mother nodded too quickly. "She's right," she said. "The past is gone."

"Sure," I said. "Unless it decides to come back."

Emily gave me a polite, puzzled look before excusing herself to help a child choose a book.

"She seemed nice," I said when we left.

"She is nice," my mother said sharply. "Not everyone in this town is hiding something."

"Of course not," I said. "Just most of them."

Carolers began to sing again. "O Come, O Come, Emmanuel," their voices trembling in the cold. Lights blinked overhead. Laughter returned, louder this time, like everyone was trying to smother what they had just witnessed.

I bought cider and pretended to enjoy it. The sweetness turned my stomach. I forced myself to smile for my mother's sake, to hum along with the music, but every time I blinked, I saw Mrs. Caldwell's face—the terror, the guilt, the clarity that didn't belong to confusion.

We walked home through the quiet streets. The market lights glowed faintly behind us, distant and unreal. Snow began to fall in thin flakes, melting as they touched the ground. My mother's steps quickened.

When we reached the house, she paused at the door, her hand on the knob. "Let's not speak of that again," she said softly.

"Of Mrs. Caldwell?"

"Of any of it."

She went inside. I stayed on the porch, watching the snow dissolve into black pavement. The market music had faded, but I could still hear it in my head; thin, trembling, desperate.

I thought of Mrs. Caldwell's voice, cracking through the cold like a warning no one wanted to hear. The truth burns until someone lets it out.

And for the first time, I wondered how many fires this town had really put out.

The Fourth Candle

December fourth arrived sharp, the air hard as glass. You could feel it in the way people walked, stiff and watchful, like the cold itself was warning them of something. The whole town moved as though waiting for a storm only they couldn't admit was coming.

By evening, the square was strung with more lights than the night before, a desperate attempt to outshine unease. The garlands glittered, the bulbs blinked, but the cheer felt forced, a play put on for some invisible audience.

Mayor Evelyn stepped forward, flawless in her fur-trimmed coat, her voice honeyed and clear. "Tonight, we light the fourth candle—a symbol of faith, of hope, of Greenridge standing together."

The words skimmed across the crowd like stones on frozen water. The applause that followed was brittle, polite, thinner than paper.

Then the choir began the carol again. Ashes tell the secret's name. That line cut straight through the air, and I watched shoulders stiffen, jaws lock, eyes dart. It was a town flinching in unison, pretending not to. Nobody moved. Nobody dared leave.

The flame caught, tall and steady, throwing shadows against the church wall. Sheriff Collins stood off to the side, arms crossed,

38

scanning the faces with the grim patience of a man who expected trouble and hated not knowing where it would come from. His jaw worked like he was chewing something sour.

We went through the motions—hot cocoa passed around, hands clasped, brittle smiles exchanged. All of it felt like pantomime. When it was finally over, people drifted home, shoulders hunched, whispers clinging to the dark.

I thought the night was over.

It wasn't.

Hours later, the sirens split the silence wide open.

The smell hit first, acrid and heavy, sliding down my throat until I coughed. Burning wood. Burning history. My mother and I ran, slippers crunching on frost, our breath clouding in the freezing air as if the world itself was gasping.

Murphy's General Store was ablaze. Not just a fire, an inferno, a monster chewing through wood and shingles. Flames belched from the roof, windows bursting outward in violent puffs. Sparks rained over the crowd like furious confetti.

Neighbors screamed. Some shouted for water. A bucket line formed, even though the fire crews were already on it, hoses blasting futile arcs against the heat. The blaze roared back, defiant, a living thing refusing to die.

Mrs. Murphy wailed on the curb, held upright by neighbors, her voice cracked and animal, keening like her grief alone might drown the fire.

"They say it started in the wiring," someone muttered behind me, the words spoken with the confidence of someone repeating a script.

"Old building," another voice chimed in, quick, relieved, as if the phrase itself were a charm against fear.

But then came a third voice, lower, sharp as a snapped branch: "Bad luck."

The crowd shifted, uneasy. It was the same chorus I'd heard after the shed burned, after the graffiti was scrubbed away. Wiring. Old building. Bad luck. The holy trinity of excuses. The town clung to them like catechism, repeating the lines until they almost sounded true.

Except they weren't. They couldn't be. Wires don't leap from building to building like vengeful ghosts. Old timber doesn't smolder on cue with each candle. And bad luck doesn't have handwriting neat enough to paint scripture across church walls.

These weren't explanations. They were lullabies, hummed to keep the town asleep.

And Greenridge loved to sleep.

Sheriff Collins barked into his radio, words clipped, face tight. He moved like a man trying to prove control he didn't have. When his gaze swept the crowd and landed on me, my stomach dropped. He knew. Or maybe I only wanted him to.

The heat pressed against us in waves. Children cried. Men cursed. A man shouted about losing his Christmas layaway—because of course, in this town, possessions mattered more than people. The mayor clasped Mrs. Murphy's hands, voice rising sweet and solemn, promising help, promising rebuilding. Her tone was honey poured on ash, too smooth, too practiced.

I forced myself forward, tried again to believe in the ritual of togetherness. I joined the bucket line, pails sloshing, water spilling down my gloves, soaking through to my skin. My muscles strained with each useless toss. It was pointless, symbolic at best, but I wanted to believe for one minute that effort mattered. That Christmas spirit mattered. That something did.

It didn't. The flames climbed higher, mocking us. The bitterness curled tight in my chest until it hurt to breathe.

Back home, my mother collapsed into her chair, pale, trembling. "Terrible," she whispered. "Just terrible."

"Which part?" I asked. "The fire or the silence?"

Her hand pressed to her forehead. She didn't answer. Her own silence spoke louder than anything.

I went to the window. The glow still pulsed faintly over the rooftops. Smoke spiraled upward, curling into the night sky like a signal no one wanted to read.

And then memory surged, not softened by time but sharpened, as if the fire outside had lit it up again.

I was seven. Standing on the curb as the orphanage burned. The night choked with ash, kerosene, screams muffled under crackling beams. The air seared my throat. I remembered the coughing of children, sharp and desperate. I remembered their cries. It was the sound of helplessness, etched into bone.

And Mr. Murphy, arms folded, jaw set, refusing to move the water truck he owned. He had the only working one in town, but he wouldn't budge. "Liability," he said. "Not my problem."

I remembered tugging on my father's sleeve, begging him to do something, anything. He hushed me, eyes fixed on the fire, voice steady and sanctimonious: "It's in God's hands now."

God's hands. That's what he always said. A man of faith, they called him. To me, he was a man who let children burn and called it holy.

He left me there, standing on the curb, while he went to "soothe" the town. His voice carried over the smoke, preaching calm while the walls collapsed and flames devoured everything inside. Beds. Toys. Books. Children. By morning, nothing left but ash.

And now Murphy's store was gone too.

Coincidence? This town adored coincidence. It wrapped denial in ribbons and called it tradition. But my skin prickled with the truth.

Graffiti. A shed fire. Brake failures. Now this. Each one a candle, each one pointing back.

The orphanage.

I tried once more to participate, to belong. I lit a candle at home, set it carefully in the kitchen window. Told myself it was for peace. Told myself this was what normal people did. The wick sputtered, gave off a thread of smoke, then died in seconds.

Figures. Even the wax didn't believe me.

The fourth candle hadn't lit hope. It had lit a pattern.

And maybe I was the only one willing to see it.

CHAPTER 5

Shadows of the Fire

The house carried the smell of laundry detergent and lemon polish, but it couldn't mask the heaviness in the air. My mother folded clothes at the kitchen table with the precision of someone trying to fold herself shut. Every towel was creased sharp, every sheet tucked perfectly, as if neatness could keep the nightmares from spilling out.

I made tea and slid into the chair across from her. The mug warmed my hands, but the chill in the room didn't ease.

"You didn't sleep," I said.

She pressed her lips together. "I did."

"Then the shadows under your eyes are just festive?"

Her hands stilled. She smoothed a towel once more, though it didn't need it. "Nightmares."

The word was so quiet I almost thought I'd imagined it.

I leaned forward. "About what?"

Her jaw worked, her eyes flickering as though weighing whether she could trust me with the truth. At last, she whispered, "The fire."

The room seemed to constrict. It wasn't often she acknowledged it—none of them did. The fire lived in shadows, half-buried under hymns and casseroles, dragged out only when the town needed a reminder of how much it had survived.

"You've never talked about it," I said carefully.

"There's nothing to talk about."

"Mother." I softened my voice. "People died. Children. Pretending doesn't make that vanish."

She flinched as though I'd slapped her. "I see them," she said suddenly, voice cracking. "In the smoke. In the windows. Reaching."

The kettle hissed in the silence. I reached across the table and touched her hand. She didn't pull away, but she didn't hold on either.

"What else do you see?"

Her eyes snapped up to mine. For a moment, the dam looked ready to break. Then she said, very quietly: "Your father knew more than he told me."

The words landed like glass shattering between us.

I froze. "What do you mean?"

Her mouth opened, then closed. She shook her head hard, as if trying to shake the words loose from reality. "Nothing. Forget it."

"Forget it?" I laughed, but it sounded bitter. "You can't throw that out and expect me to just move on. What did he know?"

"I don't know."

"You just said—"

"I don't know!" she snapped, the sound sharp enough to echo against the walls. Immediately her face crumpled, ashamed of her own outburst. She lowered her gaze. "I only know…he wasn't the man everyone thought. He carried sins with him. More than sermons and smiles could cover."

Her voice trembled. I stared at her, trying to read what she wasn't saying. The mother I'd grown up with rarely let a word slip if she didn't mean to. If she had cracked this far, there was more underneath.

The silence stretched until it felt suffocating.

I pulled my hand back. "Then maybe it's time I found out what those sins were."

Her head jerked up, eyes narrowing in fear. "Hannah, don't—"

"Don't what? Ask questions? Look at what's right in front of us?"

"You don't understand."

"No," I said. "I think I do. People have spent years burying this, and it's still rotting underneath. Maybe that's why everything is falling apart now—because someone decided it's time to dig it back up."

She pressed her palm to her forehead, as if the weight of it all was too much. "You don't know what you're saying."

But I did.

Later, when I tried to distract myself by stringing a few pitiful garlands around the living room, even that betrayed me. The lights sputtered and blinked unevenly, mocking my attempt at cheer. The tinsel looked cheap, like it knew it was a stand-in for joy.

I stared at the artificial pine branches, at the ornaments that still smelled faintly of cardboard after decades in their boxes and thought about all the Christmas mornings my father had preached about hope while hiding the rot underneath. I remembered the way he'd gather us around the fire, his voice smooth and measured, saying, "The light always drives out the dark."

But I was old enough now to know better. Sometimes the light just revealed what was hiding.

And it wasn't just him that had stolen faith from me. My work had done its share too.

I had held children's hands as their heart rhythms slid into chaos on the monitor. I had shouted "push one of epi!" while a mother sobbed into her coat in the hallway. I had pressed my palms against tiny chests, counting compressions, until sweat ran down my back and still—flatline. Pupils fixed. Code called. Time of death: 02:17.

Tell me where the light was in that.

Tell me how to pray after carrying those bodies to their parents, after handing them loss wrapped in blankets.

Faith wasn't stolen in a single night. It was eroded, grain by grain, by the silence of God in rooms filled with the sound of alarms.

Now it was my father's legacy and my own nights on the ward braided together, twisting tighter, choking whatever belief had once lived in me.

That thought followed me upstairs later, sticking like a burr: there was more to the orphanage fire than anyone admitted. More than the sermons, the handshakes, the hollow reassurances. My father's sins weren't only his. The whole town carried the guilt.

And if no one else would face it, then maybe I would.

It wasn't a plan yet, just the shape of one. A direction. A resolve.

But it was enough.

The Fifth Candle

December fifth arrived brittle and gray, the kind of day where sound carried too far, too sharp.

By evening the square looked like a stage set dressed in desperation. More lights than ever had been strung across the lampposts, over the church roof, looped through every tree that would hold still. Frost glittered on the wires like tinsel, but instead of making the scene magical, it made it fragile, as though the whole square could shatter under the wrong breath.

Children shuffled their boots on the frozen cobblestones, their laughter pitched too high, their movements stiff as if they'd been warned to behave. Parents gripped their hands tighter than usual. Everyone smiled, but the smiles were strained, fixed, like masks starting to crack at the edges.

The choir gathered in their heavy coats, clutching songbooks as if scripture alone could anchor them. Their voices rose, but even from the first line, it wavered.

Keep the watch, keep the flame; ashes tell the sinner's name.

The line rang across the square, cold as sleet. I could feel the crowd stiffen, the way you feel a body go rigid under your hand before the seizure starts. My stomach knotted. Whoever had written that graffiti knew exactly what they were doing. They'd turned an old carol into a weapon, and now every verse landed like a threat.

The new pastor, Lewis, barely older than me, with the perpetually distracted air of a man who'd rather be grading papers than saving souls—stood off to the side. He offered a polite smile, clapped at the right times, but his eyes never lifted from his watch. My father would have been at the center, booming his way through every verse, commanding the town to believe in his version of light. This one just looked like he wanted to get home.

Mayor Evelyn stepped forward, flawless in fur trim, her voice trained for reassurance. "Tonight, we light the fifth candle, a symbol of faith, of hope, of Greenridge standing together."

Applause fluttered, thin as paper, already dying before it could build.

Sheriff Collins stood stiffly near the edge of the crowd, scanning faces with the grim patience of a man waiting for a drunk uncle to ruin Christmas dinner. His hand never strayed far from the radio at his belt.

The fifth candle was lit, flame steady despite the wind. The people clapped, because not clapping would have meant admitting they were afraid.

But something had shifted. I felt it immediately. People's eyes slid away when they passed me. Conversations clipped short as I walked by. A woman from the pastry shop, who used to press an extra cookie into my hand when I was a kid, pretended not to see me. Another woman crossed herself quickly when I got too close.

And then I heard it. A whisper just loud enough to sting.

"Her father."

Another voice, tight with disapproval: "Mark's girl."

The words rippled through the crowd, bouncing back and forth like sleigh bells with the clappers knocked out. They weren't looking at me, but they didn't have to. Every whisper felt like a finger pressed between my shoulder blades, reminding me whose daughter I was.

Beside me, my mother stood rigid, chin lifted, eyes locked on the flames. Her posture said she didn't hear a thing. But I knew better. She heard every syllable. She just refused to give them the satisfaction of seeing her break.

By the time the ritual ended, and people dispersed with their paper cups of cocoa, my chest ached from biting back retorts. I wanted to scream at them: Yes, my father was a sinner. Maybe worse. But so are you. Instead, I carried their silence like a stone in my gut.

We walked home through streets strung with lights. Every decoration mocked me. Plastic reindeer with bulb-glowing noses, cheerful wreaths with velvet bows, windows filled with nativity scenes so tidy they looked staged for catalogues. I used to love those sights as a child, craning my neck to take in each glittering detail. Now they all looked cheap. Paper-thin armor against rot.

For a moment, I tried to summon one good memory. One Christmas where my father wasn't a fraud, where the hymns actually felt holy. But every memory I reached for twisted in my hands. Even the night he read the Nativity story aloud, his voice smooth and commanding, I could see the way he glanced at the clock, eager for the applause of the midnight mass. He gave himself to the town first. We were an afterthought.

Back home, we drank cocoa in silence. My mother excused herself early, retreating upstairs as though she could outrun the whispers that had followed us home.

I sat by the window, mug cooling in my hands. That was when I heard it—light, quick, like a child's step on the porch.

I set the mug down and opened the door.

At first, there was nothing. Just the sharp night air, pine needles scratching against the eaves. Then I looked down.

A small shoe sat on the welcome mat. Scuffed leather, lace broken. A child's shoe.

For a long moment, I just stared. My pulse thudded in my ears. Then I crouched and reached for it.

The instant I touched it, the spiders came. Hundreds of them, spilling from the hollow like a living tide. They poured over the boards, their legs a frantic tapping rhythm that sounded like static.

I stumbled back, nearly tripping over the threshold. The shoe dangled from my hand as my skin crawled. I shook it hard, and something slipped free—a folded scrap of paper.

Heart hammering, I kicked the last of the spiders into the snow, their dark shapes disappearing into the cracks of the porch. Then I unfolded the note.

The handwriting was jagged, but worse than that, it was identical to the graffiti sprayed across the church wall days ago. The same block letters, sharp and purposeful. Whoever wrote this wasn't hiding. They wanted me to know it was the same hand.

It read:

Keep the watch, keep the flame. Ashes tell the sinner's name. The fifth light burns for debt unpaid.

The words blurred as my vision narrowed. I looked at the shoe again. Worn, the leather cracked. It was the kind the orphans had been given, lined up in pairs by the door like soldiers waiting inspection.

That old memory tore through me once again. Seven years old, standing on the curb, choking on smoke as the orphanage burned. I saw their shoes in the windows, dangling from tiny feet. I remembered tugging on my father's sleeve, begging him to do something. His hand pressing down on mine, his voice smooth: "Hush, Hannah. It's in God's hands."

But he hadn't looked stricken. He'd looked resigned.

I hated him for that. Hated him for leaving me with the sound of children crying in the flames. Hated him more for how the town still treated him as a savior afterward.

And now, decades later, I was still paying for his sins.

This wasn't gossip. This wasn't coincidence. This was deliberate.

The town thought the debt was mine now. His daughter. His legacy.

I dropped the shoe back onto the porch. It left a dark indent in the snow, a hollow print like a ghost refusing to vanish.

I should have been terrified. And maybe I was. But beneath the fear was something colder. A certainty.

The fifth light burns for debt unpaid.

Not his debt. Mine.

If the fire left ghosts behind, they weren't his to haunt. They were mine now.

CHAPTER 6

The Files and Mrs. Caldwell

The attic had always smelled like cedar and sermons. A cramped space under a slanted roof, half storage and half shrine. Dust clung to the rafters, stirred into clouds when I pulled the chain for the single bulb. It flickered weakly before settling into a tired amber glow that turned everything the color of old parchment.

Boxes sat stacked like pews, lined up in careful rows. Old Christmas decorations filled one corner, plastic holly sprigs with brittle leaves, tinsel half crushed in their boxes, a porcelain nativity scene with Joseph's nose chipped clean off. My mother must have shoved them up here after my father died. He had always treated the season like holy theater, every ornament placed with priestly precision. Now the relics of his devotion were covered in dust, the baby Jesus wrapped in last year's newspaper.

But I was not here for Christmas.

I crossed to the far corner where a trunk rested beneath two crooked hymnals. The metal latch resisted, but not well. One twist with a screwdriver from the tool jar by the stairs and it gave way with a tired sigh.

Inside lay his life in paper form. Manila folders in neat, suffocating order. Sermons. Council minutes. Correspondence. Dozens of them, labeled in my father's blocky handwriting. His priesthood archived, filed, and forgotten.

I pulled one out at random. Advent Homily, 1997. Beneath the title, his familiar scrawl underlined three times. The light drives out the dark. I pushed it aside.

Another folder. Then another. And then I saw Mrs. Caldwell's name.

My pulse stumbled. I opened it.

Letters spilled into my lap. Thin, yellowed pages typed on a machine that must have rattled through a hundred prayers and warnings. Caldwell's words were crisp even through age. Each letter was addressed to the council, each one begging for the same thing, repairs for the orphanage.

The wiring in the west wing shorts frequently. I worry for the safety of the children.

Several alarms are broken; replacements needed before winter.

The back stairwell exit remains locked due to a warped frame. This could trap us in case of emergency.

Each note was clinical, desperate, detailed. Every sentence sounded like she was pleading through paper.

And there, in the margins, my father's handwriting. Tight. Dismissive.

Deferred. Not urgent. Handled.

Handled. The same back exit Caldwell said was sealed shut. The alarms that never worked. The wiring she begged them to fix before Christmas.

He had read these. He had known. And that Christmas, he had stood in the pulpit preaching that the children were safe in God's hands.

I stared at the pages until the words blurred. My throat burned. The papers trembled in my grip. The man who had lectured me about grace could not be bothered to fight for a fire alarm.

No wonder Mrs. Caldwell cracked in the square. No wonder her eyes were haunted. She was not crazy. She was guilty. And so was he.

I stacked the letters carefully, lined them up, slid them back into the folder, then held it against my chest for a long moment. The pages felt warm from my palms, like they were alive. Evidence. Confession. A sermon he never gave.

The bulb above me buzzed, flickered, then steadied into a faint hum. I shoved the folder into my bag, climbed down the ladder, and closed the attic hatch behind me.

Downstairs, the air was heavy with cinnamon. My mother had left a candle burning in the kitchen again, her attempt to sweeten the cold. I paused in the doorway, watching the flame tremble in its glass jar. For a second, I thought about showing her what I had found. About forcing the truth into daylight. But then I saw her in my mind, her hands folded at the table, eyes hollow with old devotion, and I stopped. She already knew. Maybe not the details, but enough.

So, I put on my coat and stepped into the cold instead.

The air outside had the clean bite of a new blade. The sky was washed gray; the kind of color that makes the town look honest. I walked to the end of the porch and rested my hands on the rail. The wood was cold enough to sting my palms through the gloves. Across the street, a neighbor's inflatable snowman nodded in the wind like he was trying to agree with everyone at once. Greenridge loved a mascot. It saved people from having to be one.

I stood there and let the cold set the edges of my thoughts. The letters in my bag pressed against my hip like a heartbeat. I could feel the shape of my father's script through the folder. Deferred. Not urgent. Handled. Three little verdicts that had grown up into a tragedy.

The house behind me hummed softly. My mother moved in the kitchen with that careful choreography she used for everything, cupboard, kettle, cup, sugar, stir. She had a way of making tiny rituals stand in for courage. When I was a child, it looked like devotion. As an adult I saw it for what it was, a life built out of the smallest choices because the big ones had already been decided for her.

A memory rose before I could push it away. I was eight, maybe nine. He was rewriting his sermon at the dining room table because a deacon had corrected him on a date in front of the choir. He had smiled through it and come home brittle. Mom set a bowl of soup in front of him and said the smallest thing, that it would be all right, that people forget details. He lifted his eyes slow and flat, then went quiet. That quiet was worse than yelling. It felt like a pressure drop before a storm. She folded the dish towel and refolded it and refolded it until her fingers trembled. Later she apologized to him for making light of his work. He accepted. He always accepted. She brought him coffee, and he did not look at her when he took it.

I had watched the whole scene from the stairwell with a stuffed rabbit pressed to my chest, trying to figure out which words in the house were safe and which ones came with a cost. Afterward she climbed the stairs and found me there and said that sometimes peace is the right choice even when truth is nearby. I did not understand what she meant. I thought truth was always right. That was before I learned about church politics and fundraising and men who were soft in public and stone in private.

Another memory found its way back. I was sixteen and had stayed out later than curfew because my friend's father had a heart scare and we followed the ambulance to the hospital. I came home raw with adrenaline and grief. He waited in the living room with a Bible open, the ribbon marking a verse about obedience. He did not ask where I had been. He told me what the rules were. Mom stood by the doorway, hands tucked into her sleeves like they were cold, and she nodded along. Later she sat on the edge of my bed and smoothed my hair and whispered that she knew I had a good heart. I asked her why she had not said anything downstairs. She said there are moments when your words only make the fire hotter. I stared at her and felt something important tilt. I did not want to be the kind of person who chose a quiet room over a right thing.

The wind shifted and brought me the scent of our neighbor's dryer vent, lavender and heat, a domestic miracle. My cheeks ached from the cold. My eyes stung for a reason that was not the wind.

Mom opened the front door. She peeked out like she was worried the air would bite her. She had tucked her cardigan tight around her and pulled a scarf over her hair. She held a mug of tea by the rim so she would not burn her fingers. That was her all over. She knew where to hold a thing so it would not hurt, even if it meant her hands looked awkward.

"You should wear a hat," she said.

"I am all right." My voice came out soft and wrong.

She stepped onto the porch and stood beside me. We watched a pickup glide down the street like a ship on a quiet sea. The driver lifted a few fingers off the wheel in that small town salute that says I see you and that is enough for now.

"You have been in the attic," she said.

I looked at her. "Yes."

Something in her face shuttered and then opened again. Not surprise. Not even fear. The expression of someone who hears a truth she has been avoiding and recognizes it like an old hymn.

"It is a mess up there," she said, pointless as a towel in a flood.

"He kept everything," I said.

"He believed record keeping was a virtue." She tried a smile, and it failed. "We are good at records in this town."

I wanted to lift the bag and show her the letters and the marginalia and the sentences that added up to a failure of duty, but I also wanted to protect her from the thing she had refused to look at for twenty years. Those two wants pushed on each other inside my chest until I felt bruised.

"You know," I said.

She flinched. It was so small I might have missed it if I had not lived on these nerves since childhood. "I know what kind of man he was," she said.

"That is not the same as knowing what he did."

Her eyes filled and then cleared. She looked over the porch rail like the street might help her choose. "He served the town," she said. "He kept things steady. People needed that."

"People also needed working fire alarms," I said.

She pressed her lips together and I saw a decision hover over her like a moth over a flame. "Do not make me say out loud what you want me to say," she whispered. "If I say it, I cannot forgive him later."

The honesty of that almost knocked me back a step. I wanted to argue. I wanted to shake her. I wanted to tell her that forgiveness that requires ignorance is not forgiveness, it is surrender dressed for church. But I also knew the part of her that had been a girl in a pew

53

believing a man at a pulpit and how hard it is to unwind a belief that grew into the shape of your spine.

"You are not stupid," I said, and my voice broke. "You were never stupid. You saw. You always saw."

"I saw." She nodded and kept nodding, as if the motion could keep her upright. "I also wanted a life that was calm. I am not brave like you."

The words landed like a bad diagnosis, accurate and cruel. I stared at her and hated the part of me that wanted her to transform right here on the porch into someone who would march with me to the mayor's office with the files in our hands and shame on our tongues. I hated that I wanted to rewrite her when she had been written by a lifetime I did not have to live. Letting go of that desire felt like tearing a bandage off a wound that never closed.

"I do not know if I am brave," I said. "I am just angry."

She gave a tired little laugh. "Anger can look like bravery from a distance."

We stood without speaking. A crow hopped across the neighbor's roofline, black against the gray. The world held still.

There had been other times I tried to change her. I remembered a night in college when I came home for winter break and made a speech about boundaries at the kitchen table. I told her she did not have to host the deacons every Sunday afternoon for three hours of small talk and backdoor decisions. I told her she did not have to make three casseroles for funerals where the widower had said something ugly to her in the receiving line. I told her she did not have to pretend she liked the woman who whispered about our family into her glove at the grocery store. She listened. She made me a grilled cheese. The next Sunday she laid out cookies in the church hall like a general stocking a supply line. She was not stupid. She was tired and trained.

I took a breath that hurt my ribs. "I want to fix you," I said, because honesty deserved at least one clear line. "I want to push you into saying what you know. I want to snap you out of that old church in your head."

"I know," she said. She slid her arm through mine and rested her head against my shoulder the way she used to when I was little, and we watched storms from the same porch. "And I want you not to have to carry what I could not."

A car door slammed a street away. The sound echoed against the houses like a gavel.

"You cannot change me," she said finally. "And I cannot change who he was. We can only decide what we do next."

I closed my eyes and let the truth land. Letting go felt like stepping off a curb you thought was a stair. There was a jolt and then there was balance.

"Next," I said, and opened my eyes. "I take these letters to someone who will not pretend they are old business."

Her face pulled tight. "The sheriff."

"Maybe." I thought of Collins and his careful eyes and his allegiance to order, not truth. "Or the mayor. Or both. And then the paper, and then the whole state if I have to."

She made the smallest sound, half fear and half relief. "Will you be careful," she asked, "even if you are brave?"

"I will try," I said. "Trying is what I have."

We went back inside because our fingers had gone numb. In the kitchen the candle had burned a small moat around its wick. She poured tea and I watched the steam rise. We did not talk about the letters again, but the knowledge sat between us like a third-place setting at the table. Not hostile. Not welcome. Real.

After tea I carried the bag to my room and set it on the desk. The folder inside it felt heavier than paper. I opened it again, as if the words might be different in this light. They were the same. Deferred. Not urgent. Handled. A trinity of negligence.

I copied the dates into my notebook, one by one, because writing makes things true for me in a way thinking does not. I marked the earliest letter. I marked the last one before the fire. I underlined the sentence about the locked back stairwell until the ink bled a little and made a dark pool at the tail of the final letter.

A sound drifted up from the street, the faint ring of a bicycle bell even though there was too much ice for riding. It made no sense, which meant it belonged here. I rubbed the heel of my hand over my eyes and let my shoulders drop. Anger had carried me up the ladder. It would not carry me forever. I would need something steadier. Not the kind of faith my father sold, glossy and loud. A quieter one that still told the truth.

I closed the folder and slid it back into the bag. The zipper caught for a second, then moved. When I looked up, the mirror above the desk held my reflection. I looked like my father around the eyes. I hated that. I looked like my mother around the mouth. I loved that, and it hurt.

I sat there a long time, listening to the house. Pipes clicked in the walls. The furnace exhaled. The candle in the kitchen went out with a soft chuff that sounded like a body giving up a last breath.

I stood and picked up the bag. I felt the ache of wanting to save someone who did not want to be saved and the equal ache of deciding to love her anyway. Both aches belonged to me. I would carry them along with the letters and the truth inside them. I would carry them to the square tonight when the sixth candle burned. I would carry them until a person with power had to choose between pretending and speaking.

In the hallway his photograph waited. I did not look away this time. I looked straight at him and said what my mother could not. You were wrong. And now I am going to tell it.

The house did not move. The light outside thinned to a winter blue. I put on my coat again. I tucked the bag under my arm. I went down the stairs and out into the cold.

The Sixth Candle

56

The sky hung low and gray by the time I reached the square. The Christmas market was half asleep, stalls shuttered until nightfall. I walked past the post office, my bag heavy against my side, and caught sight of a small, bent figure near the curb.

Mrs. Caldwell.

Her white hair whipped in the wind. One mitten dangled from her wrist, the other gone entirely. Her coat was buttoned wrong, collar twisted. She shuffled along the sidewalk, muttering, her grocery bag swinging in rhythm.

People glanced her way, then quickly looked elsewhere. Kindness in Greenridge had limits, and she'd long since crossed them.

I slowed as I came closer.

"We told them," she whispered. Her voice rasped like brittle paper. "We told them. They never listened."

Her words hit me harder than the cold. The same phrases were burned into those letters upstairs—typed warnings, pleading for repairs, ignored by men who claimed holiness.

I wanted to stop, to tell her I'd read everything, that I believed her. But when I opened my mouth, nothing came out. She clutched her bag and moved on, muttering the same litany like prayer beads. We told them. We told them.

A carol drifted from the church tower. Hark the Herald Angels Sing. The notes were too bright, too forced, scraping against the wind.

I turned away. The lights strung across the shops blinked like anxious eyes. A child's laughter rang out, sharp and brief, before being swallowed by the cold.

By the time I reached home, I felt the weight of the attic pressing on my back.

***

That evening, the town gathered again.

The square glowed like an over-dressed stage, strings of lights sagging under the frost. People huddled close, breath fogging the air. If the town thought enough brightness could erase the past, they were wrong.

Mayor Evelyn appeared in her crimson coat, hair lacquered into obedience, smile sharp enough to slice through glass. "We come together," she said, her voice amplified through the microphone, "to honor our faith and our hope."

Hope again. The town's favorite word.

Sheriff Collins stood off to the side, arms crossed, eyes restless. He scanned the crowd the way a man looks for fire he can't see yet.

The choir lined up, voices shivering in their scarves. They sang the next verse of that eerie carol.

Keep the watch, keep the flame; ashes tell the sinner's name.

The words crawled up my spine. Not a hymn anymore. A threat.

"Three, two, one," Evelyn counted.

The sixth candle flared to life, tall and steady despite the wind. For a moment the flame bent sideways, then straightened as if daring anyone to blink.

Applause followed, brittle and delayed. The sound of people pretending everything was fine. My mother's mitten found my hand, her grip trembling. Her pulse raced like a trapped bird.

We stayed for cocoa, for conversation that meant nothing, for the polite choreography of normal life. But the warmth never reached anyone's eyes.

By midnight, shouting tore through the quiet.

I was halfway to sleep when it started. A crash, voices, then the sharp edge of sirens. I threw on my coat and followed the sound, boots slipping on frost. The air reeked of smoke long before I reached the school lot.

A small crowd had gathered near the chain-link fence. Mrs. Thomas—Mia, the new nurse—stood beside her car, hands over her mouth. The vehicle was ruined. Tires slashed. Windshield shattered.

The back seat stuffed with hymn books, each one torn, shredded, and set alight.

Ash floated through the air like snow. The smell of burned leather and paper filled my lungs.

People whispered.

"Kids."

"Mischief."

"Too much eggnog."

The same excuses. The same lies.

I moved closer. The hymnals weren't just burned—they were arranged. Laid in a ring before fire took them. This wasn't random. It was deliberate. Ritual.

Sheriff Collins barked orders, but even he looked unsettled. Mrs. Thomas sobbed quietly while someone draped a blanket around her shoulders.

My gaze caught on the charred paper. A verse still legible near the edge of the circle: Light the way, though shadows stay.

And then it clicked.

Back in the attic, in the margins of my father's notes, I'd seen a name: Councilman Thomas. Mia's father. One of the men who voted against the orphanage repairs. His signature lay beneath the word Denied.

Now, decades later, his daughter's car sat in ashes.

This wasn't vandalism. It was accounting.

Each incident, each fire, each act of destruction—it wasn't chaos. It was a list being checked, one by one.

The sixth candle burned in the square, but its twin had already been lit here.

I stood among the onlookers, coat drawn tight, heart thudding like it wanted out.

Because for the first time, I realized this wasn't about haunting the town.

It was about reckoning.

And I was standing right in the middle of it.

CHAPTER 7

Echoes or Illusions

The morning broke with the kind of gray light that made the whole town look like it had been dipped in ash. The snow from the night before had hardened into a slick crust, and everything beyond the kitchen window shimmered dull and lifeless. The kettle had stopped whistling ten minutes ago. My tea sat cooling in front of me, the thin skin forming on top like a second silence.

I had been sitting there for over an hour, staring into it, waiting for the thoughts to line up in some way that made sense. They never did.

Because they weren't thoughts. They were ghosts.

I'd been seven the night the orphanage burned. Seven, standing barefoot on the curb with smoke in my hair and fear in my lungs, clutching the hem of my coat in hands too small to do anything. People always said children forget things, that the mind protects itself by blurring the sharp edges. But some memories stay bright. Some are carved deep enough that even time can't sand them down.

The first thing I remembered was the sound. Fire didn't roar like they said in books. It screamed. It shrieked when it hit wood, when it devoured air, when it reached the parts of the building that still held life. I remembered that sound, rising and falling like a choir gone mad. I remembered the windows glowing white-hot before shattering, sending shards across the snow.

And I remembered the voices.

Children crying. Coughing. Screaming. Then silence, sudden and absolute.

That was when I saw him.

Murphy.

He had been standing near his truck, the one with the water tank mounted on the back. His arms were folded, his face lit by the fire, and behind him the tank glinted, full. He could have helped. He could have done something.

Even as a child, I had known that.

And I had heard him. His voice cutting through the crackle and chaos, flat and calm.

"Not my problem."

It had haunted me for years, that moment. It sat behind every sermon my father ever gave about sin and mercy. It whispered behind every Christmas carol that filled this town like perfume over rot.

But lately, I wasn't sure anymore.

Had I really heard him say it? Or had I written the words into the memory myself after finding my father's files?

Because there it was, in black ink, in my father's hand.

"Murphy refuses liability."

"Water truck not available."

Those lines sat in the margins beside Caldwell's letters, and his handwriting was as certain as ever. My father didn't make mistakes. He wrote the truth he wanted others to believe.

But my memory—the child standing in the dark, the sound of those words—was too vivid to be fiction. And that was the problem. The closer I looked at the past, the less I trusted myself.

What if the town had been right all along? What if I was inventing patterns where there were none?

I rubbed my hands over my face, pressing my palms to my eyes until stars bloomed behind them.

But then again...

Murphy's store had burned last week. Thomas' daughter's car had been destroyed. The hymnals blackened to ash.

Coincidence was the word Greenridge liked best. It excused everything. But this town didn't deserve coincidence.

And lately, I had begun to wonder something darker.

What if I was next?

61

The list of names in my father's files was long. Most were men who had signed their names under words like "Denied" and "Deferred." Many of them were already gone—some dead, others ruined, others punished in quieter ways. But some were still alive.

And here I was. The daughter of the man who had let it all happen. The one who wrote the denials. The one who smiled from the pulpit while the orphanage fell apart.

If vengeance had finally come for Greenridge, then I was not exempt.

The thought crawled cold and steady beneath my ribs.

Upstairs, I heard my mother moving. The floorboards creaked in the same rhythm they had all my life, two steps and a pause, the sound of her body deciding whether it had enough strength to face the day. I listened to drawers open, the faint clatter of jewelry, the squeak of the wardrobe door. When she came down, her scarf was already tied, her tote bag slung over one shoulder like armor.

She stopped short when she saw me.

"You look pale," she said, voice clipped but not unkind.

"I didn't sleep."

"Then rest," she said. "You'll make yourself sick."

She poured herself coffee, stirred it twice, and sat across from me. The silence between us stretched. Her hands trembled only slightly, but enough for me to notice. I wondered if she shook from age or guilt.

"Mother," I began carefully, "I found more files."

She froze mid-sip.

"Caldwell's letters," I continued. "All the ones about the orphanage—the alarms, the wiring, the locked stairwell. Father signed off on every denial."

Her lips pressed into a thin seam; the same one she used when she didn't want to lie but couldn't tell the truth.

"You knew," I said. My voice cracked in the middle, betraying me. "You've always known."

Her eyes dropped to her coffee. "Some things," she said quietly, "are buried for a reason."

The words hit like a door slamming. Final. Cold.

"You think burying it will keep us safe?" I snapped. "Look around you. Fires. Accidents. Vandalisms. People are paying, one by one. You think silence will save us?"

Her breath came out slow, almost steady. "You don't understand."

"I understand more than you think."

But she didn't look at me again. She tied her scarf tighter and stood. The chair legs scraped against the tile like a warning. Without another word, she left the house, her footsteps fading into the quiet.

The front door closed with the same soft finality she'd used my whole life.

I sat there for a long time, staring at her empty chair.

Then I stood.

If she wouldn't give me the truth, I'd take it.

Upstairs, I dragged the folders onto the bed, their edges rough against my hands. Dust rose in little golden clouds under the thin morning light. I spread them open, page by page, letter by letter, lining them up like bodies.

Murphy. Thomas. Peterson. Miller.

Each name written in the margins of my father's notes, each tied to some decision, some refusal. My pen dug into the paper as I copied them into my notebook, carving a list so sharp it almost cut through the page.

When I finished, I sat back and looked at it. A ledger of sin.

Murphy's store—gone.

Thomas' daughter's car—burned.

Frank Miller's car—tires slashed.

Coincidence had been murdered long ago.

I closed my notebook and rested my hand on it, feeling the pulse of my own heartbeat through the cover.

And the thought came again, quieter this time, but certain.

If someone was crossing names off this list, they would reach mine soon enough.

The house felt smaller suddenly, the air heavy. I looked around my old room, the wallpaper faded, the curtains drawn tight. It still smelled faintly of lemon polish and my father's books, that sharp mix of ink and old paper that never went away.

I pulled the curtain back and looked out the window. Across the street, Mrs. Keegan was sweeping her porch, pretending not to look toward the church. People in Greenridge didn't gossip. They observed. They stored. They waited.

And they remembered.

That was what scared me the most. Not what I didn't remember—but what I did.

The Seventh Candle

By evening, the snow had begun again. Thick, slow flakes drifted from the gray sky, falling with a kind of tired grace. The town square glowed from every direction, each lamppost draped in garlands and gold ribbon. The air held that false cheer that Greenridge was famous for, the kind that could make you forget what was rotting underneath if you didn't look too closely.

The choir had gathered beneath the platform, their scarves pulled tight, their breaths puffing in clouds as they tuned their voices. I stood a few rows back, close enough to feel the heat from the lamps, far enough to vanish into the crowd. My coat was zipped to my chin. My mother stood beside me, her hands folded, her posture rigid. She looked carved from marble, and the expression on her face was one I had seen a thousand times in church pews — reverent, obedient, unseeing.

The mayor's voice rose above the chatter. "Tonight, we light the seventh candle," she announced. "A symbol of perseverance and hope."

Hope. That word again. It had become a currency in this town, traded so cheaply that it no longer meant anything.

64

The choir began.

Keep the watch, keep the flame; ashes tell the sinner's name.

The words cut through the air like needles. Each verse fell heavier than the last. Even the children, usually squirming by now, were still. Only the snow moved, whispering down onto coats and hats, soft as dust on old bones.

When the seventh candle finally flared, it looked fragile, its flame bending under the wind. But then it steadied, strong and defiant. The crowd clapped, the sound hollow and rehearsed.

I clapped too, my gloves muffling the sound. Inside my pocket, my fingers brushed the folded list I carried everywhere now. The names burned against my palm like coals.

My mother clapped once, twice, then lowered her hands. Her face was still; her eyes fixed on the candle as if staring hard enough could undo the past.

Cocoa was passed around next — the same bitter mix every year, ladled from silver urns by volunteers with frozen smiles. Children darted between the stalls, laughing too loudly, their joy sharp-edged and wrong. The adults smiled because they were supposed to. Fear hung over the crowd like smoke no one wanted to name.

I turned to look at the church. Its stained-glass windows glowed softly, the colors blurring into gold and crimson halos. For a heartbeat, I imagined the orphanage still standing. The smell of soap and cinnamon rolls from Mrs. Caldwell's kitchen drifting down the hall. The echo of laughter, small feet thudding across the old floors. Then the image twisted, warped by heat and memory, until I saw flames again — swallowing curtains, licking up the walls, consuming everything that had once been innocent.

My throat tightened. I looked away.

"Are you all right?" my mother asked, her voice low.

I nodded. Lying came easily when she was watching.

We stayed until the mayor began her yearly speech about unity and faith. I couldn't listen. Her words floated on the cold air, empty, familiar. I slipped away before the applause.

The streets were quiet, the kind of quiet that pressed against your ears. My boots crunched softly against the ice. Every window I passed flickered with light; candles on sills, Christmas trees glowing behind curtains, families pretending everything was fine.

By the time I reached our house, my fingers were numb. Inside, the heat hit me too quickly, bringing that dizzy feeling between relief and guilt. I poured tea, but it cooled untouched again. Sleep came only in fragments.

When I woke, it wasn't to silence.

It was to shouting.

At first, I thought it was a dream; muffled voices, hurried footsteps, the echo of panic carried through the cold. But then the sound grew clearer, closer. I pulled on my coat and ran outside.

The air was sharp, biting through the layers. An orange glow pulsed against the clouds. I followed it down the street, my boots sliding on the slick ground.

By the time I reached the churchyard, half the town was already there. People stood in clumps, their faces lit by the fire. The nativity display — Greenridge's pride, rebuilt every December, Donahue's masterpiece — was burning.

The wooden manger had collapsed inward, sparks leaping into the night. Painted shepherds blistered and cracked. Mary's porcelain skin split down the middle, one arm snapping off as she toppled into the snow. Joseph's figure folded onto itself, blackened and empty. And the baby Jesus, so small, so perfect every year, lay buried in the ashes, his porcelain hand cracked clean away.

The smell of burning pine and paint filled the air, clinging to coats and hair, seeping into skin.

A child began to cry. Another screamed. Parents pulled them back, shielding their faces. Someone tried to start a prayer, their voice trembling, but it was drowned out by the crackling of fire and the hiss of melting snow.

"Kids," a man whispered behind me. "Some damn prank."

But no one believed it. The word prank hung there like an insult.

I moved closer, drawn by something I couldn't name. The heat hit my face, sharp and dry. I squinted through the smoke.

The arrangement was deliberate. Even beneath the ruin, I could see it. The figures had been placed just so — the manger centered perfectly, the flames consuming them in a pattern that radiated outward, as if someone had planned every inch of it.

It wasn't chaos. It was choreography.

And I recognized the craftsmanship beneath the ashes. The careful lines, the hand-sanded edges. Donahue's work. Always his work.

I saw his name in my father's files again — right beneath the word Denied.

A chill ran through me despite the fire.

Behind me, the sheriff barked orders. "Everyone step back! Keep back!"

His voice was steady, but his hands weren't. He waved for the volunteers to bring water, though he knew it was too late. Mayor Evelyn appeared beside him, her fur-trimmed coat gleaming in the firelight, her expression the same polished calm she wore at every disaster.

"It's under control," she said. Her tone was smooth, deliberate. "Everyone please return home."

No one moved.

The fire hissed louder, devouring what was left. The crowd's faces flickered between orange and white, fear carving lines deeper than age ever could.

I turned slowly, scanning the people gathered. Pastor stood near the back, his hands shoved in his coat pockets, his face unreadable. The Keegans whispered to each other, their eyes darting toward the church. The Doyles held each other, trembling.

And at the edge of it all, my mother.

Her scarf was pulled tight under her chin, her face pale as the snow falling around her. She met my eyes only once, but that was enough. There was no shock in her expression. Only understanding.

She knew this wasn't the end.

When the last embers finally died, people began to drift away, murmuring their theories into the dark. Kids. Drunks. Vandals. Satanists. Anything but the truth.

I stayed.

I stayed until the cold turned cruel, until my breath came in short, painful bursts. I stared at the smoking remains of the nativity, at the scorch marks spreading across the snow like black veins.

Someone had done this with purpose. With precision.

And if the pattern held — if every act was retribution — then Donahue's name was just one more crossed off the list.

The seventh candle had been lit in the square that night. Now this.

Two flames. Two acts of faith turned to ash.

When the crowd had gone, I circled the scene once more. The wind had died down, leaving only the faint crackle of cooling wood. My boots left prints in the snow that filled slowly behind me.

At the base of the church steps, I saw something half-buried. I crouched and brushed the snow away.

A scrap of paper. Soot-stained, the edges curled from heat.

It was a hymn.

Or what was left of one.

O come, O come, Emmanuel...

The ink had bled, but the handwriting wasn't printed. It was written — fast, urgent, familiar.

My father's.

My hand went cold.

The sheriff's voice carried behind me. "Miss Mark, you should get home. It's not safe out here."

I folded the paper quickly, slipping it into my pocket. "I'm fine," I said.

He hesitated, studying me. "You shouldn't be near this. Let us handle it."

"Like you handled the last fire?" I asked.

His jaw tightened. "You think I don't know what's happening?"

"I think you're pretending not to."

He stepped closer, lowering his voice. "You want to help? Then stop talking. Go home."

There was no kindness in his tone. Only exhaustion.

I left before I said something that would turn his exhaustion into anger.

The walk home felt endless. Snow drifted thicker, muffling the world into a soft hum. Every streetlight flickered. Every window glowed too warmly. The whole town looked peaceful from a distance, the kind of peace that made you forget what it cost.

By the time I reached the house, the clock had struck two. My mother was awake, sitting at the kitchen table with a blanket around her shoulders. The light was dim, her face pale, her eyes hollow.

"It was the nativity," I said quietly. She didn't flinch. Of course, she already knew.

"Donahue's work," I added. "He was on the council. He voted against the repairs."

Her eyes flicked toward me, then away. "You should sleep."

"How can you say that?"

"Because nothing good happens when you talk too much at night."

I laughed under my breath, sharp and humorless. "You sound just like him."

That got her attention. Her jaw tightened, but she didn't argue.

I leaned against the counter. "You knew this would happen, didn't you? You knew the past wouldn't stay buried."

Her voice came out low. "You think I wanted this? I lived under your father's roof. I learned what happens to people who speak too loudly."

There it was — the smallest crack in her armor.

For a second, I saw the woman she might have been once. Brave. Capable. Then the moment passed. She looked down at her hands, folded tightly in her lap.

"I kept quiet to survive," she said. "That's all."

I wanted to shake her, to make her see that silence was the same as complicity. But I didn't. I just nodded, because arguing with her felt like arguing with the wind.

Later, in bed, I unfolded the hymn page. The ink had smudged across my glove. I smoothed the paper, tracing the letters that still showed through the soot.

Rejoice, rejoice…

The same verse from the seventh carol.

69

Coincidence, the town would call it.

But I knew better.

The seventh candle had been lit that night.

And now another fire had followed.

Someone, somewhere, was keeping count.

And I had the sickening feeling that when the final candle burned, they would reach me.

CHAPTER 8

The Weight of Signatures

By the time dawn cracked through the curtains, the town felt hollowed out. The snow had turned to gray slush on Main Street, streaked with tire tracks and footprints that led nowhere. Every time I caught my reflection in a shop window, I also caught the way people's eyes slid off me like water over glass. Mothers pulled their children closer, and men lowered their voices mid-sentence. The baker, one of many who used to slip me extra gingerbread as a girl, stared so intently at his tray of pastries that his breath fogged the glass.

This time, I caught the whispers clearly, sharp as bells with the clappers knocked out.

"She's the pastor's daughter."

"She brought it with her."

"Ever since she came back…"

They weren't subtle anymore. It was like being circled by wolves that had stopped pretending to be sheep.

I clutched my bag tighter. Inside were the folders from the attic, Caldwell's letters, my father's rejections, the neat signatures in the margins. I'd spent half the night building a list in my notebook, line by line, in handwriting so tight it barely looked like mine. Murphy. Thomas. Donahue. The man from the power company. Every "accident" lined up perfectly with one of those names.

The pattern was obvious, to me. And only to me.

Everyone else walked around pretending. Pretending the fires were coincidences, the vandalism just mischief, the fear just winter blues. Either they were blind or they chose to be. Both options were equally infuriating.

And underneath all that, another question itched at me. My memories—seven years old, the night of the fire, the smell of smoke and soap—were tangled with the lines in my father's files. I could see Murphy's face in my head, the glow of the orphanage flames reflected in his eyes, but maybe I'd invented that. Maybe I'd filled in the blanks to make sense of what no one else would explain.

The more I read, the less I trusted what I remembered. But if I was going to understand, I needed someone who'd lived through it, someone who wouldn't hide behind sermons or small-town niceties.

So, I went to the sheriff.

***

The station squatted at the edge of town, the bricks weathered and stained by years of frost and smoke. Inside, the air smelled of burnt coffee and cleaning solution. A radio murmured from somewhere down the hall, the low hum of a town trying to sound calm. Sheriff Collins sat behind his desk, papers scattered in front of him, a pen balanced behind his ear.

He looked up when I entered, his brow creasing. "Miss Mark." He stood, smoothing the front of his shirt. "You don't usually stop by."

"I didn't plan to," I said. "But I couldn't sleep."

He gestured toward a chair. "Sit. You look like you've seen a ghost."

"Maybe I have." I sat down, my bag heavy against my knees. "I've been reading my father's files."

His eyes flickered to the bag. "Dangerous hobby," he said, trying for a joke.

"It's not a hobby." I leaned forward. "It's a reckoning."

He studied me for a moment before asking quietly, "What did you find?"

"Letters from Mrs. Caldwell," I said. "Dozens of them. She begged for repairs—the alarms, the wiring, the stairwell that wouldn't open. And every one of you signed off on the denials. My father, you, Councilman Thomas, Donahue and many more. You all knew how unsafe it was."

His smile faded. "That was a long time ago."

"Children died," I said. "That doesn't expire."

His jaw flexed. He leaned back in his chair, folding his arms across his chest. "You don't know what it was like back then. There were budget meetings, inspections. The orphanage wasn't just the church's responsibility; it was the whole council's."

"I know what I've read," I said, my voice rising. "I've seen his notes. 'Deferred.' 'Handled.' 'Not urgent.' He wrote those words in his own hand. You expect me to believe you didn't notice?"

Collins slammed his palm on the desk. The sound cracked through the room like a gunshot. "Watch it," he said. "You're talking about a man who did more for this town than most people combined."

"He did more for its image," I shot back. "He preached charity on Sundays and ignored the letters that could've saved lives."

For a long moment, neither of us spoke. The clock on the wall ticked like a countdown.

Finally, Collins exhaled, his voice low. "You think you're the first to ask those questions? I asked them, too. Back then."

That stopped me. "You what?"

He rubbed the bridge of his nose. "I was deputy then. Younger than you are now. I filed reports, asked questions, but the council didn't want a scandal. The priest's name carried more weight than mine. I was told to keep my mouth shut. So, I did."

He looked up, and for the first time, I saw something in his eyes that wasn't just defensiveness. Regret. Maybe shame.

"And now?" I asked.

He shrugged. "Now there's no proof left. No files that'll hold up. No witnesses people will believe."

73

"I don't need proof," I said. "I just need the truth."

"Truth won't help you here." His voice dropped lower. "This town doesn't survive on truth, Hannah. It survives on forgetting."

"Then maybe it doesn't deserve to survive."

His eyes snapped to mine, sharp and searching. "Be careful saying things like that."

"Why?"

"Because people here are already scared. And scared people look for someone to blame. Your father's not around anymore, which makes you the next best thing."

I felt the words like a shove to the chest. "You think I don't know that?"

He sighed, leaning forward. "Look. I'm not saying you're wrong. I'm saying you need to tread lightly. Whatever's happening—fires, accidents, vandalism—it's stirring up more than you realize. You think you're hunting the truth, but maybe someone's hunting you."

The words hung between us. He didn't seem to mean them as a threat, but they landed like one anyway.

I stood. "Then you'd better figure out who it is before another person ends up dead."

"Hannah—"

But I was already halfway to the door.

Outside, the air bit hard against my face. The sky hung low, pressing down on the rooftops like a lid. I pulled my coat tighter and started walking. The sheriff's warning echoed in my ears, but I didn't want to believe it. He'd sounded almost sincere—and that scared me more than if he'd laughed in my face.

The snow was falling again, thin flakes twisting in the wind. The main street stretched quiet and gray, the shopfronts still shuttered. I turned toward the long road leading home, boots crunching in the slush.

Halfway down, I saw a figure standing outside the church. For a second, I thought it was Collins somehow, but when the man turned, I recognized the collar. Pastor Lewis.

He was younger than I remembered, barely out of his thirties, with a kind of fragile confidence that came from sermons more than life experience. His breath misted in the cold as he smiled at me, uncertain but eager, like a man who still believed small talk could fix anything.

"Miss Mark," he called. "I was hoping to see you."

I hesitated, then walked closer. "You saw me last night," I said.

He laughed lightly, rubbing his hands together. "Yes, well, I was hoping to see you properly. The ceremony… it was quite something, wasn't it?"

"That's one word for it."

His smile wavered. "You think it's connected, don't you? The fires, the vandalism. People are saying—"

"People always say things," I interrupted. "Especially when they don't understand them."

He nodded, looking chastened. "I suppose you're right. I just wish I could do something to help. Your father always knew how to calm the town. He'd—"

"Don't," I said sharply. "You didn't know my father."

He blinked, taken aback. "I meant no disrespect."

"I know. You just think repeating his name will make everything sound righteous again." I stepped closer, lowering my voice. "Let me give you some advice, Pastor. Stop trying to save this town. It doesn't want saving."

He opened his mouth, then closed it again. For a moment, the only sound was the wind knocking loose flakes from the church eaves.

"I'll pray for you," he said finally.

I almost laughed. "Of course you will."

I turned and started walking again. Behind me, I heard the soft squeak of his boots on the snow as he went back toward the church.

By the time I reached home, the windows of the house glowed faintly. My mother was probably inside, pretending the world outside didn't exist, folding laundry into neat piles as if order could keep chaos away.

I stood on the porch, looking out across the town; the same streets, the same faces, the same silence dressed in Christmas lights. The list of names in my pocket felt heavier than it had that morning.

Collins could pretend this was bad luck. Lewis could hide behind his sermons. My mother could keep cleaning the same spotless kitchen until her hands bled.

But I wasn't built for pretending.

The truth was here, buried beneath signatures and prayers and the ashes of old fires. And whether the town liked it or not, I was going to dig it up.

The Eighth Candle

By evening, the square no longer pretended at cheer. Stalls were open, but people moved like shadows, their voices clipped. Strings of lights glared too bright against the frost, as if wattage could beat back dread.

Children clung to their parents, eyes wide. The choir clustered together, songbooks clutched like shields. Their voices trembled on the carol:

Keep the watch, keep the flame; ashes tell the sinner's name.

Even Mayor Evelyn's smile was brittle. Her voice rose above the hush: "Tonight, we light the eighth candle — a symbol of faith, of hope, of Greenridge standing together."

No one clapped. The flame flared steady against the wind, daring anyone to breathe too loud.

Sheriff Collins stood off to the side, scanning faces, his hand hovering near his radio.

The whispers rippled through the crowd like dry leaves:

"What's going to happen next?"

"Whose turn is it?"

"Should we even be here?"

The ritual had become a countdown, and everyone knew it.

When the service ended, no one lingered for cocoa. They scattered, pulling scarves tighter, casting looks over their shoulders.

***

The sirens came an hour later.

I ran toward them with half the town. The power company's brick office roared with fire. Sparks sprayed into the night. Smoke curled black against the December sky.

Half the grid was already down. Streetlights dark. Houses black. The church glowed brighter than ever, the only light in town.

Neighbors shouted. Firefighters fought the blaze. The cold bit at my cheeks, but the heat from the flames pushed back harder.

And then — the side door burst open.

The man who ran the power company stumbled out, coat scorched, coughing hard. In his arms he clutched a cardboard box like it was his child.

Firefighters rushed to him, but he waved them off. "I'm fine! I'm fine!"

Someone yelled, "What's in the box?"

He looked at me, at us, his eyes wide, face pale. "They sent it," he rasped. "No return address. Just—" He lifted the lid.

Inside: children's shoes. Small. Scuffed. Laces broken. The same kind that had been left on my porch.

The crowd gasped. Whispers cut the night.

"They're sending warnings."

"Who would—?"

"She's the pastor's daughter—"

I froze, stomach ice-cold. This wasn't chance. This was ritual. Someone was reenacting the fire's ghosts, one warning at a time.

The man stumbled further, still clutching the box. One shoe spilled into the snow with a soft thud. Tiny. Worn.

"I didn't even open it until now," he whispered.

No one moved. The fire roared higher. The power lines hissed above.

I felt a gaze on me. Sheriff Collins. Across the crowd, lit by the fire's glow. For the first time, there was no dismissal in his eyes. Just grim recognition.

Our eyes locked. He didn't nod, didn't speak — but I knew. He saw it now.

This wasn't kids. This wasn't bad luck.

It was real. It was deliberate.

And for the first time, I wasn't the only one willing to see it.

CHAPTER 9

The Unfinished Business

The next morning, frost crawled over the windowpanes like veins, delicate and cold. The kind of morning where even the air felt brittle enough to break. Light filtered weakly through the kitchen curtains, pale blue and colorless. My mother stood at the stove, stirring oatmeal she wouldn't eat, her movements slow and mechanical. The smell of cinnamon drifted through the room, soft and misleading, as if pretending hard enough could make things right again.

The house was too quiet. Even the furnace seemed hesitant, clicking once before sighing back into silence. I sat at the table, watching steam rise from my untouched tea. My mother's cardigan hung off one shoulder, her hair pinned in a lopsided twist that spoke of a sleepless night. She hadn't looked directly at me since I came downstairs.

Then came the knock—three firm, deliberate taps. Not frantic, not polite. The sound of someone who already knew they were expected, even if they weren't invited. I felt the weight of it before I reached the door.

Sheriff Collins stood on the porch, his breath rising in clouds. His coat hung open, and his eyes were red at the edges like he hadn't slept. The man who always carried himself like a wall suddenly looked like one that had begun to crack.

"Morning," he said quietly, rubbing the back of his neck. "Didn't mean to come so early."

"You did," I said, and stepped aside anyway.

He gave a faint nod, the kind that wasn't apology so much as surrender, and came in, stamping frost from his boots. My mother turned from the stove, startled but composed.

"Sheriff," she said. Her voice was steady, though her hands weren't.

"Ma'am." He tipped his head, polite but cautious, like he wasn't sure which of us might shatter first.

He sat at the table without waiting for permission. The chair creaked under his weight, and for a long moment, the only sound was the oatmeal bubbling softly on the stove. Then he sighed, a low sound that carried more weariness than breath.

"I went through the council archives last night," he said.

I straightened. "And?"

"And half the files are gone," he said. "The rest might as well be ashes. Pages missing, reports unsigned. Someone's been cleaning house, or time did it for them. Doesn't matter. What's left is enough."

My pulse quickened. "Enough for what?"

"To know your father wasn't the only one ignoring Caldwell." His voice was low, roughened by exhaustion. "He wasn't even the worst of them."

I leaned forward. "Then who else?"

He gave a hollow laugh. "You name them, they're there. Murphy. Doyle. Thomas. Evelyn's husband before he passed. Everyone who mattered had a hand in it. Council signatures, budget cuts, decisions buried under polite minutes." He looked up at me. "It was all of them."

I wanted to feel vindicated, but all I felt was sick. "You're telling me every person in this town who preached faith and charity knew the orphanage was a fire hazard?"

"They knew," he said. "And they signed their names anyway."

My mother turned off the stove with trembling fingers. "There were reasons," she said, her voice too calm. "The roof repairs, the water bills, the donations—"

"Stop," I said sharply. "Don't defend them."

80

She didn't look at me. She was staring at the oatmeal as though it might tell her what to say next.

Collins rubbed a hand over his face. "Look, I'm not saying this to defend your father," he said. "I think I'm finally starting to see what he was up against. He had power, sure. But not all of it. The council had its hands in everything. He might've wanted to fix things, but it wasn't just his decision."

"That's generous," I said bitterly. "He had a pulpit and a town full of people hanging on his every word. He could've shamed them into action if he'd wanted to."

Collins met my eyes. "Maybe. But shame doesn't fix a wiring budget. I was a deputy then, still wet behind the ears. I asked questions once—just once—and the next morning, your father came to my office. Told me to focus on living cases, not the dead ones."

I swallowed hard. "And you listened."

He didn't flinch. "I did," he said simply. "He was the town's conscience back then, and I didn't have the authority to go against him. But I do now." His eyes hardened, and his tone shifted. "And I'm not making that mistake again."

My mother turned slowly, a dishcloth still in her hand. "Some things are buried for a reason," she murmured, almost to herself.

Collins looked at her. "Ma'am, with all due respect, that's exactly what he used to say."

Her shoulders stiffened. The dishcloth twisted in her hands until her knuckles went white. For a long moment, the three of us sat in silence, the past pressing in like fog.

"Sheriff," I said finally, my voice low. "If we start digging, there's no turning back. You can't half-unbury the truth."

He nodded once, slow and deliberate. "Then maybe it's time we stop pretending we're not already standing on the same grave."

Something in the air shifted then. It wasn't peace, exactly, but a fragile truce. My mother's gaze met his across the table. It wasn't friendship, or forgiveness. It was something heavier— acknowledgment. A silent understanding that none of us could walk away now, not when the past was already clawing its way back through the dirt.

"It's time to act," Collins said softly. "While we still can."

***

By afternoon, I needed air.

The streets of Greenridge were dressed in denial. Children dragged sleds across half-melted snow, their boots squeaking as they went. Shop windows glowed with lights, ribbons, and plastered-on cheer. The butcher leaned in his doorway, pretending not to glance toward the blackened outline of Murphy's store. Every corner of town reeked of fear disguised as festivity.

I walked until my fingers went numb inside my gloves, passing the church, the post office, the row of old homes that hadn't been repainted since before I left. The same decorations, the same people, the same pretense. Greenridge never changed—it just decayed politely.

When I reached the market square, I saw Emily Hill arranging oranges at her stall. Her hair was tucked into a gray wool cap, cheeks flushed pink from the cold. She looked up as I approached, and her smile came quickly—too quickly.

"Hannah," she said brightly. "Out for supplies?"

"Trying to pretend I have a normal life," I said. "It's not working."

Her laugh was small and careful, the sound of someone hoping laughter might make danger less real. "I don't think it's working for anyone lately."

I picked up an apple, turning it in my gloved hand. "You must've heard about Mrs. Murphy."

Her fingers hesitated mid-arrangement. "I did. Terrible," she said, her tone clipped, rehearsed.

"And before that? The Thomas family car. The school fire. You're a teacher, Emily. You see patterns."

Her throat worked. "Patterns?"

"Yes," I said, steady and quiet. "Every accident has a name attached. Murphy. Thomas. Donahue. People who signed those papers, ignored Caldwell's warnings. It's not random."

Her voice wavered. "That was decades ago."

"Time doesn't erase guilt."

She darted a look toward the other vendors, then back to me. "You shouldn't say things like that out here," she whispered. "People are on edge."

"I think they should be," I said. "Maybe fear is the first honest thing this town's felt in years."

The edge in my tone made her step back slightly. She fumbled with a crate of fruit, her fingers shaking. "The new orphanage isn't like the old one," she said quickly. "It's better now. Safer. The children are happy."

"Are they?" I asked softly. "Or do they just know not to speak?"

Her eyes flicked to mine, wide and uncertain. "You don't know what you're talking about," she said, her voice tight. "That was before my time."

"I know," I said. "You moved here later. You didn't grow up in this mess."

She hesitated. "Three years ago," she said finally. "That's all. I came for the job. I didn't even know what happened until people started whispering."

"People whisper a lot here," I said. "But never the truth."

Her throat worked. "I just teach the kids, Hannah. I keep my head down. I don't ask questions I can't live with."

I studied her. "That's the problem. No one ever asks. Everyone just adjusts to the silence."

She looked down at her hands, fingers trembling around the fruit. "You think I'm part of this," she whispered.

"I think you're afraid," I said quietly. "Like the rest of them."

Her jaw tightened. "Whatever's happening, I just want it to stop."

She turned away then, pretending to rearrange the oranges. One slipped from her grasp, rolling across the cobblestone until it hit my boot. I bent to pick it up, but when I looked up again, she was gone—her stall half-abandoned, the empty space behind it already swallowed by the crowd.

The orange was cold in my hand, its scent sharp and bitter. I stood there, staring at the spot where she'd been. The market hummed with uneasy energy—music too loud, smiles too wide, laughter too brittle.

I let the fruit fall. It hit the ground softly, splitting open. A thin smear of red bled into the frost.

The wind shifted, carrying the faint toll of church bells through the square. Somewhere beneath the noise, beneath the pretense of normal life, something older stirred.

Unfinished business never stayed buried in Greenridge.

The Ninth Candle

By nightfall, the air felt charged, brittle with tension. It wasn't just cold; it was expectant, like the whole town was holding its breath. The square was half empty when I arrived. People stood closer together than usual, their coats drawn tight, their breath rising in thin white ribbons that hung in the dark. Snow whispered against the cobblestones, soft but relentless.

The mayor stood at the podium; her fur collar powdered with frost. Her lipstick was too bright, a violent red against the pallor of her face. The microphone crackled when she began.

"Tonight," she said, forcing cheer into her voice, "we light the ninth candle—a symbol of perseverance and hope."

Her words floated into the air and went nowhere.

No one responded. No murmured "Amen," no polite applause. Just the quiet shuffle of boots on frozen ground. She tried again, louder this time. "Greenridge has faced hardship before. We endure. We always endure."

She smiled, but it wavered, unconvincing.

Someone coughed in the crowd. Someone else muttered a prayer.

The mayor gave a small laugh—thin and strained—and said, "Guess the weather's frozen everyone's sense of humor, hm?"

The sound was swallowed by silence. Even the children stayed still, their gloved hands buried in their parents' coats. The choir fidgeted behind her, their sheet music fluttering in the wind like nervous birds.

She cleared her throat, her voice smaller now. "All right then. The ninth candle."

Pastor Lewis stepped forward, his fingers trembling as he struck the match. The wick hissed, sputtered, then caught—a tiny thread of gold against the endless white. The light flickered, weak at first, then held.

The choir began the verse, voices low and uncertain.

Keep the watch, keep the flame; ashes tell the sinner's name.

The sound barely carried past the first row. It wasn't a song anymore—it was a warning whispered into a void.

I looked around at the faces beside me. Pale. Hollow. Eyes that refused to meet one another. Some mouthed the words mechanically; others stared at the flame as if waiting for it to accuse them. Even Pastor Lewis seemed lost, glancing toward the mayor for some sign that this was still the ceremony he'd rehearsed.

The applause that followed was polite but thin, a habit more than a gesture.

Across the crowd, I found Collins watching me. His shoulders were stiff, his face unreadable, but his eyes met mine. A small shake of his head. Nothing new. No progress. Just more fear.

Something was coming. We both felt it.

That night, the bakery burned.

I smelled it before I heard it—the sickly sweetness of sugar turned to smoke. I was still half-dressed when the first siren cut through the night. By the time I reached Main Street, the air glowed orange and black, light and ash fighting for dominance.

Mrs. Doyle's Bakery was a furnace. Flames leapt from the windows, ribbons of fire licking at the painted sign above the door: Fresh Every Morning! It cracked, curled, and fell, scattering embers across the street like confetti.

The air was thick with smoke and cinnamon, the kind of sweetness that makes your stomach turn.

People gathered on the sidewalk, helpless and dazed. Buckets passed from hand to hand, the water hissing into steam before it even reached the flames. A child cried somewhere behind me. The crowd pressed closer, drawn by the awful beauty of destruction.

The firetruck's siren screamed as it tore into the square. Firemen jumped down, shouting over each other, dragging hoses into the heat.

Mrs. Doyle stood barefoot in her nightgown, robe clutched tight, her hair wild with static and smoke. The light made her look ancient, her skin gray and wet from melted snow. She wasn't crying. Her lips moved soundlessly, over and over, like she was praying, or confessing.

When Collins arrived, he didn't waste a second. His voice cut through the chaos. "Back up! Everyone back!"

But no one moved until he pushed through himself, barking orders until people obeyed out of sheer instinct. When he saw me in the crowd, his jaw tightened, but he didn't tell me to leave. Maybe he knew by now I wouldn't.

The fire raged for what felt like hours, though it couldn't have been more than thirty minutes. When it was finally beaten down, the building was a shell. Charred wood and smoke. The windows had melted into glassy puddles that reflected the night like small, distorted mirrors.

The air reeked of yeast and ash, thick enough to taste.

Mrs. Doyle sat on the curb, wrapped in a blanket someone had given her. Her eyes were wide and empty, her hands shaking as she tried to clutch the blanket tighter.

Collins crouched beside her, speaking low. I couldn't hear what he said, but after a moment, she looked straight at me.

Her voice cracked the silence like breaking glass. "It wasn't supposed to happen again," she said.

I froze. "What do you mean?"

She didn't seem to hear me. She just stared at the smoldering bakery, whispering, "We did what we were told. We did what they asked." Then she started to sob, rocking back and forth like a child.

The sound carried through the smoke, hollow and desperate.

Collins tried to calm her, but she pulled away, shaking her head. "We did what we were told," she kept repeating, softer and softer, until the words became nothing but breath.

I wanted to ask her who she meant—who "they" were—but the ambulance arrived, and everything dissolved into noise. Paramedics lifted her to her feet. Someone shouted about the ovens. The wind shifted, carrying the scent of burned sugar and grief down the street.

***

Later, Collins and I stood beside his patrol car. The red lights spun lazily across the soot-streaked snow, throwing his face into flashes of color. The firemen worked in silence now, their movements slow and mechanical, like they were afraid to disturb what remained.

He rubbed a hand over his face. His voice was quiet, almost lost in the wind. "You know what Doyle's name was doing in those old council files?"

87

I nodded. "She was one of the signatures on the vote to discredit Caldwell."

He shook his head. "It was more than that. She didn't just sign the papers. She led it."

"What do you mean?"

"She organized the campaign against Caldwell," he said, his tone flat. "Convinced the council to label her unstable. Said she scared the children. There's a petition in the archives—Remove Caldwell from Office of Care. Doyle gathered the signatures herself."

I stared at the ruins. "And that destroyed Caldwell's reputation."

He nodded slowly. "It made her a pariah. No one believed her after that. When she begged for repairs again, they called her hysterical."

"And now?" I said. "Now her bakery burns."

Collins didn't answer. He didn't have to.

We stood there for a long time, the silence between us filled with the hiss of cooling embers.

"She's on the list," I said finally.

He nodded again, his breath clouding in the cold. "Looks that way."

The word list hung between us like smoke. We didn't need to say what it meant anymore. Not superstition. Not coincidence. It was deliberate. Precise.

Someone was keeping score.

He looked down the street, toward the church steeple glowing faintly against the night sky. "You think whoever's behind this will stop?"

"No," I said. "I think they're just getting started."

The wind cut between us, carrying the faint echo of sirens down the empty street. Collins exhaled slowly, the sound more sigh than breath.

"Then we'd better move faster," he said.

I looked back at the ruins, at the scorched beams still smoldering in the snow. The smell of charred sugar clung to the air, sweet and sickening. Somewhere deep inside, the ovens still glowed faintly, stubborn against the dark.

The candles in the square burned to offer hope. These fires did the opposite.

As I turned to leave, I glanced at the blanket Mrs. Doyle had dropped on the curb. The edges were singed, blackened in places, and something dark stained one corner—soot, maybe, or blood.

Collins picked it up carefully, folded it once, then met my eyes. "What if they're not trying to destroy things?" he said quietly. "What if they're trying to send a message?"

I thought about the rhythm of it all. The names. The order. The precision.

"Maybe they are," I said. "But I don't think anyone's listening."

He looked back at the bakery. The last spark winked out, leaving nothing but smoke and silence.

And I couldn't shake the thought that maybe these fires weren't punishment anymore. Maybe they were confession—every name burned into the night, one by one, until the truth had no choice but to show itself.

The ninth candle had been lit.

And Greenridge was running out of names.

CHAPTER 10

The Paper Bones of a Tow

The attic light always made everything look older, as if the bulb itself remembered too much and cast that memory onto whatever it touched. I pulled the chain and the yellow cone jittered over the rafters, the old trunks, the boxed nativity with Joseph's nose taped back on, the jar of bent nails that my father would never throw away because "you never know." The cedar smell had thinned to something drier—dust and time—and underneath it today was the faintest sting of smoke that I couldn't tell was real or imagined.

I told myself I was only going to skim a few folders, just enough to keep the anger simmering instead of boiling. A nurse's trick: control your own adrenaline or it controls you. But the first box slid open like a jaw and all the neat teeth of manila inside were stamped with the same red mouth: DENIED. RETURN TO SENDER. Some had both, as if the first "no" wasn't hearty enough.

Caldwell's letters were thinner than I remembered. Typing paper from an old machine, the ribbon running dry midway through a paragraph, so the vowels faded to a ghost of themselves. She had written like a person who didn't have time to waste on style. Dates, defects, signatures. The west stairwell door sticks, not passable in an emergency. Wiring in the north dormitory intermittently shorts. Three of six alarm bells nonfunctional; request immediate replacement. The paper quivered when my hands did.

In the upper right corner of most pages was a set of initials in my father's small, severe hand—M.L.—and a slash mark that meant the same thing every time: handled. Except it hadn't been. It had been filed. Which is different.

I stacked the worst ones in a neat pile because order helped me breathe. My mind kept trying to slip sideways into other rooms that smelled like antiseptic and adrenaline: night shift, harsh lights, someone yelling code blue down a hallway that always felt too long. I hadn't worked in weeks, not since I came home "for a little while." At first, I thought I was just taking leave. Then the town started unraveling and the idea of returning to the hospital became something that lived far away, on another planet where I could pretend that all tragedies were random. My badge was still clipped to the inside of my suitcase pocket like a relic. I pictured myself putting it back on. My stomach pitched. I can hear myself asking the unit clerk to put me back on nights—I'll ease in, I'll float, it's fine—and then the monitor screams and the parents arrive and I'm back to pressing two fingers into a wrist that doesn't want to pulsing, whispering come on, baby, come on, and you cannot go back from that empty sound when hope stops. Not yet. Maybe not ever.

I let out a breath I hadn't realized I was holding and made myself look at the next file.

"Come on," I said to the papers, like coaxing a stubborn IV into a vein. "Give me something clean. One thread that doesn't tangle."

Halfway down the stack I found a thick envelope that didn't belong with the rest. No stamp. No official letterhead. Just Orphanage—Supplemental written in pencil that smudged my thumb. Inside: clippings, meeting agendas, a printed email from fifteen years ago when someone in the town offices had finally learned to attach PDFs. And at the bottom, a brittle photocopy of a list titled Evacuation Log. Names, ages, notes. Some lines ended with deceased stamped hard enough to bruise the paper.

I traced the list with my finger. Twenty-two names. Two columns. Under the second to last: Unknown (female), approx. 8–11, transported—status unspecified.

Status unspecified.

My heart thudded. I flipped the page, hoping a second sheet would tell me where she had been transported, to whom, by what car or what hand. The next sheet was nothing more than a blank back page, the copier's black edge smearing one side like a tire mark.

"Damn it," I whispered, too loud for the quiet room. The rafters swallowed the word and handed it back.

I dug again. More DENIED stamps, more initials. A council memo whining about budget overruns for snow plowing that winter. The minutes from a special meeting held two days after the fire, in which the board agreed that "in the interest of preventing panic" all communication should be centralized through the church. My father, chairing. The kind of sentence that looks responsible until you place it under the right light and it becomes what it is: a muzzle.

Bottom corner of the box: a warped file with a rusted clip. Photos spilled into my lap—black-and-white, then the new glossy kind from the drugstore. Children stood in rows under a crooked banner that read Thank You for Your Donations. Their faces were solemn in that way kids get when you tell them to smile, and they don't quite know how. At their feet: pairs of shoes, all the same make, the same scuffed leather, the same narrow silhouette.

I lifted one photo closer. The shoes were identical to the one left on our porch—the little creases, the cheap thin soles that wore down at the toe, the laces that frayed even when you tied them soft. The sight made my scalp prickle. I imagined someone opening a modern box in a fluorescent mailroom, those old shoes inside like a time capsule of accusation.

Keep the watch, keep the flame.

I pressed the photo to my knee and closed my eyes. Try not to see the other pictures, I told myself—the ribcages rising and falling under thin blankets, the emergency room that looked the same whether you were seven or seventy, the nurse at two in the morning pretending not to cry behind the med cart. Try not to hear yourself saying time of death. Try not to think of the families who never got the chance to bring those children home, to hold them, to take care of them, to love them, because the fire had done the holding for them. The attic steps creaked. I shoved the photos under a file reflexively, as if I'd been caught doing something private.

"Hannah?" my mother called. "You've been up there long enough to grow roots."

"Coming," I said, and my voice came out rough. "Bring the board up."

I'd been thinking about a board for days—something to make the mess visual. Nurses build boards all the time; you lay out a problem and the edges of it show themselves. I wasn't sure if it would comfort me or scare me to see it.

They brought an old corkboard we used to hang Christmas cards on, minus the twine and clothespins, plus a box of pins and a stack of index cards. Sheriff Collins came up with it, his boots careful on the narrow steps. He looked like a man who had not slept and didn't expect to. My mother carried a thermos and three mugs as if you can armor a person with tea.

"Your attic's colder than my garage," the sheriff said. "And my garage could make a polar bear shiver."

"Then work fast," my mother said, because she has never believed in complaining when you can be doing. It is one of the things I love most and hate hardest about her.

I gave them the shorthand: files here, the worst of Caldwell here, the evacuation log with the blank line here. The shoe photo I left facedown until I could decide if I was ready to show it.

We started with names. Murphy. Thomas. Donahue. Doyle. The former treasurer. The pharmacist. The librarian who had sent a memo that no one read. The old fire marshal whose signature lay like a blessing across forms that blessed nothing. We pinched index cards to the cork. We drew lines in red thread my mother pilfered from her sewing basket and said she didn't miss. In the center I wrote THE ORPHANAGE and below it, smaller, Unknown Girl.

"Unknown?" the sheriff said, leaning in, breath clouding the cold air. "What girl?"

I handed him the evacuation photocopy and waited for his face to change. It did, slowly, something like surprise and something like relief, as if a loose thought he'd been refusing to think had finally gotten a name.

"I didn't know," he said. He looked genuinely stricken. "I swear, Hannah. Your father—no one let me see this. We were told there were no survivors beyond the count we listed."

He said my name, not Miss Mark. Somewhere between the attic files and the bakery fire, the distance between us had burned away. He didn't even seem to notice the change, but I did. It wasn't just habit—it was acknowledgment.

Ever since that day at the station, when I'd gone to him with what everyone else called superstition and he finally saw it for what it was—truth—something in the air between us had changed. The formality fell first, then the doubt. By the time the reports piled up and the fires stopped feeling random, I realized we weren't working against each other anymore. We were carrying the same weight, standing on the same side of something neither of us could name.

Whatever wall the town had built between law and truth, between him and me, had started to crack—and neither of us had the strength or the will to rebuild it.

Maybe it was the shared exhaustion, or the quiet horror of realizing we were both standing in the ruins my father had left behind. Whatever it was, it had made us allies, however temporary.

"You were told a lot of things," my mother said. It wasn't kind; it was true.

He took the hit like a man who knew he deserved it and then said, steady: "All right. Then from this second, I know. And we treat it like the center of gravity."

We moved around the board as if orbit could generate heat. My mother's hands were sure, more so than mine. She pinned Caldwell's letters under the names of the people who had stamped them back. She took a strip of masking tape and wrote PATTERN and placed it under the row of recent fires, and another that read WARNING under the delivered shoe.

The sheriff pinned a copied budget sheet in the corner. "Diversions," he said. "Money meant for repairs sent to other line items. Always signed off by a cluster of the same names."

"And my father," I said.

He paused. "Yes."

The attic was so quiet you could hear the pushpins scrape cork. The board looked like a city seen from above at night—lines of light connecting tiny, merciless truths.

My mother leaned her hip against the trunk and cradled the thermos in both hands. "I didn't know about a child," she said. "I would have… I don't know what I would have done. But I wouldn't have slept."

"You didn't," I said softly. "You just told yourself you did."

She nodded once, the kind of nod a person makes when she forgives herself for the first time and it stings.

I flipped the shoe photo over and set it below the WARNING tape. The sheriff crouched to see, his knees popping, old habit of a man who's searched floors for spent casings and small truths.

"Same make," he said. "Same wear." His voice went odd. "Someone kept these for years."

"Or someone tracked them down because they knew what they would say," I answered.

We stood close enough that I could see the red veins in his eyes and the shaving nick he hadn't noticed near his ear. He seemed suddenly more human than sheriff: a man who had been young when it mattered and is no longer, a man who could finally make something right because time had gifted him authority he didn't have then. He glanced at my mother. She met his look and didn't flinch.

"It's time to act," he said, low. "Now that we can."

I thought of the hospital again—the way morning looks through the seventh-floor windows, the gray light that always felt cleaner than night, the polite beeps that are mercies compared to the alarms. My leave paperwork had a date on it. I'd said I'd be back by then. I could already hear the charge nurse asking me if I was ready, if I wanted to ease in on days first. I wasn't. And this—the fire and the board and the eyes of the town on my back—was not helping. I tried to picture walking into a patient's room and not seeing the orphanage in the reflection of the IV pole. I tried to picture saying I'm your nurse, Hannah, and not tasting ash. The picture wouldn't hold.

"Okay," I said out loud, to the board and to the attic and to the version of me who used to be able to stand in a room of people grieving and not break. "We act."

We worked until our knuckles ached from the cold and the pins. By the time we clattered back down the stairs with red fingertips, the board looked like a confession. The house smelled like the faint cinnamon my mother brushed onto everything when she didn't know what else to do.

"Eat something," she said. "Then nap."

"Later," I answered, and both of us knew later rarely arrives when it should.

The Tenth Candle

By dusk the sky had dropped lower, a lid pressing on the square, the cold turning everyone's breath to speech bubbles that said nothing. Fewer people came. The ones who did kept space between themselves as if guilt were catching. The mayor stood at her podium and looked like a woman who had spent an hour in the mirror trying out expressions and chose the wrong one. Her smile was the kind that belongs to fundraising breakfasts, not funerals.

"Greenridge," she said, and her voice bounced oddly off the empty corners, "tonight we light the tenth candle. Ten nights closer to Christmas, ten nights of holding to what is good."

Someone near the front coughed. The choir huddled in their coats, the hymnbooks damp around the edges from other nights, other breaths.

The mayor tried for folksy. "We've had our share of mishaps this week, haven't we?" She let out a little laugh, waiting for a warm ripple that didn't come. "But if there's one thing I know about this town, it's that we are—"

"What went wrong at the orphanage?" a voice called from the back. A woman, sharp and high, the sound of a string snapping.

The mayor's mouth opened and closed. She was a politician caught without a script. "This isn't—tonight is for—"

"Answer her," a man called.

Pastor Lewis took a step forward as if he might help, then thought better of it and stepped back, face pale. The mayor fumbled her note cards, looked at the candle lighter as if he might rescue her with flame.

"Let us pray," she blurted.

No one bowed.

But the candle was lit anyway—the tenth wick catching, small and stubborn against the wind. The choir tried the verse, and it sounded wrong, like a lullaby sung over sirens:

Keep the watch, keep the flame; ashes tell the sinner's name.

I stared at the flame and thought of the board in our living room, the red thread pulsing in my head like vessels. Ten nights. Fifteen candles left. I tried not to do the math of how many names remained on the list. I failed.

People didn't linger for cocoa after. They left in eddies, whispering, some openly angry now. A man said cowards under his breath and didn't care who heard. A woman sobbed into her scarf and kept walking. The town had run out of denial the way you run out of salt—you can cook without it, but nothing tastes like itself.

We had almost made it back to our street when the first scream came.

It was the kind of sound that shears through everything—the thickness of winter air, the pretense of calm—and every head turned as one. Sheriff Collins was already moving, running back toward the square, hand to his radio. I ran too because running toward the worst is a habit I haven't unlearned.

The crowd funneled into a narrow lane between the barbershop and the stationery store. In the alley, a woman stood with her hands to her mouth, keening. "He was right here. He was right here." The words came out like steam.

"What happened?" the sheriff demanded. He kept his voice level the way you talk to someone who is hanging by a thread.

"My son," she gasped. "We were walking. I turned to answer— he was right there—" She pointed uselessly at the ground, where tiny boot prints stuttered and then disappeared into the frost scuffed by an adult stride.

Everything in me narrowed. Time does that when need arrives. The alley bent into a rear parking lot where the lamplight failed. "How long?" I asked.

"Two minutes," she sobbed. "Three? I don't—"

"We'll find him," the sheriff said, and made it sound like fact. He sent deputies to fan out, voices on radios overlapping—east lot, west lot, canvas doors, check behind dumpsters. I started knocking on the backs of shops without permission. My mother stood with the woman and murmured a rhythm of comfort that kept panic from splitting into pieces.

Minutes are teeth. They bite differently when they're chewing on a child.

We found him twenty-eight minutes later. The deputy's shout cracked the night, and people poured toward the old municipal shed behind the hardware store. He was curled in the doorway like something left on a doorstep, face streaked with dirt, eyes blown so wide he looked almost blind. He wasn't crying. He was beyond that, his mouth open on silent breaths, body shivering so hard the buttons on his coat clacked.

I dropped to my knees without thinking and put my hands up the way you do with a cornered animal. "Hey," I said softly. "Hey, sweetheart. You're all right." The part of my brain that counts checked: airway clear, breathing fast but not labored, circulation—fingers cold, cap refill slow; shock was courting him with greedy hands. "I'm Hannah. Can I—" I didn't finish the sentence because he leaned into me like gravity had decided to be kind. I wrapped my coat around him and felt his bones.

His parents pushed through the cluster. The mother broke into sobs so raw I looked away because there's a decency to grief, too; you let people have it without witnessing more than you must. The father made small animal sounds I have heard in hospital rooms in every language of loss.

The sheriff cleared space, the way you keep a sterile field from being contaminated. "Give them room," he ordered, and people obeyed because even fear respects certain commands.

I pulled the child back a little so I could see his clothes. My stomach cinched. The shirt was wrong. The pants were wrong. They were too thin, too old-fashioned, a fabric I recognized from photographs in the attic—the kind of rough cotton children wore in institutional halls. The hem of the shirt was stamped with a faded laundry mark: G.O.—Greenridge Orphanage.

Someone gasped when they saw it. Someone else said a prayer without meaning to.

"Who gave you these?" I asked, voice as gentle as I could make it. He shook his head, a violent, shocked little motion, and buried his face in my chest. He didn't have to answer; the clothes already had.

The sheriff's jaw went tight. He took out a handkerchief and wiped the boy's cheek carefully, as if the small dignity of being clean could be returned there in the alley. Then he looked up and found the parents' faces, steadying them with his own.

"We've got him," he said. "He's safe."

Safe is a word nurses learn to use honestly. It doesn't mean forever. It means for now. It means this breath, this minute.

By the time we reached the square again, people were gathering without being told. The mayor started to speak, thought better of it. Pastor Lewis looked smaller than he had any right to be. Someone in the crowd shouted, "This isn't bad luck. Say it." Another voice added, "We know what you did," but the you was not one person; it arced over all of us and landed where it wanted.

The boy's father lifted him, holding him as if the child might vanish if someone blinked too slowly. He turned to the sheriff, face ash-pale. "My father signed those forms," he said, not loud, not soft—just true. "He was the fire marshal. He stamped safe and slept just fine after."

The words rolled through the crowd like a new weather system.

The mayor tried to climb the podium and take control back with sentences. "Let's all—please—we must stay calm, we're investigating—"

"No," someone said, and then many someones, a sound like a wave pulling stones.

For a breath I thought the square might break open into something uglier than fear. Then my mother stepped forward without invitation and stood beside the sheriff. She did not speak like politicians speak or pastors; she spoke like a woman who has buried the version of herself that believed easy things.

"We will tell the truth," she said. Her voice carried. "All of it."

It wasn't an answer to who had done what, not yet, but it was a promise, and sometimes a promise is the only bridge you can build between a disaster and the next morning.

The sheriff nodded once, a small motion that somehow mattered more than the mayor's thousand words. He looked at me over the heads of the crowd, and the look said we are past pretending. The board in our living room pulsed in my mind like a diagram whose labels were beginning to resolve.

The tenth candle burned in its glass. The little flame wavered and held.

On the walk home my body did that thing it does after a code—everything shakes once the adrenaline lets go. I thought of the unit again, of the badge tucked where I could not see it, of the doctor who had told me two months ago to come back when the nightmares stopped waking me up. I imagined phoning the hospital tomorrow and saying put me back on nights, and I heard myself hang up before the sentence could end. I wasn't ready. None of this made me more ready. And yet there was a part of me, traitorous and true, that missed the narrow clarity of a monitor that either spikes or flatlines. Towns don't present like that. They smolder.

At our door, my mother squeezed my hand so hard the bones clicked. "We keep going," she said.

"We keep going," I echoed, and the words tasted like ash and something else—salt, maybe. Or the start of clean.

Inside, the house felt too small for the board we had built. The red lines waited on the cork, taut as if they could pluck sound. I pinned one more card at the bottom and wrote in block letters TURNING POINT. It looked melodramatic. It also looked true.

I stood in front of it long enough that the cold from the attic seeped through my socks. Then I turned off the hall light, leaving the board in a square of darkness where the threads still glowed in my mind. Outside, somewhere, someone was keeping watch, and not in the way my father had meant.

In bed I lay awake and listened to the winter settle—the house ticking as it cooled, the wind stitching itself into the eaves, the distant murmur of a town that had finally run out of silence. When sleep came, it came with the image of a girl without a name being carried out of a burning building and set in a car with no destination written on the windshield. In the dream I ran beside the car, banging on the window, shouting that I could give her one, I could give her a name, but the driver's face was made of smoke, and the road didn't end.

I woke before dawn to the cold and the honest knowledge that tomorrow would be worse. I made tea and stood alone at the window while the snow started again, very fine, like the air had decided to practice being gentle. Then I went to the board, and with a pen that wouldn't stop trembling, I wrote beneath Unknown Girl: Find her.

The flame in the square had burned down to nothing hours ago. But a house can make its own candle when it needs to, and resolve, I've learned, throws light farther than you think.

CHAPTER 11

The Things That Don't Burn

The morning after the last night's disaster felt heavier than snow. Even the air seemed to hang differently, like it had absorbed the smoke and decided not to let go. The town was quiet in that way it gets when people are pretending things are fine; doors opening just a crack, blinds twitching, conversations ending the second footsteps approach.

By noon, Sheriff Collins came by. I heard his truck before I saw him, the slow crunch of tires over frost. My mother was pruning her dead hydrangeas in the front yard, scissors snapping in neat, sharp bursts. She didn't look up when he walked up the path, but I saw her shoulders tense.

"Morning," he said. His voice sounded rougher than usual, like he hadn't slept.

"Morning," I echoed, crossing my arms.

He hesitated before taking off his hat, running a hand through his hair. "Didn't think I'd be back here so soon."

"Didn't think the town would keep burning," I said.

He tried for a smile, but it didn't stick. "You got coffee?"

I gestured toward the house. "Always."

Inside, the kitchen smelled like cinnamon and dust. My mother had baked earlier—stress therapy, her version of control. Half a loaf of bread cooled on the counter, unsliced, untouched.

Collins sat at the table, elbows on his knees. For a long time, he didn't say anything. When he finally did, it came out on a sigh. "You were right."

I blinked. "About what?"

"This isn't random. Whoever's behind this—fires, letters, the shoe—it's not a kid or some drunk with a grudge."

"That's new," I said. "You admitting it."

He nodded, weary. "Doesn't mean I can prove it. But I've been digging through old reports, and it's a mess. Records missing, others sealed under your father's name."

Something twisted in my chest. "Of course."

He looked up at me. "You don't want to know what your father signed, Hannah."

That was his warning, not a threat—soft, but loaded.

I met his gaze evenly. "I think I do."

He leaned back, studying me. "You're serious about this."

"People are in danger. Maybe they deserve it, maybe they don't. But if I can stop the next one, I'll try."

"Stop it?" He frowned. "You sound like you know what's coming."

"I don't. Not exactly. But every time another candle's lit, someone on that list ends up buried under ashes. My father's list, not mine."

He went still. "You made a real list?"

I hesitated, then nodded. "Everyone who denied Caldwell's requests for repairs. Everyone who helped bury her warnings. Murphy. Thomas. Doyle. The fire marshal. Every single one of them has paid for it."

He sat back, the air between us thick. "And you think you're next."

"I know I am. My name's tied to his. To everything he did."

He rubbed his temples. "You realize how this sounds, right? A nurse returning home, finding fires following her around—people are already whispering that you brought it with you."

"I know," I said, voice low. "But if someone's keeping score, I'm already on the board."

We sat in silence. The only sound was the tick of the old kitchen clock and the wind against the windowpane.

My mother came in then, wiping her hands on a towel. She froze when she saw him, like she forgot she saw him coming in. "Sheriff."

"Ma'am."

They looked at each other for a moment—two people bound by things unspoken. She broke the silence first. "You found anything?"

He shook his head. "Not enough. But maybe it's time to start acting instead of reacting."

She met his gaze squarely. "It's about time."

Something passed between them—mutual regret, maybe, or quiet resolve. Then she looked at me. "Whatever your father built, we'll unbuild it together."

That was the closest she'd ever come to admitting guilt. It hit harder than I expected.

We spent the rest of the afternoon clearing space in the living room. The dining table became a command center—files spread out, newspaper clippings pinned to corkboard, a half-finished jigsaw puzzle shoved aside. The evidence board took a new shape slowly: photos, maps, strings connecting names, each line leading back to the orphanage at the center.

When I stepped back, it looked like a spiderweb.

My mother traced one red line with her finger. "It always comes back here," she murmured.

Collins nodded. "Every name tied to that building."

We stood there together, three people who'd spent too long pretending the past was buried.

After he left, I stared at the board until my vision blurred. My body ached from sitting too long, my neck stiff. For a second, I thought about work—about the hospital waiting for me to call and say I was ready to return. I wasn't. Not yet. Not while my hands still remembered the heat of skin cooling beneath them, the silence after the monitor stopped beeping.

This town had its own kind of triage.

By evening, I needed air. I went to the market for groceries and noise. The sky was flat gray, the kind that promised snow but never delivered it.

Emily Hill was there by the produce stand, choosing apples with careful precision. Her hair was tucked under a knitted hat, her smile small when she noticed me.

"Hi, Hannah," she said, too bright.

"Hi." I grabbed a bag, started picking through bruised fruit. "Rough night, huh?"

Her fingers froze mid-reach. "You mean the child from last night?"

"Among other things."

"Terrible," she said quickly. "I—uh—I'm trying not to think about it."

"I wish I could," I said. "Hard to, when it keeps happening."

Silence. The wind moved between the stalls, rattling the empty crates and stray bits of tinsel.

"Everything okay at the orphanage?" I asked. The last time I'd seen her, I'd let my anger do the talking, and she hadn't deserved it. This time, I tried to sound like a decent human being.

She nodded. "Yes. It's… better now. Safer. We have regulations, alarms, drills."

I looked at her. "You sound like you're trying to convince yourself."

She flinched. "I'm not. I just—don't like revisiting the past. The children need stability. They need people who aren't… haunted."

The way she said haunted made something in me still.

Before I could ask more, she turned, mumbling an excuse about lesson plans, and hurried off toward the register.

I watched her go, heart thudding. Something about her fear wasn't the fear of someone who didn't know. It was the fear of someone who remembered.

The Eleventh Candle

By the time evening arrived, the square looked hollow. Fewer people came each night now. The ones who did showed up out of habit, not

105

hope. Their breath rose in pale clouds, their hands buried deep in their pockets as if holding themselves together.

The choir stood in their usual place, scarves wound tight, voices subdued. Even the music sounded different—hesitant, brittle, as if afraid of echoing too far.

When Mayor Evelyn stepped up to the platform, her smile looked painted on, the kind that cracked if you looked too long. Her fur collar was dusted with frost, her gloved hands trembling slightly around her cue cards.

"Tonight," she began, her voice trembling, "we light the eleventh candle—a symbol of endurance and community... of standing together through hardship."

Her tone wavered, searching for something to catch on. It didn't.

No one responded. Not even polite applause.

Someone near the back muttered, "What's left to stand for?"

The words spread through the crowd like static.

The mayor tried to laugh, but it came out thin and forced. "Oh, come now. It's just been a rough few weeks, hasn't it? But we've got cocoa, and carols, and—well—faith."

No one laughed with her.

The sound of the match scraping the wick echoed louder than it should have. When the flame caught, it flickered weakly before straightening, gold against the black.

The choir began their verse, voices shaking against the cold.

Keep the watch, keep the flame; ashes tell the sinner's name.

The words floated through the air, hollow now, stripped of comfort.

I stood near the back, coat pulled tight, my heart sinking with every note. The crowd looked wrong—faces drained of color, eyes darting toward the rooftops and alleys. The whole town felt like a matchbox waiting for one careless spark.

Sheriff Collins was across the square, half-shadowed beneath a streetlight. He wasn't watching the stage; he was scanning the edges—the crowd, the rooftops, the darkened windows above the shops. His hand hovered near his belt, not quite ready to draw his weapon, but close. When he met my eyes, he gave a small shake of his head. Nothing yet. But something was coming.

I believed him.

The hymn faltered before it finished, voices thinning until the last note just... died. The mayor fumbled for her closing line, her cue cards shaking in her hands.

"Greenridge endures," she said, her voice cracking. "We always endure."

No one clapped.

The crowd began to break apart, scattering faster than usual. Parents pulled children close, vendors packed up without speaking. The mayor stood alone on the stage for a few seconds before her aide rushed forward to lead her away, her face pale and drawn beneath the lights.

I lingered.

The single candle burned in the center of the platform, its small flame bending toward the wind but refusing to die. Snow had started to fall again—thin, restless flakes that melted before they touched the flame.

Something inside me twisted.

***

By nine o'clock, I was back home. The house smelled faintly of smoke from the woodstove and old paper. The dining table was buried under some other files Collins found in the archive—half-destroyed pages, warped binders, and folders stamped Council Records.

Some of them were water-damaged, others smelled of mildew, but the ones marked Orphanage were spotless. Untouched. Someone had taken time to protect them.

I spread them across the table, tracing the ink with my fingertips. Budgets. Memos. Rosters. Line after line of signatures, most of them familiar. My father's handwriting appeared over and over at the bottom of pages—looped, confident, final.

"What are you trying to tell me?" I whispered. "Why leave these behind?"

The house creaked around me. The clock ticked too loudly.

Then—

A sound split the quiet. A scream.

It came from somewhere outside, sharp and panicked, cutting straight through the cold. I froze, listening. Then another scream followed, farther away but rising.

Not sirens. Not an argument. Real fear.

I was already moving before I realized it—grabbing my coat, nearly tripping over a stack of papers on the floor. When I opened the door, the night hit me like a slap.

The sky glowed orange.

People were pouring into the street, half-dressed, clutching coats and blankets. Their voices clashed—shouts, confusion, crying. Smoke curled up over the rooftops in the distance, thick and dark against the snow.

At the far end of Main Street, flames were clawing their way out of the town hall windows.

"The archives!" someone screamed. "The archives are burning!"

The words tore through the crowd.

My breath caught.

I ran. My boots slipped on the frozen pavement, the air tasting like ash before I even reached the square. The smell of burning paper filled the street—sweet, chemical, suffocating.

When I rounded the corner, the full sight of it hit me. The entire front of the town hall was alive with fire. Glass exploded outward in bursts of orange light. The sign above the entrance—Greenridge Council Chambers—buckled, then collapsed, sparks raining onto the crowd below.

"Back up!" someone shouted.

Then Collins's voice—loud, commanding. "Get the hoses around back! Keep people clear!"

His truck was parked sideways across the road, blocking traffic. He jumped out, shouting orders to the firefighters as they dragged the hoses toward the hydrant. The red lights of the fire engine cut through the smoke, flashing against the stone walls.

The heat hit me next—thick, searing, alive. It rolled across the street like a wave. My scarf did nothing to stop the sting in my throat.

But amid the chaos, something glinted.

A flicker of light—not firelight, but metal.

I turned toward the steps.

There, just beyond the reach of the flames, sat a steel filing cabinet. It was tilted slightly to one side, drawers open, papers stacked neatly inside. The labels were still legible, perfectly written in neat, black ink.

Caldwell Correspondence.

Council Minutes.

Orphanage Ledger.

Every single file we'd been searching for—intact.

The fire burned around it but not across it, like someone had drawn an invisible circle in the snow and told the flames to stay out.

My pulse hammered.

Someone had dragged that cabinet out before the fire began. Someone had made sure it would be seen.

The crowd's noise dimmed around me. All I could hear was the low, hungry crackle of fire and the faint whine of sirens echoing through the valley.

Collins appeared beside me, his face streaked with soot. He followed my gaze to the cabinet. For a second, neither of us spoke.

Then he said, quietly, "They didn't burn it."

My throat tightened. "They saved it."

He nodded once, eyes narrowing. "Then whoever's doing this isn't trying to erase history."

I looked back at the flames curling along the hall's roofline. "They're curating it."

The word came out like a confession.

The roof gave way then, collapsing inward with a sound like thunder. A burst of sparks shot into the sky, scattering like a swarm of fireflies. People screamed, covering their faces. Some crossed themselves, others whispered prayers that sounded more like apologies.

The firefighters worked in near silence, their faces grim behind masks, the hoses roaring as they unleashed water into the inferno. Steam hissed up in thick clouds, blurring the streetlights, coating everything in a damp, sooty mist.

I couldn't stop staring at that cabinet. The fire's reflection danced over its surface, a twisted mockery of the candlelight ceremony from earlier.

This wasn't destruction. It was presentation.

When the last of the roof crumbled, the clock tower fell too. Its bell crashed through the wreckage, landing half-buried in ash. The sound it made wasn't a chime. It was a groan—a long, low note that seemed to come from the earth itself.

Someone behind me whispered, "It's a message."

Another voice answered, trembling, "But from who?"

I turned to Collins. His jaw was set tight; eyes locked on the fire. "They're telling us what we missed," he said. "Everything they tried to bury."

The firefighters finally got control of the blaze, the water dousing what little remained. The flames shrank, turning the air gray and heavy with steam.

When the smoke thinned enough to see, the cabinet was still there—untouched, gleaming faintly beneath a layer of falling snow.

I moved toward it before Collins could stop me. My boots crunched over ice and debris. The air was still hot, the smell of wet ash clinging to every breath.

Up close, the papers were exactly as I'd imagined them—old, yellowed, fragile. Each one marked with names and signatures that once meant authority, now reduced to ghosts. I brushed my hand across the top drawer. The metal was warm.

I looked back at Collins. "Someone wants us to read this."

He gave a grim nod. "Then we will."

110

We stood there for a long time, the fire trucks idling in the background, the crowd slowly dispersing. Snow fell in thick, uneven flakes now, landing on my shoulders, in my hair, on the edges of the papers inside the drawer.

Across the square, the eleventh candle still burned. The flame wavered, bent, almost went out—then caught again, stronger than before.

Its reflection flickered in the wet pavement, in the metal cabinet, in my eyes.

I didn't know if it was faith or fury keeping it alive.

But one thing was certain now: whoever had started these fires didn't want silence. They wanted confession. And they were willing to burn every lie in this town to make sure no one ever looked away again.

CHAPTER 12

Echo of Locked Doors

Sleep had become a place I didn't trust.

Every time I closed my eyes, the dreams found me—children pounding on doors, the clang of metal against metal, smoke pouring through the cracks. Sometimes I saw faces pressed to the glass, gray and ghostly, their mouths forming my name. Sometimes I woke with the smell of burnt wood still in my throat.

I'd learned to live with bad dreams before. Hospitals will do that to you. But this was different. These dreams didn't fade with daylight—they followed me downstairs, clinging to the smell of coffee and old wood polish, whispering through every room of the house like they'd been here all along.

I kept telling myself it was exhaustion, that the nights of smoke and sirens had finally caught up with me. But every morning, when I passed the evidence board we'd built in the dining room, I saw the faces again. Names scrawled under the photos. Caldwell's letters pinned like accusations. Arrows connecting deaths, fires, signatures. The orphanage in the center—our rotten sun—and all the town's orbiting sins around it.

The sheriff came by before noon, coffee in hand, his uniform jacket buttoned halfway, the fatigue plain under his eyes. My mother sat at the table already, her hair pinned back, looking both composed and fragile—like a porcelain cup that had already cracked but still held tea.

"Morning," Collins said, setting his hat on the counter.

"Morning," I replied. "Or whatever's left of it."

He gave a short laugh, but it didn't reach his eyes. "You didn't sleep."

"Did you?"

"Not much." He rubbed the back of his neck. "I keep seeing that fire from last night. And then there's Doyle's bakery. A dozen families depended on her. And she—"

He didn't finish. He didn't need to.

My mother looked up from the notes she was sorting. "Has anyone spoken to her?"

"She's with her sister out of town," he said. "Not saying much. I think she's in shock."

"She'll remember soon enough," I said quietly. "They always do."

Collins gave me a look that was half sympathy, half warning. "Let's not assume too much."

But I could tell he didn't believe it either.

We stood there in silence for a while, the kind that fills up the air until you start hearing things that aren't there.

Finally, he said, "There's someone I want you to meet."

***

The janitor lived in a one-story house near the edge of town, past the woods where the old railway used to run. His name was Frank Lawson. I remembered him vaguely from childhood—stooped, quiet, always smelling of bleach and pipe tobacco. He opened the door before we could knock twice.

"Hannah," he said slowly, studying me with clouded eyes. "You look just like him."

I stiffened. "That's not much of a compliment these days."

His mouth twitched—almost a smile, almost regret. "No, I guess it isn't." He stepped aside. "Come in."

The house smelled of mothballs and wood smoke. Newspapers lined the counters. A crucifix hung above the fireplace; its brass tarnished with age.

He led us into the kitchen, where two mismatched mugs waited. "Coffee?"

We declined.

Collins leaned against the doorframe, letting me take the lead.

"I wanted to ask about the night of the fire," I said carefully. "You were working at the orphanage then."

He nodded, his hand trembling as he lit a cigarette. "Maintenance man, yes. Caldwell was my boss. She ran that place tighter than any man could've. She cared for those kids more than anyone ever did. But the council…" He blew out smoke. "They didn't care for her much."

"Because she wouldn't shut up about safety," Collins said.

Lawson looked at him. "Because she wouldn't shut up about truth."

I unfolded a copy of one of Caldwell's letters, the one about the locked stairwell. "You remember this?"

He squinted at the page. His fingers brushed the edge like he was touching a ghost. "Yeah," he said. "She told me to unlock it. Said if there was ever a fire, it'd be their only way out. I had the key. I was going to do it."

"But?"

"But your father found out." His eyes shifted to me, guilt and fear tangled in the same stare. "He took the key. Said Caldwell was stirring rebellion. Said faith meant obedience. He told me God would protect the children, not doors."

The words punched the air out of my lungs.

"Did you tell anyone?" I asked.

"I tried," he said softly. "No one wanted to hear. He was the pastor. People thought questioning him was the same as questioning God."

My mother's voice came from behind me, quiet but trembling. "He said the same thing to me."

I turned. She stood in the doorway, her coat still on, eyes glistening. "I begged him to listen to Caldwell," she whispered. "To fix the wiring, the exits. He told me faith was about obedience, not action. That to doubt him was to doubt the Lord."

114

Her hand pressed to her chest, trembling. "I believed him. God forgive me, I believed him."

The room fell still.

Collins stepped forward and placed a steadying hand on her shoulder. "You did what anyone would've done in your place," he said gently. "He had the whole town under his thumb."

I swallowed the lump in my throat. "Well," I said, forcing my voice steady, "he's not under anyone's thumb now. And we're not either."

Lawson exhaled smoke. "Then you'd better move fast," he said. "Whoever's doing this isn't slowing down."

We left him standing in the doorway, the smoke from his cigarette curling into the cold air like a prayer that never reached heaven.

Back home, I stared at our board again—the lines, the faces, the arrows. The list was growing. Murphy. Doyle. Thomas. Every one of them tied to a decision that had cost the orphanage something: a safety measure ignored, a complaint dismissed, a plea denied.

And yet, the real story was buried under years of worship and fear. My father had built his ministry on silence, and silence had kept this town standing.

Until now.

I felt Collins's eyes on me. "We'll get to the truth," he said.

"When?"

"When we're ready," he said. Then, with a small, grim smile: "It's time to act now that we can."

My mother looked up from the board and nodded once.

For the first time, the three of us stood together, the air between us heavy but clear.

Later, when the sheriff left, I stayed up for hours. I couldn't stop thinking about the children—their locked doors, the stolen key, my father's calm certainty that God would sort it out.

Faith without action. Belief without mercy.

The Twelfth Candle

By the time the twelfth night came, the air itself felt tired. Even the snow had given up pretending it could cover what they had done. The sky held that flat winter gray that made color look embarrassed to be seen. Light leaked early from the shops along Main, weak and apologetic, as if the bulbs had learned the town's habit of speaking softly and saying nothing.

The square was smaller than it had ever been, not by distance but by courage. People kept to the edges, heads down, hands stuffed into pockets, shoulders turned so their faces would not meet one another full on. The few who carried hymnbooks held them like shields. Every laugh sounded wrong, too quick, and stopped halfway. Even the vendor with the kettle drum of cocoa had turned down his flame so low the steam looked hesitant to rise.

I stood with my mother near the back where the snow was still untrampled. The first eleven candles burned in their tall iron holders, a ring of gold around the wreath, their wax caught in frozen drips. The flames bent toward the wind and then straightened again like stubborn spines. People had started to look at the fire the way you look at a dog you do not trust. Admire the beauty, keep your distance, do not meet the eyes.

The choir came out from the church steps and sorted themselves into a half circle. The smaller children had red cheeks and noses that ran, and the older ones tried to stand tall but kept glancing at the adults as if reassurance could be borrowed. Scarves were wrapped twice and three times. Mittens bumped music folders. A boy tapped his foot too loudly and looked ashamed.

Mayor Evelyn climbed the two steps to the low platform. The red of her coat should have read festive. Against the gray it read warning. Frost dusted the fur collar and sparkled around her ears. She had cue cards in one glove, and she kept shifting them, as if shuffling the order would change the script she had been stuck in for days.

"Tonight," she said, and her voice cracked on the first syllable. She swallowed and tried again with a second breath. "Tonight, we light the twelfth candle. A reminder of hope." Her smile reached only one corner of her mouth. "Of faith in each other."

No one applauded. Even the few who still applauded as a reflex had learned to keep their hands still.

A gust skimmed the square and set the lanterns clinking against their hooks. The garlands rasped along the railing. For a second every flame shivered. I thought the ring might go dark all at once. It did not. The fire steadied, gold with a thin blue heart, and the sound the town made was not relief. It was the collective breath of people who had already started to expect the worst and found it disappointing to be wrong.

Music rose, thin at first, then fuller when the choirmaster lifted two fingers and insisted. The carol came out like superstition more than worship. You could hear the fear in the vowels. You could hear the stubbornness in the consonants.

Keep the watch, keep the flame; ashes tell the sinner's name.

The last line fell apart in the mouths that tried to hold it. Some sang it, some did not, and the words broke on the cold like glass.

Across the square Pastor Lewis stood near the base of the platform with his hands clasped. He looked even younger than usual, a man who had been handed a ship in a storm and a map that ended at the shore. He nodded along as if agreement could count for leadership. When the first verse ended, he looked around for a signal that was not coming and lowered his head as though prayer might pass for direction.

My mother's mitten found mine for a second. She did not squeeze. The touch was a check of presence, proof that we were still two bodies in the same place. When she let go, I rubbed the stiff wool along my palm and tried to remember the last time this square had felt like anything but a stage.

The match scraped against the twelfth wick. The scratch sounded too loud, a single hard note in all that padded quiet. The flame took with a stutter and then a rush. The twelfth candle lifted itself into the circle and cast a new slice of gold across the faces around us. People blinked as if the light hurt. Someone in front of me began to cry without sound. The mayor held up her cards, but her hand had begun to tremble, and she had to set them down against the podium to steady herself.

The cocoa vendor banged his ladle against the rim of the pot and called out that the first cups were free tonight. No one moved. When a few finally stepped forward, they did it like penance. Take a cup, say thank you, pretend your hands are warmer, pretend your heart is not afraid.

The ceremony ended without an ending. No benediction, no last hymn, no mayoral flourish. People left in twos and threes, boots squeaking on the packed snow, conversations beginning and then dying. I stayed by the railing until the square thinned, and the candles had the space to glow. The church windows behind them were stained with color that the night made richer. I tried to hold the glass the way I had held it as a child. Angels, shepherds, a blue so deep it felt like a lake you could fall into. All I could see was fire reflected in every pane.

I turned to go when Sheriff Collins brushed past at the edge of the steps. He did not stop. He did not need to. The look we exchanged said enough. Stay alert. Do not believe the quiet. I tucked my scarf higher and led my mother home through the side street where the snow lay clean. When we reached our porch, I looked back. The ring of twelve held, stubborn as a promise that had run out of breath but refused to lie down.

***

The scream yanked me out of sleep as if someone had pulled a string tied to my ribs. It was not a siren. It was a human sound. It hit the inside of the window like a hand.

I was already out of bed and in my coat before I knew where my feet were going. The cold in the hallway felt like a wall I had to push through. I pulled on boots without socks and did not feel the laces bite. My mother called my name from her room, not a question, just the fact of me moving through the house. I shouted that I would be careful and was outside before I could hear her answer.

The sky had a low orange bruise along the horizon. The glow pulsed, brighter, then duller, and the air tasted like iron. Collins's car took the corner of our street with the back end skidding and corrected in a spray of dirty snow. He did not see me wave. I ran toward the park by the river, breath turning to smoke, lungs burning. The footprints ahead of me multiplied. Half the town was awake now, pulled out of doors by that same string.

The heat met us before the flames did. The old playground stood at the far edge of the park, the place where summer used to sound like laughter and the metallic screech of ungreased chains. Tonight, it sounded like wood giving up. The slide had softened into a silver fold. The merry-go-round had buckled into a question mark. The see-saw lay at an angle in the snow like a broken limb. The smell was a complicated ache. Paint and rubber and pine and the old rot of beams that had already survived one fire and were now doing it again.

Someone near me whispered that the lumber had come from the orphanage after demolition, because the town could not bear to throw away anything that might redeem itself. I remembered the dedication ceremony, the blue ribbon, the cheers when the first child climbed the ladder and slid into a future that looked simple. My stomach pulled tight. The past had a way of finding its own shape no matter how you tried to sand it smooth.

Police tape went up in a shaky line. People obeyed it because they needed to be told where to stand. The firefighters worked with that quick, practiced rhythm that tries to be calm and cannot quite manage it. Water turned to steam and then to frost along the edges of the equipment. The mist made everything look softer until the wind moved and the truth snapped back into focus.

Collins came to the tape and lifted it for two of his crew. When he saw me, he did not pretend to be surprised. He did not tell me to leave. He tipped his chin toward the burned center where the swing set had been. His face had emptied out, that particular expression men get when they are setting aside their own feelings to make room for a task.

"Started fast," he said. His voice was flat to keep it from breaking. "No way this is an accident."

We stood together and watched the chain of a swing drip black onto the snow in slow taps. You could hear boards splitting somewhere inside the mound of heat. It sounded like bones if you let your imagination run. I could not stop mine.

A shout broke the rhythm. One of the firefighters stepped back and pointed with the heavy hand of a man in thick gloves. "Here," he called. "Chief, here. You need to see this."

The crowd pressed forward against the tape and then recoiled when it hummed under strain. Collins ducked beneath, and I followed before I had time to think about rules. The heat slapped my face. Snow wet my boot and then refroze. The air shimmered, and for a second, I could not tell what I was looking at. Then the smoke shifted like a curtain drawn by a cautious hand.

Letters. Not carved. Arranged. Someone had stacked the charred planks and beams in lines before the fire reached them, and the flame had done the rest. The blackened wood framed lighter troughs in the dirt, and the embers in those grooves still pulsed red like veins.

The time has come.

The words sat there in the middle of everything that had melted, patient and sure of themselves. For an instant the message seemed to lift a little, as if it breathed. The hair along my arms rose. The fire popped and settled. A child whimpered behind us and the sound cut straight through the heat and lodged behind my heart.

Collins swore in a voice that did not carry. It sounded more like a prayer someone had forgotten how to aim. He looked at me, and I knew we were having the same thought. Whoever had done this was not hiding. They wanted to be understood. They wanted the town to read.

The murmurs behind the tape thickened. Someone said the words aloud and then covered her mouth as if saying them had given them power. A man made the sign of the cross with a hand that shook. Another man said that vandals had no respect and another told him to shut up. Pastor Lewis stood with his hat in his hands and stared as if the sentence might tell him what to preach on Sunday. The mayor was not there. The square coat and the cue cards were probably folded neatly on a chair while she sat awake with her hands on her knees and listened for the phone.

I crouched because my legs had started to shake, and that was the only way to hide it. The heat licked my face. The ash had that delicate lift it gets, like breath, like a whisper, and then fell back into its own darkness. If I reached out, I could smudge the message with one sweep of my glove. I did not move.

"It is for us," I said. I did not mean me and Collins. I meant all of us. The town. The names in the files. The margins in my father's hand. The children who never grew up to hate the winter. The children who might have been adopted and stubborn and alive.

Collins nodded once. "They are ready to finish whatever they started." He kept his eyes on the words, as if they would blink and give him a clue. "We do not get many more warnings."

The last ember in the E went dark and then flared again as the wind changed. The firefighters began to rake the edges, turning wood to gray with the gentle care you give to an injured animal. The tape shivered. The crowd thinned. People had begun to feel the cold again now that the shock had found places to sit inside their bodies. Boots ground grit into the snow. Breath clouded. Someone started to hum a carol and stopped after three notes. It sounded wrong without accompaniment.

"Do you remember when they built this place out of the old beams," I asked, still crouched, "and called it redemption."

Collins's mouth went sideways. "I remember the speeches. I remember the press photo. I remember how relieved everyone looked that they had found something polite to do with guilt."

Behind us Pastor Lewis moved closer to the tape as if proximity could help him understand. He caught my eye and gave a small nod that said he was sorry for something, maybe for the fact that he did not know what to do. His collar looked too white in the smoke. He was the sort of man who might become brave in ten years. We were fresh out of ten years.

The wind carried the smell of the river under the smoke, that cold, metallic scent. A siren that had been wailing somewhere else went silent and the night felt bigger. I stood and brushed my knees with a useless little motion that made ash lift and fall. The words blurred for a heartbeat and came back into focus.

We stayed until the last visible ember surrendered. Snow began again in a patient sift, small flakes that caught in my hair and melted when the heat found them. The sentence slowly dulled as the ash cooled. It did not disappear. It took its time sinking, letter by letter, as if it wanted to be sure we had read it well. I turned away when the last spark in the M winked out. The dark looked deeper than it had when I arrived.

On the way home the streetlights made dull halos on the ice. The town had not gone back to bed. Windows glowed with television light and with the bluish square of phones held in both hands. People sat at kitchen tables without speaking. A dog barked and would not stop. Somewhere a child cried and was told to hush, please, for once, it is late.

At our porch my mother met me with a blanket. She put it around my shoulders without a word. We stood and watched the orange at the edge of the park fade to a tired pink and then to ordinary dark. Collins drove past, slower now. He lifted two fingers off the wheel. It was not a wave. It was acknowledgment. He would not call me Miss Mark in the morning, or ever again. Names change when people begin to carry the same weight.

Inside, I sat at the table and stared at the notebook where my list lived. I did not open it. I could feel the names through the cover anyway, like the way you can feel a splinter beneath skin before it breaks the surface. My hands smelled like smoke even after I washed them. I lay down and the dark behind my eyes filled with red. The playground with its soft summer sounds flickered once, like a film, and then the image burned. I waited for sleep the way you wait for a bus in a storm. It took its time coming and when it arrived it was already full.

The twelfth candle still burned in the square. I knew it without seeing it. I could feel the small, stubborn heat of it somewhere behind my ribs. I did not know if that was faith or fury. I did not know anymore if there was a difference. All I knew was that the message had been set down in fire and ash so that even the people who did not want to read would have to.

I lay there and listened to the house settle and the distant sound of plows, and I understood that whatever was coming would burn hotter than anything before. The town would not walk away untouched. I did not know if I would walk away at all. I closed my eyes and saw the sentence one last time, bright as if written on the inside of my skull.

The time has come.

CHAPTER 13

Lessons in Light

The morning air carried the brittle chill of a town holding its breath. Frost edged the windowpanes like lacework, delicate and sharp. I'd barely slept—my dreams had been tangled knots of smoke and footsteps, children's voices echoing down halls that no longer existed. When I woke, I could still smell the faint burn of the playground, as if ash had lodged itself somewhere in my lungs.

The sheriff had told me to rest, to "slow down before you burn yourself out too," but rest was a luxury I couldn't afford. Every night brought a new fire, a new accident, every dawn another piece of Greenridge reduced to soot. And still the pattern held—the names, the council, the denials.

By midmorning, I was walking toward the new orphanage.

It sat on the far edge of town, past the old mill road, a squat brick building surrounded by frostbitten hedges. Someone had tried to make it cheerful—murals of smiling suns and stick-figure angels covered the walls—but the winter light drained the color, leaving everything pale and tired.

Children's laughter drifted from behind the building. It wasn't the laughter of fear; it was light, real, the kind that cut through the cold for a moment.

I rounded the corner and stopped. Emily Hill stood near the playground, a bright red scarf looped twice around her neck, hair pulled back in a neat ponytail. A boy of maybe eight stood in front of her, shoulders slumped, his mittened hands twisting nervously.

Emily crouched down so their eyes met. "When you knock someone down," she said softly, "you don't just say sorry and walk away. You help them stand again. That's how people learn we mean what we say."

The boy sniffled. "But he called me a liar."

"Then show him what truth looks like," she said. "Be kind anyway."

The boy hesitated, then shuffled off toward a group of children by the swings.

Emily straightened, brushing snow from her coat. That's when she saw me. For a moment, surprise flickered across her face, but she recovered quickly, smiling with the calm of someone who'd practiced grace her whole life.

"Hannah," she said, walking toward me. "I didn't expect to see you here so early."

"I wanted to talk," I said. "If you have a minute."

"Of course." She gestured toward a wooden bench near the fence. "Though I warn you, the bench bites back. It's colder than it looks."

I sat anyway, my breath forming clouds between us. "I've been reading through my father's files. Caldwell's letters. The council's denials. The people who ignored her are the same ones losing everything now."

Emily's expression didn't change, but her fingers tightened around her scarf. "You think these fires are connected."

"I don't think," I said. "I know."

A shadow crossed her face, faint but unmistakable. "You're not the first to look for meaning in tragedy. It's human nature to want order. But sometimes..." She exhaled, a thin stream of white in the air. "Sometimes chaos doesn't have an author."

Her words were careful, deliberate, but I heard what she wasn't saying. She didn't believe that.

"I saw you with the children," I said. "You're good with them. You care."

"I have to," she said simply. "The children I have now need me. I won't fail them like others did."

Her voice broke slightly on that last word—others. She noticed it too and smiled quickly to hide it.

"You're a teacher," I said. "But you sound more like a soldier."

She laughed softly. "Maybe that's what teaching is—fighting a war against what the world does to people."

Her eyes drifted toward the orphanage windows. Inside, I could see a string of paper stars taped to the glass, each one marked with a child's name in uneven handwriting. Hope spelled out in construction paper.

For the first time in weeks, something inside me loosened. Emily's calm wasn't a mask of denial—it was survival. She believed in the goodness that could be built, even here, even after everything. And for a fleeting moment, I envied her for it.

"How do you do it?" I asked. "Keep believing people can be better?"

She tilted her head. "I don't know if I do. But the children believe it, and that's enough to keep trying."

Her words shouldn't have hit as hard as they did. But they did.

A gust of wind sent frost scattering from the eaves. Somewhere, a bell rang—the lunch bell, maybe. The sound made me flinch.

Emily turned toward the door. "I should go. It's reading time."

"Emily," I said before she could leave. "If you know something about the fires—about what's coming—please tell me. You could help stop this."

Her smile faltered, just for a heartbeat. Then she said quietly, "The children of this town have had enough loss for one lifetime. I won't let them suffer again. I'm not getting involved in whatever war the adults of this town want to fight."

"But—"

"No." Her tone was gentle, but firm. "You're brave, Hannah. But bravery can look a lot like self-destruction when no one's beside you."

And with that, she walked inside.

I watched her through the frosted glass. She knelt beside the boy again, helping him open a book. He smiled. She smiled back.

She was everything I wanted to believe still existed in the world—steady, kind, unbroken.

126

And yet something about her words lingered like the smoke from an old fire.

***

By the time I got home, the sheriff's cruiser was parked in front of the house. He stood by the porch steps, coat collar turned up against the cold, hands shoved deep into his pockets.

"Morning," he said.

I raised an eyebrow. "It's past noon."

"Yeah, well, time's a blur when you're chasing ghosts."

Inside, my mother was sorting through old photographs at the kitchen table. She gave the sheriff a faint smile. "Coffee?"

He nodded, and for a few moments, the three of us just sat there, the smell of brewing coffee filling the quiet.

I told him about Emily—her insistence on staying uninvolved, her devotion to the kids, the way she made me feel like maybe there was still good left in people.

He nodded slowly, eyes thoughtful. "She moved here a few years back," he said. "Didn't have much family left, from what I gathered. She said this town gave her purpose again. People like her... they find light where most of us stopped looking."

I traced the rim of my mug. "She said the children believe people can be better."

"Then maybe that's enough," he said. "For her. For them."

I looked up. "What about for us?"

He smiled faintly. "We'll see."

I leaned forward. "You think I should stop?"

"I think," he said, "you should breathe. Whoever's behind this — if there even is someone—they're already miles ahead of us. You'll only burn yourself out chasing shadows."

I stared at him, and for the first time, I saw how tired he truly was. His eyes were rimmed red, his stubble dark against pale skin. He'd aged a decade in a week.

But I couldn't stop. Not now.

"Every night another accident," I said. "Every name another connection. You can't tell me that's coincidence."

He sighed. "I can tell you that I've been here long enough to see how grief eats people alive. Maybe this town deserves the reckoning it's getting. But I don't want you caught in it."

Too late, I thought. I was already in it, neck-deep.

Outside, the church bells began to toll. Another evening, another ritual.

The Thirteenth Candle

The crowd had thinned to barely a quarter of its usual size. Even the choir looked reluctant, their voices small and brittle as glass. Frost clung to the railings, to the hems of coats, to the edges of eyelashes.

The air smelled faintly of smoke. It always did now.

Mayor Evelyn stood on the dais, face powdered too pale against the dark night. She shuffled her notes nervously, the paper trembling in her hands.

"Tonight," she began, "we light the thirteenth candle. A symbol of... of endurance, and of unity in difficult times."

No one spoke. No one smiled.

Her eyes darted over the silent crowd. "You know," she tried, her voice lilting into false cheer, "when I was a girl, we used to fight over who got to light the Advent candles at church. Now I'd pay someone not to volunteer."

A hollow laugh escaped her—alone. The silence that followed was merciless.

She coughed, adjusted the mic, and finished her speech in half the time.

The candle was lit. The flame bent once in the wind, then stood tall, bright, defiant.

I watched it burn and felt the heat of it against my face, though I stood yards away.

When it was over, people drifted off wordlessly. Even the children didn't beg for cocoa anymore.

The sheriff met me at the edge of the square. "You heading home?"

"Soon," I said.

He hesitated. "Stay alert tonight."

The words sat heavy between us.

***

I was halfway through organizing my father's files again when the sirens started.

It was near midnight. I dropped the folder in my hands and ran to the window.

An orange glow bled through the fog, distant but unmistakable.

I didn't need to ask where.

By the time I reached Main Street, half the town was already there. Smoke poured from the pharmacy, flames chewing through the roof, licking the brick with greedy fingers. The sign out front—Greenridge Apothecary—glowed like molten glass before collapsing inward.

The heat was unbearable.

"Everyone out?" I shouted.

A woman near me nodded, tears streaking down soot-stained cheeks. "He wasn't inside. Thank God."

The sheriff's voice cut through the chaos. "Keep back! Let them work!"

He caught sight of me and strode over, face streaked with ash. "You shouldn't be here."

"Who was it?" I demanded.

He hesitated, jaw tight. "Pharmacist. John Doyle."

I blinked. "Mrs. Doyle's husband?"

He nodded. "The same. He was on the committee that signed off on the orphanage's medical inspection reports."

The fire hissed and cracked, sparks raining like gold dust.

"Falsified," I said quietly. "They said the kids were healthy when half of them were coughing their lungs out."

He didn't answer, but he didn't have to.

We stood there, side by side, watching the flames eat through the last of the roof.

Another name crossed off the list. Another sin burned clean.

I should have felt satisfaction. Closure. Instead, I felt hollow.

When the last ember died, I turned to him. "How many more, do you think?"

He looked toward the church, where the thirteenth candle still flickered in the distance. "As many as it takes," he said quietly, "for whoever's doing this to think they've saved what's left of this town."

And for the first time, I wasn't sure whether he meant to stop them—or join them.

CHAPTER 14

The Weight of Forgiveness

The morning began with silence. Not the comforting kind, but the heavy sort that sits in your chest and waits for you to breathe wrong. I stood at the window, mug cooling in my hands, and watched snow drift down over the empty street. Even the birds had stopped coming to the feeder. They knew something was wrong in Greenridge.

Behind me, the Sheriff coughed softly. "You ready?"

I turned. He was already at the kitchen table, sleeves rolled up, papers spread across the surface like a surgeon preparing for a long operation. My father's signature was everywhere — the same looping M.L. that used to sign birthday cards and sermon notes. Now it marked re-routed budgets and canceled repairs.

"I don't think you ever get ready for this," I said.

"Fair," he muttered. "But we need to finish."

He handed me another folder. The town seal was stamped across the front in faded ink. Inside were transfer slips, each with a tidy line item: Emergency fund → Community festivities. Safety budget → Holiday lighting. Over and over. The handwriting approving it was neat, deliberate, familiar.

"My father," I whispered.

Collins nodded. "He moved everything meant for the orphanage. Every last dollar."

The words slid through me like cold water. "For banners. For candles. For carols." I looked up. "For vanity."

He didn't argue. "For appearances," he said quietly. "That's what the council wanted. He gave them what they wanted."

I dropped the folder onto the pile. The pages fanned out, a paper storm. "You realize this means he wasn't some bystander. He orchestrated it."

"I know."

The admission didn't comfort me. It hollowed me out. My father had always said sin begins with small compromises — one lie, one omission. I wondered if he ever realized he'd become the example.

My mother entered then, slow steps, bathrobe pulled tight. She looked smaller lately, as if each revelation had taken something from her. She glanced at the mess on the table but didn't speak. Collins greeted her softly; she nodded without meeting his eyes.

I watched her move toward the counter, where she poured herself coffee she wouldn't drink. "You knew," I said. It came out harsher than intended. "Didn't you?"

Her shoulders stiffened. "I suspected. Not this... not like this."

"Then why didn't you stop him?"

She turned. "Because I loved him."

"That's not an answer."

"It's the only one I have." Her voice trembled, but she didn't cry. "He believed obedience was faith. He thought questioning meant betrayal. I didn't know how to fight that."

The Sheriff cleared his throat, giving her a small mercy. "We're tracing where the money went," he said. "If we can prove the council benefitted, it shows intent. Fraud, at minimum."

My mother nodded absently, her gaze fixed on a water stain spreading along the ceiling. "Intent," she murmured. "He always had plenty of that."

I sat down beside the Sheriff. "How many names so far?"

"Eight." He pointed to a sheet. "Thomas, Murphy, Doyle, the mayor's husband, a few others. All signed the same approvals."

"Everyone who's suffered since the candles started," I said.

He nodded. "Every one."

The coincidence was gone. It was a pattern, carved in ash.

I traced my father's initials with my fingertip. The loops were too perfect, too calm. "He thought faith would save him," I said. "But it only hid him."

"Maybe that's the same thing," Collins replied. "For people like him."

I looked up sharply, but he didn't flinch. He wasn't accusing; he was tired of excuses. I respected that.

For the next hour we worked in near silence, cataloguing transfers, circling amounts, connecting dates. The sound of pencil against paper was steady, rhythmic, almost soothing. For a moment it felt like control — fragile, borrowed, but real.

My mother finally spoke again. "When you find everyone responsible," she asked, "what happens then?"

"We tell the truth," I said.

"And after that?"

I didn't answer. Because truth never fixed what it exposed.

***

By noon the kitchen smelled of dust and cold coffee. We'd built another evidence board along the wall — newspaper clippings, photos, red string connecting one signature to another. My father's picture from a church bulletin sat in the center. The smiling face of a man who preached salvation while signing death warrants disguised as budget cuts.

Collins stepped back and studied it. "You know," he said, "for a small town, this is one hell of a conspiracy."

"Not a conspiracy," I said. "A congregation."

He gave a humorless laugh. "Maybe both."

The clock ticked toward one. My mother finally sank into a chair. Her fingers toyed with her rosary. "Do you think God still forgives men like your father?" she asked.

The Sheriff didn't answer. He knew the question wasn't for him.

I took a breath. "Forgiveness requires confession."

Her eyes lifted to mine. "And if the sinner's dead?"

"Then the burden's ours."

She closed her eyes, whispering a prayer I couldn't hear. The beads clicked softly. The sound used to comfort me; now it reminded me of counting bodies.

I gathered the files into neat piles. The motion steadied me. "He once said faith was endurance," I murmured. "Maybe endurance is just another word for punishment."

The Sheriff gave a small nod. "Maybe."

When he left, the house felt even emptier. I stayed by the window, watching him walk down the street, his figure shrinking against the snow. My mother moved behind me, her reflection blurred in the glass. She placed a hand on my shoulder — gentle, trembling.

"You can't carry all of this alone," she said.

"I don't know how not to."

Her hand lingered, then fell away. "Then at least don't forget why you're doing it."

I watched her walk back toward the kitchen, her robe brushing the floor, and I thought: maybe she's the only one still trying to believe there's something holy left to save.

The Fourteenth Candle

By evening, clouds rolled in from the hills, thick and low. The square looked smaller under them, swallowed by shadow. Fewer people came tonight — maybe twenty, maybe less. Their faces were hidden behind scarves, their eyes darting toward the church doors as if expecting them to open on their own.

The mayor stood at the podium again, her breath fogging in front of her face. The fourteenth candle waited beside her, its wax flecked with frost. She fumbled with the matchbox, dropping one, then another. Someone in the crowd coughed. No one laughed.

"Tonight," she began, "we light another candle… as a reminder that faith endures." Her voice cracked. "Even now."

The pastor beside her shifted uncomfortably, the hem of his robe catching the wind. He tried to lead a hymn, but the first note broke halfway out of his throat. Silence answered him. The mayor smiled tightly, eyes glassy.

She struck another match. The flame flared, small and uncertain, before settling on the wick. "For hope," she whispered.

No one clapped. No one prayed aloud. The sound of the wind against the eaves filled the gaps where singing used to be. It wasn't a ceremony anymore — it was a vigil.

I stood near the back, beside Collins. His breath came out in clouds. "You can feel it," he said under his breath. "This town's holding itself together with twine."

I nodded. "And each candle cuts another strand."

We stayed until the mayor ended it early, muttering excuses about the cold. People scattered fast, boots crunching across frozen snow. Only the candle stayed, flickering stubbornly on the platform like it refused to admit what it represented.

As we walked away, I asked, "Do you ever wonder if the person behind this thinks they're doing the right thing?"

He looked at me. "You mean justice?"

"I mean redemption."

He hesitated. "I think they believe they're balancing the scales."

I thought of the files, of my father's signature, of the coffins filled with children the fire left behind. "Then maybe they're the only one who is."

He didn't answer.

***

135

I couldn't sleep that night. The house creaked like it was remembering. My mother had gone to bed hours ago, leaving the hallway dimly lit by a single lamp. I sat on the sofa with the files again, tracing the ink, memorizing numbers. Around two a.m., I smelled smoke.

At first, I thought it was in my head — phantom scent, like the memories that came every time I closed my eyes. But then the window pulsed orange. Real. Immediate.

I grabbed my coat and ran.

The church loomed dark against the sky, but light flickered from inside. The door was ajar. I pushed it open and stepped into the silence.

Smoke curled in ribbons near the ceiling. The air smelled of wax and burnt paper. Candles had been overturned, some still glowing faintly in pools of melted wax. The altar was blackened, but not destroyed. At first glance it looked like another act of vandalism; then I saw the message.

Ash smeared across the white altar cloth, thick and deliberate. A child's handprint in the center, five small fingers pressed deep into soot. Beneath it, written in uneven strokes:

THE DEBT IS NOT FORGIVEN.

My stomach dropped. The words seemed to breathe with the draft. I stepped closer. The heat still radiated from the cloth. Whoever did this hadn't left long ago.

Footsteps echoed behind me. Collins's flashlight beam swept the pews. "Hannah?"

"Here."

He joined me at the altar, jaw tightening when he saw the writing. "Christ."

"Looks like the same message as the others," I said. "But different place."

"They're escalating."

He crouched, examining the handprint. "Small. Could be a child."

136

"Or someone wants us to think that."

He looked up at me. "You think it's connected to the money?"

"I think everything is." I gestured toward the words. "My father's debt. The council's debt. Maybe the town's."

The wind outside rose, pushing through the cracks of the stained-glass window. The Virgin Mary's face fractured under the shifting light. For a second the colored shards made her look alive — eyes glistening, mouth curved in sorrow.

I felt something tighten in my throat. "I used to sit right there," I said, pointing to the front pew. "He'd make me listen to every sermon twice — once from the pew, once at home."

Collins glanced at me. "He believed you'd follow him."

"He believed wrong."

We stood there for a long moment, letting the smoke thin. Somewhere in the rafters, ice cracked. The sound echoed like distant applause. Collins finally exhaled. "We'll keep this quiet tonight," he said. "No press. No panic."

"They'll hear anyway."

"I know."

He turned off his flashlight, letting the candlelight take over. Shadows swallowed the corners of the church. For a moment we stood in near-darkness, two silhouettes in a place meant for worship.

I reached out and touched the edge of the altar cloth. The soot came off on my fingers, black and oily. It smelled faintly of wax and iron — like the world had burned and refused to cool.

Outside, through the cracked door, I saw the fourteenth candle still burning in the square. Its light trembled in the wind but didn't die. I watched it until the Sheriff touched my arm.

"Come on," he said softly. "Nothing more we can do tonight."

As we stepped outside, snow began to fall again — soft, slow, relentless. The flakes landed on the soot on my hands, melting into gray streaks. I rubbed them together, trying to clean them, but the black lingered under my nails.

The town slept behind shuttered windows, pretending it didn't smell the smoke. Pretending none of this was real. But I knew better.

Forgiveness wasn't coming.

Not for him.
Not for us.
Not for anyone.

CHAPTER 15

Paper Ghosts

By morning the snow had crusted over, a thin, glassy shell that cracked underfoot with a sound like breaking china. I walked fast because walking slowly made the cold feel personal. The breath in front of me fogged and then vanished; if only the past could do the same.

I'd sketched a plan the way I used to prep for a night shift: triage first, then orders, then the slow, stubborn work of keeping someone alive. On paper it made sense. In the body, everything argued back. So did a town.

The "someone" we were trying to keep alive now wasn't a person, not yet. It was a thread: the surviving child. If there was a center to all of this, a living mind that remembered exactly how the orphanage was left to fail, it had to be the child who slipped through the fire when no one else did. The fires weren't random anymore. They were a map—and maps point to destinations.

Town Hall had a vestibule that still smelled faintly of wet wool and pencil shavings. The clerk on duty wore a sweater with snowmen along the hem and the pinched look of someone who'd developed an allergy to questions. She recognized me the way people do now: a flinch first, then a slow professional smile.

"I need old placement records," I said. "Child welfare. Orphanage closures. Any adoption agency that handled transfers the year of the fire."

She folded her hands. "We don't keep those onsite. You'd need county."

"County burned," I said. "We both know that."

A flash across her face, quick as static. "Then the state," she said, recovering. "You can submit a request."

I slid a form across her desk with the blank spaces already filled. The ink looked too dark against the paper. "Submitted."

She took it without looking down and buzzed a back room. While we waited, I watched a family of three stamp snow off their boots by the radiator. The child's coat had a rip at the elbow, the stuffing peeking out like a handful of cloud. He laughed when his father shook snow from his hat; the sound was a bright thing in a gray morning. I caught myself smiling and then didn't, because you don't get to keep joy in Greenridge; you borrow it and return it mostly intact.

The clerk returned alone. "County did use an intermediary for the orphanage closures," she said, softer now, as if the word itself needed cushioning. "Heartland Family Services."

I blinked. "They're still around?"

A shake of the head. "Dissolved ten years ago. Absorbed into a regional non-profit that rebranded twice since. Records are... patchwork."

"Meaning gone."

"Meaning incomplete," she corrected, which was the polite way to say the same thing.

"Who signed the dissolution?" I asked.

She rummaged in a canvas bin and came up with a thin photocopy—faded letterhead, a list of board names like dull knives. At the bottom: Treasurer: Harold P. Keller.

I felt the sheriff's presence before I saw him, that steady quiet he carried like a second coat. He slid to my side, nodding at the clerk with the sort of tired courtesy that's become its own language. "Morning."

She returned it in the same dialect and disappeared again, grateful to have something to do besides hold bad news.

"Keller," I said.

"Former church treasurer," he replied. "Signed off on 'reallocation' funds for the orphanage that year."

"Of course he did."

140

We stepped aside to let the snow-coat family pass, the child's boots squeaking on linoleum. The door sighed open; cold swirled through the lobby and settled again. For a beat, the air tasted like metal.

"Missing agency," he said, holding up a finger. "Fragmented county records." Second finger. "Aging witnesses with selective memories." Third finger. "And a church that benefits from amnesia."

"All solvable problems," I said, because bravado and hope sometimes share a closet.

We drove to the county annex where "Records" was a basement with fluorescent lights that hummed like a trapped insect. We fed coins into a microfilm machine while the clerk on duty pretended to update a spreadsheet and told me, unprompted, that her cousin's brakes had "mysteriously failed" last week. People are itching to confess fear if you look like you'll keep it safe.

On the screen, columns of names flickered past: donations, placements, transfers. I found what passed for an orphanage closure schedule—typed, then hand-corrected; strike-throughs like scars. Heartland Family Services appeared in the corner of multiple pages, chopped to HFS and once to just Heart. Over fifty records had been marked with the same stamp: REASSIGNED. Another twenty: RETURNED—INSUFFICIENT INFO. One line had no stamp, no annotation. It didn't even have a name. Just a number and a half-typed designation: F–07, female, approx. 6–8, no known family, provisional guardian— and then the type faded, mid-syllable, like the machine lost its nerve.

"F 07," I said. "She has a label and not a name."

"That was common then," the sheriff said. "Kids became paperwork. Numbers were easier to lose."

We chased the thread. F–07 popped up again two pages later, a note in different ink: pending placement via Heartland satellite office — Millers Crossing. The satellite office number was the kind that predates area codes; the date attached was a decade too old for calling it to do anything but reach some man's garage.

"Millers Crossing?" I asked. "That's three towns over."

"Now it's a storage unit facility," he said. "We raided it in '09 for forged titles. Nothing about kids."

"Heartland was dissolved by then."

He nodded. "Board signatures we know. Keller, Murphy, a few others."

We tried a different angle. The county recorder's office—deeds, property transfers, the quiet legal shuffling of a town's bones. If a child had been placed through a private adoption (and Heartland had done those, too), there might be a sealed notation paired with a change of name, a court docket that lived in a room like this—the kind no one visits unless they owe money or want to forget.

The clerk was young enough to still believe rules were a blanket. "If it's sealed," she said, "it's sealed."

"Even if it's evidence," the sheriff said.

"Is it?"

He didn't answer, which was its own kind of answer.

We left with nothing we could hold in our hands, but we weren't empty. The shape of the emptiness had edges now: F–07, Heartland, Keller, Millers Crossing. In medicine, when you can't find the problem, you chart the absences: negative tox screen, lungs clear to auscultation, no murmurs, denies pain—and in the white space between them, the truth hides. This was that. A chart of what our town refused to say aloud.

We drove to the library next because libraries remember what people work hard to forget. The reference desk clerk wore fingerless gloves and had the hair of a person who'd said, "It's just a trim" and been lied to. When I asked for old newspaper reels around the time of the fire, she made the face librarians make right before they become saints for you.

"The Herald didn't run much," she said, unrolling brittle copies on the table. "The paper owner was best man at your parents' wedding."

A chord struck in my ribs, low and mean.

"Here," she said, setting down one from the week after. The headline was a hymn to resilience. The subhead mentioned "community generosity" and "safety upgrades forthcoming." Down-column, buried like a tooth in gum, a single sentence: "Heartland Family Services to assist with temporary and permanent placements; inquiries may be directed to the parish office."

My father's face was in the photo above, framed by smoke-dimmed Christmas lights. His collar was straight. His smile was the one people called compassionate. I watched my mother's hand rest in the crook of his arm and thought about how the body learns to anchor to whatever looks steady.

"Do you have any clipping files on Heartland?" I asked.

"Someone else asked a few months ago," she said. "An out-of-town researcher. Said she was doing a piece on regional adoption histories."

"Did she leave a name?"

"No," the clerk said, rolling another reel. "But she took notes for hours. Barely drank her tea." A wistful smile. "I liked her."

"Her?"

The clerk glanced up. "Yes—her." She paused, seeing my face. "Dark hair. Early thirties. Soft voice. Sharp eyes."

The sheriff and I exchanged a look that said we heard the same thing, didn't we. I wrote the description down like I was writing an order I couldn't fill: female researcher, early 30s, dark hair, quiet, focused. The shape that had been a rumor grew edges. I was a nurse again, reading an ECG—no longer guessing at electrical disturbances but seeing a definite rhythm, unkind and real.

Outside, the day's light had stretched thin. The kind of thin that tears if you touch it wrong. We stood beside the sheriff's cruiser, each of us facing a separate corner of the same problem.

"You still think the survivor is the center," he said.

"I think all roads lead to her," I replied. "If not the hand, then the voice. Either she's speaking through these fires or someone else is speaking on her behalf. Everyone's pain is generic. Hers would be specific."

He nodded slowly. "And specific pain acts like a compass."

"Exactly."

He rubbed a gloved thumb along his jaw. "If she's the one lighting these—"

"We don't know that," I cut in, because I needed to be fair even if fairness didn't matter to flames.

"—if," he said, patient, "then she's not just settling scores. She's curating the record. Preserving what matters, burning what lies." He glanced back toward Town Hall. "You notice? Every time something burns, something else about the orphanage survives."

"Not accident," I said. "Arrangement."

He looked off down Main Street where the square sat like a stage we kept resetting with worse props. "Whoever's doing this is running out of nights," he said. "If there are twenty-five candles in a season and we're halfway there, escalation's coming."

The word worked its way into my bones. Escalation.

When we got back to my mother's, I spread everything across the table and made myself list what we knew, what we guessed, and what we feared. It's how I keep panic from fogging my hands.

Known: Heartland handled placements, dissolved under Keller. One child listed as F–07 with no follow-up name. The "researcher," recent and careful. My father's signature like a tide mark on every bad decision.

Guessed: F–07 left under a new name through Millers Crossing. If she stayed close enough to pry at the library, she's within driving distance. She's watching the town from the edges and leaving messages we're meant to read.

Feared: The fires were no longer about property. The ledger would get flesh.

My mother came in as I was shuffling the notes. She set a plate of toast beside me like an apology. "I prayed for your father this morning," she said. "Then I prayed for the child who lived."

"What did you ask for?"

"That she has a name now," she said. "That someone calls her by it."

It was the gentlest sentence I'd heard in weeks. It cut deeper than the newsprint.

"Mom," I said, "if we find her—"

144

"When," she corrected, stubborn in the way faith can be stubborn even when it's threadbare.

"When," I agreed, because sometimes love is agreeing to grammar you don't believe in. "When we find her, what then?"

"Then you listen," she said, as if that were the simplest and hardest thing in the world. "Then maybe the fires stop."

I wanted to believe her the way I had as a child when she told me thunder was God moving furniture. I knew better, now. Sometimes thunder is just weather you didn't prepare for because you hoped you wouldn't need to.

When the church bell tolled seven, the sound felt like a spoon striking a glass: time to gather. The fifteenth candle waited.

The Fifteenth Candle

The wind chased us down Main as if it wanted to see what we'd do next. The square had thinned to pockets of people huddled close enough to share breath. No one pretended this was tradition anymore. It was surveillance. We watched each other out of the corners of our eyes and pretended we didn't.

The mayor kept her remarks brief because you can hear when your voice has worn out its welcome. She didn't even try for a joke this time. The pastor's prayer snagged on the word mercy and broke. No one bothered to rescue it. A child in the front started to cry, not for any reason, just for being small and cold in a world that had stopped making sense—and every adult pretended not to hear, because comforting one child means remembering the others.

The fifteenth candle caught on the second strike. A tiny bevel of flame, then taller, like courage rehearsing. The crowd didn't sing;

they whispered, and whispering sounded worse than silence. It sounded like collusion.

We slipped away before the mayor could force us to feel blessed. The sheriff walked me halfway home, then peeled off toward the station, promising to check a storage unit lead in the morning. I watched his taillights until they turned into distant cherries and blinked away.

Snow kept falling. It softened the town into something that looked harmless until you put your hands in it and lost feeling.

I was in the kitchen winding the clock—something my father used to make me do, an old rule that had outlived the man—when the sirens punched the night. One, then two, then a chorus. The sound hit low in my spine, the way alarms do when a heart monitor goes from chaotic to flat and your body knows before your brain catches up: this one is bad.

I grabbed my coat and boots, didn't bother with gloves. My mother called my name; I shouted back stay with a firmness I didn't feel and ran.

The glow turned the snow orange two blocks before I could see the fire. It drew a crowd like fires always do—horror's magnetism.

It was Keller's place. Former treasurer. Detached garage with a loft like so many around here—cheap wood, a promise of independence for someone's grown kid who was "finding his footing," as the polite phrase goes. The main house stood a short distance away, lights on, front door yawning. The garage was the thing roared alive.

Flames licked out from the clapboard seams, a living thing pushing, testing. The loft window glowed white. Smoke stacked above the roofline in a column like a threat.

"Is anyone inside?" I asked the first face I recognized.

"His boy," the man said, not taking his eyes off the fire. "Upstairs. Works nights sometimes. Sleeps days. Keller said he was in the loft reading when the breaker popped." He swallowed hard. "Went to reset it. Then this."

"Does he have a name?" I asked, because people deserve more than "boy" when the smoke's already in their lungs.

146

"Paul," the man said, and I held the name like you hold a wrist you're about to check for a pulse.

The sheriff pushed through the ring of onlookers, his radio at his shoulder, his jaw set. He scanned for me and didn't look surprised when he found me. "Medics are en route," he said, which means not here yet.

The fire crews were already deploying, hoses snaked like veins across the snow, steam rising where water met heat. The captain shouted orders. No one wasted a motion. The loft window flashed dark for a heartbeat, then light again.

"He's up there," someone said, pointing.

I moved closer because sometimes all you can do is be the body that moves closer. Black smoke peeled down as the garage door buckled. A pair of firefighters hit the side door with a Halligan; it gave, vomiting thick gray. The air hissed like a snake.

Then I heard the coughing. Raw, animal. A human body insisting on air that kept refusing to be anything but poison.

They dragged him out six minutes later that felt like a year. Paul was tall in the heavy, slack way of a person who'd been vertical until his muscles stopped negotiating. His hair was singed; his eyebrows gone. Soot ringed his nostrils like a child's crayon misapplied. The skin at his temples was pinked and stippled but not blistered—no deep burns. That was a mercy.

The danger was inside.

"Here," I said, already moving into the space the firefighters cleared. "I'm a nurse."

I'm not sure I had the right to say it after weeks away from the floor, after nights of pretending the world wouldn't need my hands again. But my body remembered before my ethics did.

We lay him on the snow because sometimes cold is medicine, sometimes it's just a surface. His chest rose fast, shallow. The kind of respirations you get when your brain thinks air is coming and your lungs disagree.

"Paul," I said, leaning over him so he'd have a focal point that wasn't fire. "My name is Hannah. You're outside. You're safe. Breathe with me."

His eyes were wild. Sclera so bloodshot they looked painted. His pupils reacted, sluggish but present. Soot blackened his tongue. The smell coming off him was a chemical sawblade: smoke and melted plastic and that sweet almond tang I hoped I was imagining because cyanide feels like a rumor until it isn't.

"Non-rebreather," I snapped, out of habit, and one of the firefighters—blessed souls—had already grabbed an O2 kit. Mask over his face. The hiss of oxygen like a small benevolent snake this time.

"SpO$_2$ is ninety-nine," someone said, glancing at a little finger clip pulled from a jump bag.

"Worthless," I said, sharper than I meant to. "SpO$_2$ lies with carbon monoxide on board. It reads saturation, not truth." My hands moved without input: two fingers under his jaw, checking for swelling; a quick look at the inside of his mouth—black soot, no blistering in the oropharynx, good, less likely thermal injury. Breath sounds wheezy on the right, coarse on the left. "We need a carboxyhemoglobin level," I added, because wanting is a language medicine speaks even when the lab's ten miles away and closed.

Paul tried to rip the mask off. I caught his wrist, firm but not cruel. "No," I said, and my voice found the register it used for panicked parents and dying kids. "Mask stays on. That's your job. Mine is everything else."

He blinked at me, recognition not of me but of the tone. He left the mask.

A firefighter brought a blanket. We slid it under his shoulders. Another unscrewed a bottle of sterile water; I wet a cloth and wiped his eyes. Soot came away in gray streaks. He coughed a string of black spit into the snow, and it melted a small pit, obscene and real.

"Any burns?" the sheriff asked, crouching on the other side.

"Superficial at most," I said. "Big risk is poisoning. Smoke inhalation, carbon monoxide, possibly cyanide if synthetics were heavy up there." I nodded toward the loft window, where a shade fluttered in the heat like a white flag's ghost. "He was in it long enough to see God and come back."

Paul gagged, turned his head, vomited. It was all smoke and bile. I rolled him, swept his mouth with the cloth, let him retch until his diaphragm stopped fighting air and started letting it in again.

"Any chest pain?" I asked when he could hear me.

He nodded too hard. "Hur—" The rest dissolved in coughing.

"Could be from coughing," I told the sheriff, "or myocardial stress from hypoxia. He needs high-flow oxygen, monitoring, and likely a cyanokit if anyone around here still stocks one."

"Ambulance is two minutes out," Collins said.

"Two minutes is a lifetime," I muttered, then to Paul: "Hey. Look at me."

He did. Soot had settled into the lines beside his mouth at an age too young for lines.

"You're not dying tonight," I said, and believed it just enough to make it a tool. "Breathe in. Now slow out." I breathed with him—four seconds in, six out—until his shoulders loosened a fraction.

The medics pulled up with the sort of controlled hurry I will always respect. We rattled off what we knew. Vital signs: tachycardic, tachypneic, blood pressure holding, mental status improving. Soot in nares and mouth; no obvious airway burns. They started a line, hung fluids, kept oxygen where it belonged. One medic looked at me with the professional nod that says good catch on the SpO_2. I nodded back with the one that says thanks for coming when it matters.

As they loaded him, he grabbed my sleeve. His voice was ragged under the mask. "The boxes," he forced out. "Dad's boxes."

"What about them?" I asked, leaning in because truth likes to be heard close.

"Up there," he said. "All the money stuff. Records. He said not to touch 'em. Said they were church business."

Across the lot, the garage roof sighed and folded in like a lung that had decided breathing was a young person's game. A pillar of sparks leapt and died.

The sheriff's eyes found mine. We didn't need words. Boxes of financial records, destroyed. The past burning itself in effigy while we stood close enough to feel our eyelashes singe.

149

They took Paul, siren yelping twice to clear the intersection, then steady and receding. People watched with the flat faces of those who have given up on surprise.

"Anyone else hurt?" Collins asked the captain.

"Neighbors with smoke exposure," he said, "but okay. Nobody burned. Lucky."

Lucky, I thought, the way you do when your definition of luck keeps shrinking.

Keller himself wasn't in sight. Someone said he'd been at the holiday committee meeting until the power flickered, that he came home to find the garage already taking, that he ran into the yard shouting records! as if paper had lungs. The firefighters had held him back, the way you hold someone back from the grave they dug.

We stood outside the tape while the crews fought what remained. The night was so cold it ate the fire's edges. Foam hissed, snow turned gray, steam lifted and bit our faces. The loft stairs were visible through the garage door's torn mouth: blackened, half-standing, the top step gone, a momentary stairway to nothing.

"What started it?" someone asked.

"Wiring," a voice said automatically, the town's reflex. Then, quieter, guiltier: "Or not."

The sheriff spoke low. "We'll have an investigator look. But you and I know this was placed."

"Arson that eats only what it needs," I said. "Selective appetite."

"Smart arson," he muttered, as if the word itself shouldn't be allowed.

My hands had stopped shaking. It always happens like that for me—panic at the first siren, a sober clarity once the damage shows itself, the shakes later when no one's watching. I wiped the last of the soot from my fingers onto a napkin I hadn't realized I'd been holding since the medics left. The black smeared. It would be under my nails tomorrow. That's how smoke stays: little reminders in places that weren't invited.

"I need to see his father," I said.

"He's in the house," the sheriff replied. "They're keeping him back."

150

We walked there together. Inside, heat cranked so high it felt ugly. Keller sat at the kitchen table with a blanket around his shoulders, a styrofoam cup steaming between his hands. He looked smaller without the word treasurer shoring him up.

"I'm sorry about your son," I began, because decency and fury can coexist.

"He'll live," he said hoarsely, as if the phrase owed him money. "They said so."

I nodded. "He will."

His eyes slid past me to the window where a fire truck pulsed red-white-red. "All my records," he said, and I swear I heard something satisfied pushed down under the grief. "Gone."

He didn't meet the sheriff's gaze.

"Church records?" I asked evenly.

He flinched. The sheriff didn't miss it.

"I told Paul not to touch them," Keller said, a little too quickly, like he'd rehearsed it. "Old stuff. No use to anyone."

"Then why store them in a loft lined with pine and bad wiring?" I asked.

His mouth tightened. "You can leave now," he said. It was the tone of a man who used to believe people did what he said.

"We will," the sheriff said easily, and we did.

The town had drifted back to their houses by the time the last visible flame died. Steam curled from the structure like breath from a sleeping beast. The air tasted like pennies. The snow at our feet had gone gray, the way snow always goes gray around the truth.

The ambulance returned, briefly, a medic stepping out to find the sheriff. He spoke low. "He's stable. O_2 sat ninety-eight on high flow. Carboxyhemoglobin will be high—sending blood to county lab. Airway's okay for now."

"Cyanide?" I asked.

"Hard to test here," he said apologetically. "We gave hydroxocobalamin empirically—protocol on heavy synthetic smoke. Turned his skin a little pink. He'll pee red. Don't panic."

I felt something like gratitude crack my sternum. "Thank you."

He shrugged in the old medic way. "Man was on the wrong side of hot gas. He's lucky he's strong."

After he left, the sheriff and I stood in the middle of the street where the heat had carved a dry circle in the snow. The silence wasn't real; it was an accumulation of sounds we were trying not to notice: the ticking of cooling metal, a neighbor crying behind a closed door, the squeal of a hose being coiled, the church bell in the distance chiming an hour that meant nothing.

"First official casualty," he said quietly. "And it won't be the last."

The wind found my wrists where the coat didn't. "This is the turn," I said. "Whoever's doing this isn't just erasing anymore. They're willing to hurt people to underline the sentence."

His eyes flickered to the ruin of the loft. "And yet," he said, voice low, "it's still curated. Not the house. Not the man. The records. Paper first, flesh only to prove a point."

"Some points require blood," I said, and hated that I knew that.

We walked back toward the square in the kind of exhausted quiet that's almost intimate. At the edge of Main, the fifteenth candle still burned, the wick a tiny coal now, not a flame, a stubborn ember teaching itself how to last.

"People are whispering openly," I said. "They weren't before."

"They're whispering names," he said. "Yours. Mine. Keller's. Your father's. The survivor's."

"You think they know about her?" I asked.

"They don't," he said. "They believe. Belief is louder."

I stared at the candle until it guttered, flared, and then steadied, a small defiance. The town would wake tomorrow and pretend it was just another accident with better timing. We wouldn't let them. The ledger had a heartbeat now: Paul. Smoke inhalation, high-flow O_2, cyanokit in a town that shouldn't know that word and now did.

"You should go home," the sheriff said.

"You too."

He snorted. "Tell that to the paperwork."

We shared a look that was more than agreement. It was a pact carved out of fatigue. If we were going to stop this—if it could be stopped—we'd have to accept two truths at once: the person lighting these fires was writing the history our town refused to keep, and they were becoming more dangerous by the night.

At my porch, I paused with my hand on the rail. Frost glittered along the wood, beautiful and indifferent. Inside, my mother had left the hall light on. It made a warm square on the floorboards like a promise.

I could still taste smoke. It had a way of finding the soft tissues and staying, a chemical memory. I washed my hands three times anyway. The water ran gray, then clear, then gray again from under my nails.

I lay awake longer than I intended. At some unholy hour, the house creaked, and I thought of the loft stairs, of the boxes turned to soft ash, of a son calling out through smoke and the way his eyes found mine when I gave him an order, how relief felt like oxygen threading clean into blood.

F–07. Heartland. Millers Crossing. Keller. Paul.

The list wasn't just names. It was a map drawn in heat and dark.

And in the white space beside the list, I wrote what I didn't want to say aloud:

Whoever you are, we are coming. We'll bring water, and we'll bring names.

Outside, one candle's worth of light still seemed to stain the snow, though I knew it was only moon. The town slept. The fires did not.

CHAPTER 16

The Quiet Before the Ashes

The kitchen was cold enough to see my breath. The radiator had given up halfway through the night, leaving only the weak light from the window and the smell of lemon polish clinging to every surface. My father's notebook lay open on the table; pages yellowed like bruised skin. I had spent half the night reading it, trying to understand how a man could be so full of God and still let hell grow in his backyard.

His handwriting was perfect. Every word was measured, as if he feared that sloppy ink might expose something ugly beneath. The sermons began with grace, forgiveness, renewal, and slowly bled into warnings about sin, about the price of disobedience. One line stood out in thick, black ink.

Fire is both punishment and purification.

He had written that three months before the orphanage burned.

The words crawled across my mind. The more I read, the more the house seemed to lean closer, listening, daring me to keep turning pages. I found donation records next. Lists of promised repairs. Receipts marked "redirected." A scrawl in my father's careful hand: Funds reallocated for greater good. I knew what that meant. I had seen greater good before. It usually meant someone else's suffering.

My tea had gone cold long ago. The clock on the wall ticked in time with my pulse. Every sound in the house felt too loud. The scrape of my chair. The whistle of wind through the chimney. I closed the notebook carefully, afraid that if I looked any longer, I might see my father for who he really was, not who I had needed him to be.

Then, at the very back of the book, I found something different. Not sermons or council notes — but his handwriting trembling, uneven. A confession written like a prayer:

If the Lord does not forgive me, I will burn until He does.

I sat there for a long time, staring at those words until they blurred. My stomach twisted. He hadn't repented; he'd prepared himself for absolution through fire. He thought destruction would save him.

It hit me suddenly that maybe this whole town was built on that logic — everyone pretending that tragedy was a test, that pain was part of some grand design. Maybe that was why I'd left faith behind. Not because I didn't believe in God, but because I had seen how easily people used Him to excuse their cruelty.

The knock that followed made me jump. Sharp, impatient. I opened the door to find Sheriff Collins standing there, his coat dusted with frost. He looked like a man who hadn't slept in days. The lines under his eyes were deep enough to hold shadows.

"Morning," he said, though it sounded like an apology.

"Barely," I replied, stepping aside. "Come in."

He glanced at the notebook on the table but didn't sit. His gaze lingered on the handwriting. "Still digging through the past?"

"I don't have much choice," I said. "The present isn't exactly improving."

He sighed, rubbing the back of his neck. "You're making people nervous."

"People should be nervous."

"Not like this," he said. "You've got half the town whispering. They think you brought this with you."

I laughed, but it came out sharp. "That's convenient. Saves them from blaming themselves."

He stared at me the way a doctor does when they already know the diagnosis but can't say it out loud.

"You need to lay low," he said finally. "Don't leave the house tonight."

"I'm not hiding."

"This isn't about hiding. It's about surviving."

His tone softened, but I could hear fear beneath it. He was unraveling too, just slower than the rest of us. He looked older than he had a week ago—shoulders heavier, jaw tight. The uniform didn't make him untouchable anymore. He was just another man waiting for the next fire.

"I'll check on you tomorrow," he said. "Promise me you'll stay in."

"I won't promise that," I said. "You know me better."

He gave me a look somewhere between admiration and exhaustion, then left.

The house fell silent again. I sat for a long time, staring at the steam rising from my freshly brewed tea until it faded completely. The faint smell of smoke lingered, even though nothing burned.

By late afternoon, I couldn't sit still. My mother was outside again—she'd been outside more and more lately, always finding something to tend to even when there was nothing left that could grow. Through the window I could see her kneeling in the frozen dirt of the garden, her breath rising in white clouds. The rose bushes were brittle, dusted with frost. The garden looked asleep, not dead— but something about it felt wrong. Too still. Too expectant.

I pulled on my coat and stepped out onto the porch. "You shouldn't be out here," I said.

She didn't look up. "These need tending. Even in winter, they need care."

Her gloves were caked with dark soil, and her movements were slow, deliberate. I knelt beside her, watching her brush the frost away from the base of the rosebush.

"Do you really think they'll bloom again?" I asked.

She shrugged. "Hope is the only thing that still grows, even when nothing else does."

Her voice wavered. It wasn't faith anymore—it was the echo of it.

I looked around at the neighborhood. Curtains fluttered. Doors closed. A man walking his dog crossed the street rather than pass us. My mother saw it too but said nothing.

Inside, the warmth of the house was misleading. It smelled of cinnamon and disinfectant. She had been baking again—probably as a distraction. The table was set for two, though I hadn't said I'd be home for dinner.

"You knew I'd stay," I said.

"I always know," she replied softly, setting a cup of tea in front of me. "You carry your father's restlessness."

I almost laughed. "That's not a compliment."

Her lips pressed together. "He meant well."

"Good men don't let children die because a new roof costs too much."

Her eyes closed. "You think I don't know that?"

The words cracked something in her voice. For the first time, she looked her age. I reached for her hand but stopped when I saw the dirt under her nails—black and charred.

"What's on your hands?" I asked quietly.

She drew them back to her lap. "The soil's darker this year. The frost bit deep."

It was a lie. I didn't push. I'd learned that some truths only shattered what little peace was left.

We ate in silence. Outside, the sky bruised into twilight. When I stood, she followed me to the door.

"Hannah," she said, her voice trembling. "If anything happens, don't let them make you doubt who you are."

"Who am I?" I asked.

Her eyes filled with tears. "A good woman born from bad history."

The Sixteenth Candle

The square looked half-abandoned. The Christmas lights glowed too brightly against the snow, sharp and artificial. The wind carried the faint sound of bells from the church tower, off-key and lonely. I joined the small group huddled near the stage. Twenty, maybe twenty-five people. The mayor stood stiffly beside the candles, her fur collar trembling in the wind.

The choir began, but their voices cracked halfway through the hymn. One of the altos started crying and had to stop. The rest stumbled through the verse, finishing in silence. The crowd didn't clap this time. They only stared at the flame as if waiting for it to choose someone.

The sixteenth candle burned clean and tall. Its light was too steady, too calm. The kind of calm that makes your skin crawl.

When the service ended, no one lingered. People scattered like ash. I caught whispers as they passed.

"She's here again."

"Her mother's still lighting candles at home."

"It's them. It has to be."

By the time I walked my mother home, the words felt carved into my skin. We didn't speak. The snow muffled everything. Even our footsteps sounded like secrets.

The first smell of smoke reached us before the sound of sirens. My mother's house was still a block away when she froze. Her hands trembled. "Hannah," she whispered. "Please, no."

We ran.

The garden was burning. Not the kind of fire that spreads wild, but something worse. The flames were low, creeping through the soil like veins, blue and gold, almost beautiful. The roses folded inward, small, almost blooming petals curling into ash. The air was full of that familiar sweetness, the same scent that hung around the orphanage ruins.

"Help me!" I grabbed the hose, spraying the black soil, but the water turned to steam before it touched the ground.

Neighbors came to their windows, faces ghostly in the glow. None of them stepped outside. Some whispered. Others crossed themselves. One woman shut her curtains as soon as she saw me.

"Call someone!" I shouted.

No one did.

The fire department arrived after what felt like an hour, though it couldn't have been more than ten minutes. The chief crouched near the smoldering fence, shaking his head. "No accelerant. No heat source. It's like it started from underneath."

Sheriff Collins appeared soon after, his eyes darting between me and the flames. "You need to get her inside," he said. "It's not safe out here."

"Nothing's safe anymore," I said.

He looked at the crowd gathering near the edge of the yard. "They're scared, Hannah. That's dangerous."

I turned to the onlookers. "You think this was us? You think we lit our own damn garden on fire?"

No one answered. A few stepped back. One man spit into the snow and muttered something I couldn't hear.

My mother knelt in the dirt, her coat smeared with ash. She was shaking all over, whispering something over and over. I crouched beside her. "What are you saying?"

"They took it," she said, voice thin as thread. "The blessing. They took it back."

I followed her gaze. In the center of the scorched earth lay something small and glinting. I reached for it carefully. It was an ornament, half-melted, its edges fused into a swirl of glass and foil. I brushed away soot until I saw what was inside—a tiny paper angel, burned around the edges but still visible.

My mother sobbed harder. "Your father used to bless this garden every Christmas Eve. Said the earth remembered kindness."

I looked at the ornament in my hand. "Then the earth is tired of remembering."

The firemen doused the last flicker of blue flame. The soil smoked and hissed, refusing to cool. The night smelled of wet ash and betrayal. Collins stood near the gate, talking to a reporter who had arrived too quickly to be innocent curiosity. When he saw me watching, he turned away.

By the time the trucks left, a new rumor had already taken root. I heard it whispered as people walked home.

"She's cursed."

"She's bringing it here."

"It's her father's penance."

I helped my mother inside. She was shaking so badly she could barely climb the steps. I made tea, though neither of us drank it. From the window, the garden looked like a grave. The moonlight turned the smoke silver.

Outside, the street stayed busy longer than it should have. I watched figures gather in the dark — not helping, not comforting — just watching. Some stood with arms folded, others with their phones raised, faces glowing in the blue light. I could almost hear their thoughts. The pastor's daughter. The cursed bloodline. If they burn, maybe it ends.

My mother touched my arm. "They're still out there," she whispered.

"I know," I said.

She reached for my hand and held it tight. "We can't win against ghosts, Hannah."

"They're not ghosts," I said. "They're people who need someone to blame."

"Does it matter?" she asked. "They'll burn us either way."

Her words sent a chill through me deeper than the cold ever could. I stared at the window until the last shape finally drifted away.

"Maybe they're right," my mother said softly. "Maybe this is our punishment."

I stared at her. "For what?"

"For silence," she said. "For knowing and doing nothing."

I wanted to argue, but I couldn't. The truth was a heavy thing, and tonight it sat between us like a third presence in the room.

Outside, the snow began again. It fell over the blackened earth, covering it gently, as if the world was trying to forget. But forgetting wasn't forgiveness. It never was.

I watched until the smoke disappeared, until the garden looked like nothing but frost and shadow. Somewhere in the distance, I thought I heard singing, faint and off-key, carried on the wind.

Keep the watch, keep the flame. Ashes tell the sinner's name.

I closed the curtain, turned off the light, and let the darkness settle. The sixteenth candle still burned in my memory, steady and merciless.

The town had chosen its villains now.

And I had finally learned what it felt like to live inside a prayer no one believed in.

CHAPTER 17

The Weight of What's Left

By morning, I had reached the end of my father's papers. Not misplaced, not hidden, simply finished. I had read every sermon outline, every council memo, every receipt with ink so thin it looked like it wanted to vanish. I had turned each page until the room felt scraped clean of secrets. It left a strange quiet behind. Like the silence after an argument no one won.

I closed the last folder and rested my palm on the cover. The cardboard felt tired. The house felt tired too. Even the floorboards seemed to hold their breath when I crossed the hall to make coffee. I stood at the sink and watched the kettle steam and thought, I have wrung this well dry. If the dead cannot tell me more, I need to ask the living.

The living included a town full of people who did not meet my eyes anymore. It included a sheriff who had begun to move like a man trying to outrun his own shadow. It included a mayor who smiled like a statue. And it included my mother, who had started lighting candles at home like the act could stitch the world back together.

I poured coffee and took a sip. It tasted metallic. I set the cup down and looked again at the lists I had made in the spiral notebook. Names upon names, their children, their businesses, their decisions. I drew a line under the last one and stared at the white space below it. I was running out of names. The pattern was nearly closed. That felt like relief and terror at once.

Someone knocked. Three quick raps, then two. The rhythm of impatience.

I opened the door to Sheriff Collins. His collar was frosted with snow, and his eyes were bloodshot. He stepped inside without waiting for an invitation, stomped the snow from his boots, then stopped in the doorway to the kitchen and looked at the piles of folders on the table. He took in the spiral notebook. He took in my face last of all.

"You are going to have to give me more than this," he said. No greeting. No small talk. Just the verdict.

"More than what," I asked. "More than the town's history of neglect. More than signatures that tied people to the choices that burned children alive."

He winced. "You know what I mean. I need something I can hold. Something that can stand in court, not just in conscience."

"Court is not where this is happening," I said. "It is happening in basements and backyards, in the square, in the wind, in the way people refuse to say the word guilt. It is happening in the fact that you and I both know this is deliberate, and yet you are still asking me for evidence like a photo of a ghost."

He rubbed a hand over his jaw, then dropped it and looked at me hard. "Hannah, people are calling my office. They want you questioned. Some want worse. The more this escalates, the more they say your name. I need a way to turn them from you. Help me."

"Turn them to what," I asked. "To the truth that they do not want. To the memory that makes their teeth hurt."

He leaned on the back of a chair and lowered his voice. "At least act like you are not the center of this. Stop walking straight into the crowd. Lay low. Let me take the heat for a few days. You are running out of names. I am running out of town."

A laugh escaped me, quiet and ugly. "You cannot outrun a story, Sheriff. It catches you at the corner and calls you by your first name."

He looked at the spiral notebook again. "Who is left?"

"Four," I said. "Maybe three, depending on how you count bloodlines. And then me."

He shut his eyes for a long second. When he opened them, something softer had slipped through. "I am sorry," he said.

"For what," I asked.

"For the way this place makes everything a sermon or a secret." He straightened. "I will be near the square before the candle. If you get anything, call me. If you need a patrol car to sit outside your mother's place tonight, say so."

"I will keep that in mind," I said. We both knew I would not ask.

He left. The house swallowed the silence again. I looked down at the notebook and wrote one more name on the bottom margin, then crossed it out, then wrote it again. Hannah Mark. There. Truth in ink. I closed the book and put on my coat.

The wind cut through Main Street and blew the garlands out of shape. Shop windows were darker than last week, and the few stores that stayed open had hand painted signs with shortened hours. I passed the bakery, where Mrs. Doyle and two men were inside, scrubbing soot from the walls and replacing the shattered front window. A plank of fresh wood leaned against the doorway, half-painted, trying to disguise what the fire had taken. She glanced up when she saw me, then looked back down just as quickly, her hands red from the cold water in the bucket beside her. The bell above the door didn't even stir. I passed the hardware store, and the owner pretended to fix a display that did not need fixing. The square sat ahead like a bright coin pressed into a bruise.

I turned right instead. I had an appointment with patience.

Mayor Evelyn Hargrove kept her office in a tidy brick building beside the town clerk. Her receptionist had a wreath pinned to her sweater and a voice that tried to be cheery and landed on brittle. I gave my name, and before she could decide whether to tell me the mayor was out, Evelyn stepped into the doorway.

"Hannah," she said, warm and careful. "Come in."

Her office smelled like furniture polish and vanilla. A silver tree stood by the window, white lights, tasteful ribbon, not a single homemade ornament in sight. She gestured to a chair. I sat, folded my hands, and felt how tight my shoulders had become.

"You look tired," she said.

"So do you," I said.

She smiled with awkwardly. "What can I do for you?"

I looked at the framed photographs on the wall. The glasses raised at fundraisers. The crisp ribbon cuttings. The parade wave. Then I looked at her face. I chose not to be delicate.

"You can stop pretending you did not know," I said. "You can stop smiling like we are having coffee in a safer month. You can tell me why you did nothing when Caldwell brought you letters with the words locked exit written right there in the second paragraph."

The smile cracked. It did not fall, only split along an old seam. She opened a drawer, took out a handkerchief, touched the corner of one eye, and then set it aside.

"We all knew something was wrong," she said. Her voice was quiet and even. "But you cannot fight a pulpit."

I sat there without moving. The sentence rang like a bell.

She continued, very softly. "He was not only your father. He was the voice people trusted when everything else was cold. He told us the repairs would come next quarter. He told us the city fund would reallocate. He told us to be patient, to keep faith, to focus on the right kind of charity. If you stood against a man like that, you did not just stand against a man. You stood against the idea of goodness. Most people are not built for that kind of fight."

"So, you stood down," I said.

"We stood aside," she said. "Which is the same thing in the end."

The room felt smaller. Outside, a gust thumped the window, and the silver tree trembled. I thought about the old carol. Keep the watch, keep the flame. I thought about who we had chosen to watch, and what we had allowed to burn.

"Tell the town," I said. "Tell them you knew. Tell them why you stayed quiet. Say the sentence out loud into a microphone, and let it stop hiding in rooms like this."

Her face aged a year in a blink. "Do you think confession will save us?"

"No," I said. "But lies will finish the job."

She looked at the tree again. Her hand shook as she smoothed her skirt. "I will think about how to speak," she said. "I do not know if they will hear it."

"They will," I said, and stood. "They will because the wind is louder than the choir now."

On my way out, the receptionist avoided my eyes. I stepped into the cold and let it bite me awake. I walked the long way, past the river, past the dark shape of the orphanage ruins, past the charred rim of the shed that had started this run of ritual. The air smelled like iron and pine. I wanted to scrape the sky clean and see what lay behind it.

I reached my mother's house before dusk. She had lined three small candles on the sill, each one cupped in glass. Their flames flickered and threw small crowns against the pane. She was at the stove stirring soup, and the kitchen smelled like thyme and onion and the faintest hint of smoke, the smell that never left these days.

"Have you eaten?" she asked.

"Not yet," I said. "I will make a sandwich."

We moved around each other like people who have lived in the same scene a long time. She set a bowl on the table. I took bread from the tin and the knife from the drawer. She watched me for a while, then set down the ladle.

"Your father kept the town alive through winters no one remembers anymore," she said. "He closed the church for one week when the pipes burst and people came here to eat at this table. He told men who had not worked in months that the Lord saw them. He kept a list of who needed coal. He kept a list of who needed shoes."

"He also kept a list of requests for repairs and wrote Deferred in the margins," I said. I kept my voice soft. "Two truths do not cancel each other."

She pressed her fingers to her eyes and breathed. "Maybe the truth is not meant to destroy," she said at last. "Maybe it is meant to cleanse."

I set the knife down. "Cleansing burns too."

Her hands fell to the table. She nodded once, slow and sorrowful, like a woman who had finally allowed herself to agree with a sentence she hated. We ate without talking, and the wind made a thin sound around the frame of the kitchen window.

When I left for the square, she walked me to the door and touched my sleeve. "If the crowd turns ugly," she said, "come straight back."

"The crowd is already ugly," I said, but I kissed her cheek and promised anyway.

Outside, the sky had that bruised color that made every light look colder. I pulled my coat tight and walked toward the square, feeling the town contract around me. Windows glowed. Curtains shifted. Somewhere a radio tried to lift a carol, then gave up.

I was running out of names. I was not out of fear.

The Seventeenth Candle

Wind replaced the choir. It moved through the square and plucked at the garlands and rattled the wooden railing where the brass holders stood. Fifteen candles burned to nubs. The sixteenth sat stubborn and short. The seventeenth waited, pale and new and too clean.

People gathered in small knots, faces turned inward, all conversation hushed. The mayor stood at the base of the steps with a coat that looked warmer than anyone else's, her mouth a tight line that pretended to be a smile. Sheriff Collins took up a position where he could see the whole square and the street that fed into it. He nodded at me once. I nodded back.

No one sang. No instruments. Only the wind and the sound of paper programs rustling like leaves. The match hissed as it struck. The seventeenth candle caught on the first try and rose into a steady flame that did not waver even when the gusts pushed at it. People clapped out of habit, then stopped after two beats, embarrassed by the sound they had made.

A child began to whimper. The mother lifted her, bounced her, whispered something into her hat. The mayor said nothing beyond a simple sentence. Tonight, we stand together. Tonight, we keep the

167

watch. It sounded like a sentence written by a committee. The crowd drifted away faster than any other night. The square emptied until it looked like a stage after the curtain had fallen.

I walked my usual loop instead of going home. Habit can be a kind of prayer. The river sounded harder than yesterday. Ice hissed against the shore. I traced the block that held the little post office and the diner and the insurance agent, then turned toward the older neighborhood where the houses sat deeper on their lots. Lights were warm behind lace curtains. Wreaths shone like coins on every door. I saw the silhouette of a woman stringing cranberries at a kitchen table and for a moment I could pretend the town was gentle.

The sirens broke that. One, then another, then a chorus. They were headed east. My stomach went cold. I knew that direction as clearly as I knew my own name.

Mrs. Caldwell's house.

I ran. My breath turned sharp and hot in my throat. The wind cut across my face and made my eyes stream. I turned at the laundromat, cut through the alley, almost slipped on black ice, caught the telephone pole with my palm, then kept going. The smoke rose before I reached the street, thick and dark, the kind that comes from old wood and everything it has absorbed.

Flames chewed through the roof of the narrow white house at the corner. They painted the bare trees orange and made the icicles look like knives. Neighbors stood on sidewalks in coats over pajamas, faces lit by a color that does not belong on human skin. Firefighters hauled hose across the lawn where summer lawn chairs still sat under snow. A paramedic shouted for a backboard. Another called out vitals. I saw a stretcher by the curb, sheets flung back, ready.

"Out of the way," someone yelled, and two firefighters staggered through the doorway carrying a small woman wrapped in a smoke-stained blanket. Mrs. Caldwell's hair, white as frost in daylight, looked brown with soot. Her eyes were open, unfocused, lashes stuck together. She coughed and the sound made my chest seize in sympathy.

"Airway is patent," the medic called. "Oxygen on. Check for burns."

Another siren screamed to a halt. The ambulance doors opened. They transferred her with a practiced rhythm that looked like a dance no one wants to know. Her hand flailed for a second and caught my sleeve. I leaned in close.

"We told them," she rasped. The words I had heard all month, but now they sounded like blood. "They never listened."

"I know," I said. "I am listening."

Her grip loosened. They loaded her, doors slammed, engine roared, and the ambulance jolted away with its lights turning the snow the color of candy that breaks teeth.

I stood there, throat raw, and watched the fire climb a wall of family photographs. I could see them through the window when the smoke shifted. Children with paper crowns. A young nun in a dark habit. A spring festival banner. The flames rolled over the frames and the glass flashed and went black.

The crowd found its voice.

"This has to stop."

"Who is next?"

"Someone needs to do something."

Then the turn, sharp and mean.

"She was the one who kept talking to the pastor's girl."

"She dug this up."

"She wants attention."

Someone pointed. I did not have to turn to know where the finger aimed. A woman I had known since childhood lifted her chin and called out, "Hannah, why are they following you?"

The question cracked like ice. Every head near me turned. I felt a heat that did not come from the burning house climb up my neck.

"We are all being punished," another voice said. "But it started again when she came home."

Sheriff Collins pushed forward then and planted himself between me and the faces. "Back up," he said. "All of you. This is an active scene. Go home."

A man in a heavy work jacket did not move. "You going to arrest the fire, Sheriff?" he asked. "Or the curse that walks around with a last name that still smells like the church."

My fists clenched inside my gloves. The urge to step forward and say something that would scorch the night almost won. The urge to break into a run almost won too. I did neither. I stood my ground and spoke in a voice that carried because I had learned how to speak to families in waiting rooms where the worst news had to be gentle.

"She is the one person who did not look away," I said, nodding toward the house. "She wrote letters. She begged you all to listen. If you think this fire is about her guilt, you have not understood a thing. If you think it is about me, you have understood even less."

The man in the jacket took one step back. Only one. The others did not move at all. Fear is heavy. It takes a long time to set down.

Collins jerked his head toward the far corner. "Move," he said to me under his breath. "I will talk to you in five."

I did not move. I looked at the window where the flames had broken through. The frame sagged and dropped inward. Heat washed over the sidewalk. The smell changed from wood to the sickly scent of burning insulation and something else, an old chemical stink that lived in ancient paint.

On the lawn, just beyond the reach of the hose spray, something lay half buried in slush. I stepped toward it and crouched. A metal tin, scorched, lid warped. I nudged it with my fingers. It flipped open. Inside, paper curls of brown and black. The top fragment still had lines of type. A letter to the council. My stomach flipped as I read what little remained. Faulty alarms. Back stairwell door. Children. Please.

A firefighter saw me and shouted to get clear. I closed the tin and stood. The paramedic who had ridden in with Caldwell must have radioed back, because a second crew arrived with a supervisor who scanned the crowd and then looked at me like I was a match. The mayor arrived too, coat thrown over a dress, hair still perfect, eyes not. She stayed on the sidewalk and pressed a gloved hand to her mouth when the roof gave a soft moan and then folded in. A puff of sparks rose and drifted like a perverse snowfall.

The wind changed and blew smoke down the block. People coughed and pulled scarves up over mouths and noses. They did not leave. They wanted to be here for the end. It made me want to retch.

Someone whispered near my shoulder. "No one is safe now."

Another answered, louder. "Then make them leave. Run them out."

There was a murmur, then a small ugly sound that could have been agreement. I felt it like a touch. I took one step back. Collins saw it and moved closer again, putting his shoulder next to mine as if he could make a wall with bone.

"Hospital says she is stable," he said, eyes still on the fire. "Smoke inhalation. Minor burns. She is lucky."

"She is not lucky," I said. "She is being punished for failing to save a town that refused to be saved."

He looked at me for a long beat. "You need to go home."

"To my mother's," I said. "Where the garden is ash and the neighbors keep watch in the dark like they are waiting for a sign to act."

His jaw tightened. "I will have a car idle on the corner. Use the back door tonight."

"I am not a fugitive," I said.

"You are prey," he said, quietly. "Do not make me test how fast I can be."

I wanted to argue. I did not. I looked again at the house, now a hot black hump with orange at the edges. The water made a hiss that sounded like something alive trying to breathe under a heavy blanket. The wind carried embers across the street and left tiny, smoking commas on the new snow.

As I turned, the crowd parted just enough to let me through. No one reached out. No one offered a word that could be mistaken for kindness. The cold had teeth again by the time I reached the corner. My legs felt hollow as reeds.

I walked fast without running. I cut down a street with older trees and deeper shadows. My breath plumed in front of me and broke apart. Every sound seemed too loud. The creak of a porch. The slam of a car door two blocks over. My own boots. I kept my head up and my eyes forward.

At my mother's house the porch light was on. She had two mugs on the counter when I stepped inside. Her hands were steady, but her face had the pale look of a person who has read a headline and is waiting for the phone to ring. I told her what I could. I did not tell her about the crowd asking for us to leave. She already knew.

We carried our mugs to the front room and stood at the window without touching the curtain. Across the street three figures stood under the elm. They were not smoking. They were not speaking. They were doing nothing at all except looking at our door. After a minute one of them lifted a phone. A small cold light bloomed and went out. They stayed another five, then walked off in different directions, as if they had agreed to meet elsewhere and continue the sentence they had started with their presence.

My mother set her cup down. The china clicked against the saucer. "You cannot stay here," she said.

"I will not leave you."

"You cannot stay here," she repeated. "They will come back in daylight next time."

"It is our house."

"It is a town," she said, and her voice shook for the first time tonight. "And towns are louder than one house."

I thought of the mayor's sentence. You cannot fight a pulpit. I thought of Caldwell's letters turned to ash. I thought of my father writing purification like a promise to himself. I thought of the wind at the square taking the place of the choir. I thought of the seventeenth flame holding steady while everyone turned their faces away.

"The fire spreads fear faster than heat," I said.

My mother closed her eyes. "So, what do we do?"

"We tell the truth before someone else tells it wrong," I said. "We say the names. We read the letters. We refuse to let them make us the altar."

She looked at me then, really looked, and a resolve I had not seen in years returned to her eyes. She nodded. "Then we speak tomorrow."

I did not say it, but I knew tomorrow would not wait for us. The air itself felt charged, ready. I stood at the window until the glass cooled the heat on my face. Somewhere in the distance, a siren called and then quieted. Snow began to fall again, slow and heavy, the kind that blankets everything, the kind that makes a town feel muffled. The kind that hides. The kind that remembers.

I left the lamp on when I went upstairs. I lay down fully dressed and listened to the house shift and sigh. Sleep came in short stumbles. Each time I woke, I heard wind in the chimney and thought it was the choir trying and failing to find the right note. Each time I woke, I saw the stretcher and Caldwell's hand clutching my sleeve. We told them. They never listened.

When morning came, it came pale and cold. I went to the window and looked at the street. No figures stood under the elm. The snow was clean. My mother was already in the kitchen, her hands around a mug she had not yet raised to her lips. She looked up at me and tried to smile. It did not land, but the attempt counted.

"Eat something," she said.

"We will need strength," I said. "It will not be a quiet day."

In my mind the seventeenth candle still burned in the square. No song. Only wind. No comfort. Only a steady light, and the knowledge that the eighteenth would come whether we were ready or not.

CHAPTER 18

The Town Without Light

By morning, the world outside looked half-erased. The snow had turned gray overnight, streaked with soot from the fires that never seemed to stop. Windows were boarded up. Decorations hung like tired ghosts, their glitter dulled by ash. Every streetlamp hummed as if afraid to go dark.

The church bells rang just after dawn, even though no one had pulled the rope. The sound drifted over Greenridge, hollow and uneven, like someone shaking a memory instead of metal.

The mayor's announcement came over the radio before breakfast. Her voice was composed, as though she had practiced in front of a mirror. "Effective immediately, all public gatherings are suspended until further notice. This includes candle ceremonies, choir rehearsals, and town markets. Please remain home. Stay vigilant."

No one said it aloud, but everyone knew what it meant. The mayor was trying to end the ritual.

My mother turned the volume down and sat very still. "She thinks silence will keep it away."

"Silence hasn't saved anyone so far," I said.

We had spent the early morning preparing for something different. Notes covered the kitchen table. Sentences half-crossed out, questions rewritten in red ink. We had planned to speak to the town that evening, to tell them what my father had done, what the council had buried. We had believed, even for a few hours, that truth might be the cure.

Now that hope was gone. The speech was useless. The candles were gone. Even the stage had been taken down.

When Sheriff Collins knocked on the door that morning, his face said everything before his words did. He looked older, shoulders bent as though the weight of Greenridge had settled there overnight.

"She's serious," he said. "No gatherings. No exceptions. She thinks the ceremonies are feeding this thing."

I laughed without humor. "You mean the only thing keeping people together?"

He rubbed the bridge of his nose. "You're not helping by challenging her. You're giving the town a villain, and they're already picking one."

"They've already picked two," I said. "Me and my mother."

He didn't deny it.

I pushed past him and stepped into the cold. The air tasted metallic, sharp with smoke and frost. I couldn't stay still. If I did, the fear would find its way under my skin.

"Where are you going?" he asked.

"To finish something."

***

Henry Alcott's gas station sat at the edge of town, half-swallowed by snowbanks. The wind made the pump signs creak like old bones. The smell of diesel carried even through the cold.

Henry was outside, wiping his hands on a rag, his breath white in the air. He gave me a wary look when he saw me crossing the lot.

"Well, if it isn't the preacher's daughter," he said, his voice rough from years of cigarettes. "Here to save my soul?"

"Just here to warn you." I stopped near the pump, my boots crunching on ice. "You're on the list."

He frowned. "What list?"

"The people whose names were on the council's ledgers. The ones who ignored the orphanage's repair requests. Your father was treasurer then. He diverted the funds to build this place."

He laughed, but it sounded forced. "Lady, that was decades ago. My old man's been dead ten years. You think ghosts keep receipts?"

"Maybe not," I said, "but something does. Murphy's store, Doyle's bakery, Caldwell's house. Everyone connected is paying for what happened. The fires follow the names."

His eyes flicked toward the office window, then back to me. "You think I'm next?"

"I think you already know you are."

He opened his mouth, then closed it again. His hand trembled as he reached for a cigarette. "I pay my taxes," he said finally. "That's my religion."

I watched him light the cigarette. His fingers shook so badly the match broke in half.

"You should get out of town," I told him.

He gave a dry smile. "And go where? Everywhere smells like smoke now."

The wind picked up. I turned toward the road. "Be careful, Henry."

When I looked back, he was watching me with eyes that didn't look mocking anymore. They looked like confession.

***

By afternoon, the light was gray and bruised. I found my mother in the living room, sorting through old Christmas ornaments. Most of them were cracked or faded, but she handled them like relics.

"Do you really think it will stop if they cancel the candles?" I asked.

She didn't look up. "No. But people believe what makes fear smaller."

"Maybe fear isn't supposed to be small."

She sighed and set an ornament aside. "You sound like him when you say things like that."

"That's the last thing I want."

She smiled sadly. "You think you're his opposite, but you're not. You're what he should have been. A believer who isn't blind."

I sat down beside her. "I don't believe anymore."

She shook her head. "Belief isn't only about God. It's about light, too. About keeping one lit when everything else is dark."

For a long time, we sat in silence. The fire in the hearth had gone out, but the air still smelled faintly of smoke.

Then she said softly, "I had the dream again."

"The same one?"

She nodded. "The orphanage. The same night. The same cries. It doesn't change. It loops. Like the fire never ended."

I wanted to tell her it was just her mind replaying trauma, but the words caught in my throat. Too much of what she said lately had been true.

Outside, the wind rose again, carrying the faint, high sound of church bells. No one was supposed to ring them.

The day died early. The sky turned the color of unpolished steel. I watched from the window as the streetlights flickered on, one by one, reluctant and dim.

It felt like waiting for something to breathe.

The Eighteenth Candle

The square was dark that night. No carols. No cocoa. No children chasing snowflakes. The wooden stage where the candles had once stood was empty, the holders dusted with snow. Even the church door was locked.

I went anyway. My mother begged me not to, but the thought of sitting in the silence of our house was worse. Sheriff Collins found me there, standing in the center of the square with my breath ghosting in front of me.

"You should go home," he said quietly.

"I should have been there yesterday too," I said. "You think skipping the ritual makes us safe?"

He looked at the empty row where the candles should have been. "Maybe nothing does."

The wind cut between us. It wasn't a normal wind. It moved like something alive, circling the square, testing it.

I stared at the dark altar. "It feels wrong, doesn't it?"

He didn't answer.

After a while, he turned and walked away. I stayed until the cold numbed my fingers. When I finally went home, I thought maybe the air would ease. It didn't.

The explosion hit just after midnight.

It began as a low, trembling sound — then the world cracked open. The blast rattled every window in Greenridge. The sky lit up like sunrise. My mother screamed from her room.

I ran barefoot into the snow. The air burned in my lungs. Even from the hill, I could see the fire — a tower of flame twisting into the night, the glow painting the clouds red.

The gas station.

By the time I reached it, half the town was already there. The heat hit like a wave. People covered their faces with scarves, eyes wide with disbelief. Fire trucks screamed through the smoke, tires hissing on ice.

Henry Alcott was on the ground near the office, his clothes singed, his hands blistered. Two firefighters tried to hold him down, but he kept shouting the same words.

"He said light them! He said the flames were the only thing keeping it from spreading!"

I pushed closer. "Who said that, Henry?"

He didn't seem to see me. His pupils were blown wide. "The one in the smoke," he rasped. "He said the dark was hungry. He said it needed the fire to stay fed."

The firefighters hauled him toward the ambulance, but his voice carried over the sirens, high and broken. "If we stop lighting them, it'll come for the rest of us!"

I felt sick. My hands shook so badly I had to hide them in my pockets.

The explosion had gutted everything. The pumps were melted down to metal stems. The sign had collapsed in on itself. The snow around the wreckage steamed like breath.

When the flames finally started to die, the firefighters found something strange. Burn marks, dark and even, fanned out from the center of the blast. Perfect circles, each one inside the other, like ripples in a frozen pond.

Collins crouched beside me, his face ghosted by the orange light. "That's no accident," he whispered.

I didn't answer. The heat pressed against my skin, the same way the candlelight used to. It felt almost intelligent.

One of the firemen called out, "Over here!"

He held up a small metal box, warped and blackened, found near the pumps. Inside was a folded sheet of paper, half-burned but legible.

Collins opened it with trembling hands. His eyes scanned the words. Then he read aloud.

"Light the remaining candles until Christmas. Or Greenridge will burn for what it buried."

The crowd went silent. Even the fire seemed to hush for a moment.

Someone whispered, "We stopped lighting them."

Another voice, sharp with fear, said, "This is our punishment."

The murmurs grew louder, spreading like the fire had. Faces turned toward me and my mother. A woman crossed herself. A man shouted, "It started when she came back!"

179

I stepped backward, my boots slipping in the slush. The sound of panic was louder than the sirens now. Collins raised his hand to quiet them, but no one listened.

Henry Alcott was still muttering from the stretcher. "He said it had to be paid. He said it had to be even."

The mayor's car rolled up then, black against the orange glow. She didn't get out. She sat inside, face pale, one hand over her mouth.

Collins stormed toward her, his coat streaked with ash. He slapped his palm against the glass. "You'll put them back," he said, his voice rough. "The ceremonies. The candles. Tomorrow night."

Her lips moved, but no sound came. Her eyes darted between him and the fire.

I watched from the curb, the burned paper still in his hand, the fire reflecting in the melted snow.

"It isn't belief anymore," I said quietly. "It's obedience."

The mayor opened her door at last. Her face was streaked with tears. "Then we light them," she whispered. "Every night until Christmas."

Collins nodded. "And if we don't?"

She looked toward the flames. "Then it'll come for all of us."

The words sank into the air like smoke.

I stared at the burn marks on the ground. They weren't just patterns. They were instructions. The circles aligned perfectly with where the candles had once stood in the square.

Eighteen down. Seven to go.

As we turned to leave, the fire hissed and flared one last time, spitting sparks into the night. I looked back and caught sight of something glinting in the slush — a single melted match, still faintly warm.

The mayor stood beside her car, whispering into her hands. A prayer, or maybe a plea.

The town would light the candles again tomorrow.

Not because they wanted to. Because they were too afraid not to.

CHAPTER 19

The Quiet Before Smoke

Morning arrived sharp and colorless, the kind of light that made even snow look tired.

The night before, the gas station had burned until the sky turned orange, and by dawn the smell of fuel still clung to every breath. Greenridge had been taught its lesson. The note found in the ashes—Light the remaining candles until Christmas, or Greenridge will burn for what it buried—had been read aloud in whispers, passed through kitchens and stores like a prayer no one wanted to own.

They had tried to stop the ceremony. One night without lighting a candle. One night of defiance. The fire had answered before morning, loud enough for everyone to understand.

Now obedience was back on the schedule.

I stood at the kitchen window with a cup of tea I didn't remember making. The mug's warmth didn't reach my fingers. Outside, the snow had crusted into dull gray ridges, and the street was too quiet.

People didn't shovel anymore; they moved quickly from door to car and car to door, like the air itself carried a curse.

My mother was sitting at the table, her robe tied tight, rosary wound around her wrist like she didn't want to pray but couldn't let go of the tool.

She stared at the newspaper even though there was nothing new in it—just smoke photos, lists of damage, the mayor's promise to rebuild.

"They'll light it again tonight," she said finally.

I nodded. "They don't have a choice."

"Obedience isn't faith," she murmured. "It's fear dressed in the right color."

I didn't answer. She wasn't wrong.

The smell of smoke had soaked into the curtains, faint but stubborn. I pushed the window open and let the cold rush in. My breath fogged the glass. Somewhere down the street, a dog barked once and fell silent.

Greenridge had never felt smaller.

The kettle clicked off behind me. My mother poured coffee, movements mechanical. "I dreamed of the fire again," she said. "Not last night's. The old one. The orphanage. I keep hearing the windows break."

I turned. "You think that means something?"

"I think some things refuse to stay buried. Maybe that's what this is."

Before I could answer, someone knocked—three short, deliberate raps that only one man in town used anymore.

Sheriff Collins stood on the porch, face wind-burned, coat flecked with snow. He took off his hat as he stepped inside, the gesture still polite even when everything else about him looked exhausted.

"They're doing it," he said. "The mayor called. Candle's back on tonight. No music, no speech. Just the candle."

"I figured," I said.

He rubbed a hand over his jaw. His knuckles were red and raw, as if he'd punched a wall or maybe a steering wheel. "People are scared enough to behave. You can feel it. Nobody argues when they think the sky's listening."

"Do you think it'll stop the fires?" I asked.

He hesitated. His eyes found mine. "Waiting keeps people alive," he said, and for the first time it sounded like a plea. "They stopped the candles, and the gas station went up. That's the pattern now—obedience or fire."

"So tonight, we obey."

"Yes," he said quietly, "and we pray that obedience still means survival."

182

He walked to the window and looked out at the street. "No one will admit it, but half the town's relieved. They wanted someone to make the choice for them. Fear feels lighter when you share it."

"That's how control works," I said.

He turned from the glass. "You still think this is about revenge?"

"I think it started that way. Now it's about power."

He didn't argue. He looked at my mother, who had been silent this whole time, and nodded to her with the soft respect he always showed her. Then he left without another word, his boots crunching over the frozen steps.

By noon, the sky had dimmed to the color of pewter.

I couldn't sit still, so I went to the back door. The garden still looked like a wound. My mother followed me out, scarf over her hair, eyes fixed on the blackened soil.

The roses she had tended for twenty years were gone. Only the stakes remained, twisted and splintered, pointing at nothing. The smell of char and fertilizer still clung to the air.

"It's strange," she said. "It burned so clean. No accelerant, no reason. Just gone."

"Maybe it was a message," I said.

She crouched and touched the frozen dirt with her fingertips. "Then someone is writing in a language I wish I never learned."

We went back inside when our hands started to sting from the cold.

I checked my phone—no new messages from Leah. She'd promised to dig through the adoption records, to find the truth about the girl who survived the fire, the one who'd vanished into a new life.

I'd texted her the night we discovered there had been a survivor, after gathering everything I could from the files and the sheriff's notes. She'd jumped in without hesitation.

Leah had always known how to slip through the cracks of bureaucracy—she'd worked at the county clerk's office for a few years and still had friends in the right places. If anyone could uncover what the town tried to bury, it was her.

Maybe she'd find something tonight. Maybe she wouldn't. Either way, the town wasn't waiting for paperwork to decide its next step.

At four o'clock, the church bell rang once.

The sound echoed through the snow like a reminder that God might still be watching, though I wasn't sure anymore which side He was on.

My mother flinched. "That bell hasn't rung since your father's funeral."

"Maybe it's automatic now."

She shook her head. "Nothing here is automatic."

***

The town hall meeting started at dusk. People crowded inside in heavy coats and silence.

Mayor Evelyn looked smaller than usual, her confidence stripped down to the bone. Collins stood behind her, arms crossed, jaw tight.

On the table in front of them lay the scorched note from the gas station ruins, sealed in plastic. Everyone stared at it like it might start talking.

Evelyn's voice trembled when she spoke. "You've all seen it. You've all heard. We can't ignore the warning."

A man near the front said, "What if lighting the candle brings more of this?"

Evelyn's gaze flicked to the sheriff, then back. "Not lighting it brought an explosion. I'll take smoke over fire."

No one argued.

Someone in the back muttered, "It's the pastor's family. It started when she came back."

All eyes turned toward me. The heat rose under my skin.

Collins's voice cut through the murmurs. "That's enough."

184

Evelyn nodded once. "Tonight, we light the nineteenth candle. And we pray that's the end of it."

When it was over, people filed out wordlessly, like mourners leaving a graveside.

The decision had been made. Fear had a schedule again.

***

That night, as I laced my boots, my mother said quietly, "You don't have to go."

"Yes," I said. "I do."

She didn't argue. She just wrapped her scarf tighter, picked up her coat, and followed me into the cold.

The Nineteenth Candle

The square looked stripped bare, the decorations pulled down or blackened from smoke.

The brass candleholders had been polished, though, as if to remind us that ritual survives even after reason doesn't. A single box of matches sat on the table.

No choir. No music. No speeches. Just breath and wind.

The mayor stood near the steps with her hands buried in her coat pockets. Sheriff Collins watched the crowd with the same expression soldiers must wear in the last hour before surrender.

People clustered in small groups, their words muffled by scarves. Everyone watched the table.

I found a place beside my mother. Her hand brushed mine. "If fire listens, maybe mercy does too," she whispered.

Collins struck the match. The sound of it scraping the box was loud enough to startle someone in the front row. The wick took on the first try. The nineteenth candle flared, wavered once, and steadied.

No one clapped. No one prayed.

We just stood there, counting heartbeats, waiting for something to break.

The flame burned clean and tall. For the first time all month, the wind didn't move.

My breath fogged the air in short bursts. Every sound felt too close.

A child tugged on his mother's sleeve. "Is it over now?"

"Almost," she whispered.

Almost. That word sat in my chest like a stone.

When the wick burned halfway down, people began to drift away, slow and careful. I stayed until the last drop of wax pooled and hardened. The mayor nodded once at the sheriff.

"End it," she said.

He blew out the flame, and the crowd exhaled together—a single, weary sigh.

We were halfway home when the siren went off.

Not the long wail that meant tragedy. A short burst. Controlled. Contained.

Collins's radio crackled behind us, his voice low but audible. "Small fire. Church property. Another shed only. No spread."

I turned to my mother. Her face was pale but calm. "They're calling that good news now," she said softly.

We followed the glow at the end of the street.

The shed burned politely, the flames licking along the roof like fingers tracing a line. Firefighters worked with quiet precision. Buckets passed from hand to hand. The air was cold enough that the steam rose white as breath.

No one screamed. No one cried.

Neighbors stood along the fence lines, bundled in coats, whispering.

"It's small this time."

"Thank God it's only the shed."

"At least it's not the house."

Relief passed through the crowd like warmth from a dying fire. People were learning to measure mercy by the size of the damage.

Small meant forgiven. Small meant safe.

Collins walked the perimeter, eyes sharp. When he saw me, he didn't tell me to leave.

He just said quietly, "They're getting used to it."

"That's the point," I said. "You can teach people to thank their tormentor if you scare them long enough."

He rubbed the bridge of his nose. "When this ends, it's going to end ugly."

"It already has."

We stood until the last flame died and the shed steamed like a ghost trying to disappear. The Pastor stared at the ruin of his tools and nodded to himself, as though it could have been worse was comfort enough.

People started clapping him on the shoulder, congratulating him for surviving the smallest fire yet.

The sound was wrong. Too loud, too proud. Like victory after surrender.

My mother touched my arm. "Come," she said. "There's nothing to see that we haven't seen before."

Back home, the house was dark and still.

I stood at the window, watching the reflection of distant smoke dissolve into the snow.

For the first time, I understood why people stop fighting. You can't live in constant alarm. Eventually, you start mistaking fear for routine.

My mother came up beside me. "When I was a girl," she said, "we used to say that as long as there wasn't war and there was bread on the table, life was good. We never asked what the cost of that calm was."

I looked at her. "Maybe that's what we've done here. Accepted the quiet because it's easier than asking who's paying for it."

She nodded. "And who will collect the debt."

The kettle whistled. We didn't move to silence it right away.

Later, as I checked the locks, my phone buzzed.

A message from Leah. Partial match confirmed. Amy K, age seven, adopted six months after the fire. Record sealed by municipal petition, not private family. I'll find who signed it.

My heart thudded once, then twice. Someone in this town had paid to hide a survivor.

And that meant someone alive still carried the secret.

I texted back, You're close. Don't stop.

Then I turned off the lights and went to bed, though I knew sleep wouldn't come easily.

The faint scent of smoke still clung to my hair. Outside, the wind pressed against the house like a question that didn't need to be answered.

At some point after midnight, a small sound woke me—a tap, light and deliberate, against the porch rail. I rose, pulled back the curtain.

Nothing moved. But on the railing, half buried in snow, lay a single wooden match.

Unburned.

I stepped outside in my bare feet and picked it up. The wood was cold, but clean, untouched by fire.

I held it up to the moonlight and felt something shift in the pit of my stomach.

It wasn't a threat. It was a reminder.

The fire will come when we forget what fear costs.

I placed the match on the mantle beside my father's photograph and went back to bed.

Sleep came in fragments, stitched together by dreams of candles burning one after another, until only two remained unlit.

In the last dream, I stood before the orphanage again. Its windows glowed like open eyes. A child's voice whispered from the smoke.

Keep the watch. Keep the flame.

When I woke, the whisper was still in my head.

And for the first time, I wasn't sure if I'd been warned—or invited.

CHAPTER 20

Six Lights Left

Morning arrived with a sky the color of old paper, thin and tired. The square felt far away even when I could see it from the window, a pale smudge where the candle would breathe tonight if the town kept its promise. My phone sat on the table like a small machine that could decide whether the past stayed buried. I watched it the way people watch a sleeping child, alert to every twitch.

It buzzed at 8:13.

Leah: Found it. Confirmed adoptive parents. Names attached to sealed petition. Address is two towns over, off Route 17, blue house with a porch. I have the street number. I am sending details now. Be careful.

The text came in pieces, one tiled bubble after another, as if the phone needed to breathe between truths. A second later the address appeared, neat and ordinary on the screen, impossible in its ordinariness. I stared until the numbers stopped blurring.

Amy K. had been given a new last name. There was a small photo clipped to the record, the kind taken by child services long before the adoption—a little girl's face, unsmiling, with soot-dark hair and eyes too large for her years. No adult photo, nothing recent. Just that single image frozen in time, proof that she had existed before someone decided she should disappear.

There was a municipal signature on the seal. I knew the shape of the first letter. I would have recognized that flourish if you had shown it to me in a dark room. It looked like a person trying to write themselves into history with a pen that wanted no part of them.

My mother set a cup of coffee beside my elbow and took the chair across from me. She did not ask what I had; she knew. She folded her hands and waited. When I handed her the phone, she read in silence, lips moving slightly, the way she used to read Scripture under her breath while the choir rehearsed. She stopped at the address and tapped the screen with one finger.

"Two towns," she said.

"Not far."

"Far enough to feel like a decision," she said, and looked up. "Do we go?"

"Today," I said, because the answer felt like a reflex, and then it felt like a mistake. The calendar on the wall showed a week that was running out of days. Twenty squares marked and scarred by smoke. Six left. I could feel the number under my skin the way you feel a fever before the thermometer catches up.

She shook her head slowly. "You are tired. Your hands trembled when you poured the sugar. You will drive on nerves and nothing else."

"I have driven on less," I said.

"That is not a boast," she answered gently. "It is a warning."

Before I could reply, a knock came at the door. The same rhythm. Three even taps, the courtesy of a man who has never stopped asking to be let in.

Collins stepped into the kitchen, boots leaving clean outlines on the mat. He took in my face and my mother's and the way my body had leaned forward as if it might stand without me. He took his hat off and set it on the table, careful not to touch the papers that had migrated there like fallen birds.

"You have something," he said.

I slid the phone across the wood and let him read. He did not sit while he read, which told me he did not yet trust his legs. When he reached the line with the municipal seal, a muscle in his cheek ticked. He blew out a breath, quiet and flat.

"Evelyn," he said, but it was not a question.

"Her office, not her alone," I said. "A petition from the desk, not necessarily from the hand. The signature is the town's, not only hers.

191

The seal says we are all implicated even when we pretend we cannot read."

He looked toward the window where the cold had drawn a thin lace of frost along the edges of the glass. "If you go there today, you will go with the wrong mind. You will go angry. You will go hungry. You will say something you cannot unsay."

"I am past worrying about politeness," I said.

"This is not about manners," he replied. "It is about outcome. Give me the address. I will put eyes on it quietly. You and your mother stay in town until I know who answers that door."

I wanted to argue. I wanted to burn the road between here and that porch with the heat in my chest. But the picture came to me of arriving with night behind us and finding the face I had been chasing for what fells like forever, and saying the wrong first sentence because adrenaline had stolen my judgment. I had seen families do it in hallways, grief turning them into people they did not recognize. I have triaged on the edge of that kind of storm; you learn to buy one hour with a calm voice.

"We wait," I said. The words tasted like a pill you take because you believe in science, not because you expect to feel better right away.

He nodded once. "I will drive by at dusk," he said. "If there is movement that looks like flight, I will call and you will meet me there. If the house sleeps like a house, we plan for morning."

My mother poured him coffee without asking, because some rituals still mattered. He stood with the mug in his hand and stared at nothing for a moment, as if the air in our kitchen could offer a second opinion. Then he drained it, set the cup in the sink like a man who had once been taught to clean up after himself, and reached for his hat.

"Six candles," he said, glancing at the calendar. "It is strange how numbers take on personalities when you are frightened."

"They always had personalities," my mother said softly. "We were not listening."

He left us in the quiet. Outside, a truck downshifted at the corner and carried on, and the sound felt like a decision leaving us behind.

I looked back at the phone. The map app had obediently drawn a little blue line to the address. It would take forty minutes if the roads were good. Roads in December lie.

"We should tell the mayor," my mother said.

"About the address," I asked, "or about the seal on the petition that bears her office stamp."

"Both."

"She will call the council members before she calls us back. She will ask them what story to prefer. She will ask the town lawyer what to say and where to stand. By the time she meets my eyes, the truth will have a speech wrapped around it."

"You do not know that," my mother said, though she sounded like a person quoting a principle she wanted to believe.

"She has been part of the story too long to know how to walk without it," I said. "We will tell her when we can, and not before."

My mother folded her hands on the table and watched me the way she used to look at me after a twelve-hour shift, searching for the moment when the adrenaline broke and the exhaustion took its place. "Eat something," she said.

I did. It tasted like cardboard until it did not. The body always surprises you by doing the next right thing.

By late morning, the town had found its strange routine again. The butcher's shop was open, and a small grocery beside it smelled faintly of oranges and soap. The sound of the radio carried through the thin air — a Christmas hymn warped by static. People avoided meeting each other's eyes. A group of teenagers carried boxes of canned food toward the church, pretending not to notice that every window was still blackened.

And then, at the far end of Main Street, I saw Emily Hill. She walked with three of the orphanage children beside her, their scarves mismatched, cheeks flushed with cold. She was speaking softly, pointing out the Christmas decorations still hanging from the lampposts, even though the snow had half-buried them. The children listened as if the world were still capable of teaching gentleness.

A man nodded at her as she passed. A woman smiled but too quickly, as if kindness had become a reflex rather than a choice. Emily smiled back in that calm way she had, the way you speak peace into a room without asking permission. Watching her, I understood how the town managed to function at all. People needed someone to believe in, and she fit the shape of belief without ever asking for it.

I turned away before she saw me. Some faiths are too fragile to touch.

The Twentieth Candle

The square was full of breath and not much else. No choir. No brass. No decorations layered to pretend at joy. Only the rail with its row of cups and the number that mattered now. Twenty. Someone had polished the brass again. The metal caught what little light there was and pretended it was more generous than it felt.

People spoke softly the way they do at wakes. The shuffling sound of boots on packed snow had the rhythm of procession, not celebration. I recognized faces that had lost the habit of looking at me. A few nodded, small acknowledgements that carried no warmth. A few turned away and turned back, as if turning twice could erase the intention.

Mayor Evelyn stood in a dark coat with a fur collar that must have been a comfort in another life. Her lipstick had been applied with the care of a woman who believes in rituals even when they fail. She looked ten years older than she had in November. Sheriff Collins stood at her shoulder, his eyes on the edges, his posture saying there were more ways into this square than there should be.

He struck the match on the second try. The sound of the scrape went through me like a spark through tinder. The wick took and bloomed, then steadied. The light reached the faces in the first row

194

and made their eyes look wet. No one sang. The cold made our breath visible. The only music was the faint hiss of wax remembering heat.

A boy asked if he could hold the next match. His father shook his head and squeezed his shoulder until the child leaned into him. An older woman near the steps crossed herself with a hand that trembled. I felt the handprint of prayer on the air and wished I still knew how to place mine that way.

As the flame settled, a sound rose that I did not recognize at first. It took a second to name it. It was relief, low and communal, the sound people make when a ventilator kicks in after a power flicker. I had stood at bedsides for that sound. It was never grateful. It was permission to keep waiting.

When the candle burned low, Evelyn lifted her chin, and Collins leaned in with the string of a long lighter and finished the ritual the way a priest finishes a mass. The square exhaled again. People turned toward home in the same motion, like birds noticing a shadow and lifting together.

We were almost at the edge when someone shouted. The word was only a word. Fire. It always sounds like a sentence in a town like ours.

The shout came from Main Street, not the square. We pivoted. The glow rose behind the municipal building, that tidy brick box where decisions go to learn how to sound official. For one moment the glow was only a suggestion, the kind you talk yourself out of because hope is a stubborn habit. Then the roofline brightened, and the suggestion became fact.

"Move," Collins said, his voice not yet raised and somehow louder than the siren that woke a second later. The crowd turned as one body. Some ran. Some did that fast walk people do when they want to be brave and are not. My mother and I followed the heat.

By the time we reached the steps, smoke had found the seams in the building and pushed out like black cloth. A window shattered on the second floor and gave birth to a tongue of flame that licked outward and then curled back in to feed.

195

Evelyn had gone inside.

What followed would stay with me longer than I wanted.

When it was over, the mayor was alive but broken, her lungs scorched, her face gray beneath the soot. As they carried her out, she looked straight at me and rasped through the oxygen mask, "I signed it. I sealed the adoption. I told myself it was mercy."

Her voice cracked. "It was silence. That is worse."

She coughed again, body shaking in the medic's arms. "Tell them," she whispered. "Tell them we are all guilty. The fire knows it already."

No one answered. Not the crowd. Not the sheriff. Not me.

The fire behind her consumed the office where the seal had once sat. Files curled in their drawers like dying tongues. Flames reached through the windows like hands trying to pull the rest of the truth out with them.

The twentieth candle had burned quietly. But the night did not end quietly.

And for the first time, the town finally understood that no one—not even those who had built their safety out of prayers and signatures—would leave this story untouched.

CHAPTER 21

The Road Out

By morning, the snow had stopped, but the world still felt frozen in place. The windows wore a thin crust of frost, and the air smelled faintly of smoke from the night before. I moved through the house like a ghost, careful not to wake my mother though she was already awake. I could always tell from the silence. When she slept, the house exhaled; when she didn't, it held its breath with her.

She sat at the kitchen table, hands wrapped around a chipped mug, staring at nothing. The lamplight carved soft shadows under her eyes.

"You don't have to go," she said, voice thin as the morning light.

"I do."

"You've already seen enough."

"I haven't seen the truth."

She looked down at her hands, as if the answer might be hiding in the lines of her palms. "Truth doesn't heal, Hannah. It only burns."

I zipped my coat and tried not to meet her eyes. "Maybe that's what this town needs."

Her hand twitched as though she wanted to reach for me, but she didn't. "Be careful."

"Always."

"That's not true," she said, but she smiled faintly, a small ghost of the woman she'd once been.

Outside, the sheriff's truck rumbled in the driveway, clouds of exhaust drifting upward like offerings. He leaned against the door, coffee steaming in his hand. His shoulders looked heavier than usual, like the badge itself had grown in weight overnight.

"You ready?" he asked.

"I was ready five candles ago."

He gave a small, grim nod. "Then let's finish this."

We drove out of Greenridge in silence. The tires cracked over patches of black ice, and the headlights cut through the fog in narrow, trembling beams. The town receded behind us, the church steeple fading into a blur of gray.

The further we got, the stranger the quiet became. The forest on both sides looked dead, but not peacefully so. Trees leaned inward as if conspiring. Their branches hung heavy with ice, rattling faintly against each other. Every so often, we passed a patch of scorched snow where a fire had burned and then been swallowed again by the cold.

I watched the horizon and thought of my father. He had spent years teaching that fire was a form of grace. That through flames, the wicked were cleansed and the faithful proved. I used to sit in the front pew, chin on my hands, believing him.

Now, watching smoke stains stretch across the white hills, I wondered if belief was just another form of blindness.

The sheriff cleared his throat. "You think we'll find her today?"

"I think we'll find what's left of her story."

He gave a low whistle. "You always have to sound like a sermon, don't you?"

"Comes with the bloodline."

He almost smiled. "Yeah. About that. You ever think all this—" he gestured toward the pale horizon "—might be punishment?"

"For what?"

"For your father's sins. For mine. For everyone who turned their head when that place went up in smoke."

I looked at him. His eyes stayed on the road, but his grip on the steering wheel was tight enough to whiten the knuckles.

"You sound like you've stopped believing in law."

He exhaled. "Law didn't save those kids. Faith didn't either."

"Then what's left?"

He gave a humorless laugh. "Fire, apparently."

We drove on without speaking. The road curved through a patch of woods that still smelled faintly of char. Every so often, the sheriff's radio crackled, then fell silent again. Even technology seemed too scared to speak.

By the time we reached the neighboring town, daylight had thinned into a colorless haze. The place looked untouched by everything that haunted Greenridge. Decorations still glimmered in shop windows, wreaths hung straight and green, and people walked the streets as though December still meant joy. It felt obscene, almost cruel, to see normal life continuing.

The address led us to a quiet cul-de-sac. The house was small, painted blue with a wreath that matched the others on the block. A snowman stood crooked in the front yard, its carrot nose pointing down, as if ashamed.

We parked in silence.

"Ready?" the sheriff asked.

I nodded.

The first knock echoed. Nothing. He tried again, louder. The hollow sound swallowed our breath.

"No lights," he murmured. "No car in the drive."

"They're away," I said, but my stomach twisted. "Or hiding."

"Convenient timing."

I pressed my hand to the window. Inside, the curtains were drawn. I could see the faint outline of furniture, a glint of something metallic—a frame, maybe. For a second, I thought I saw movement, a figure stepping away from the window. I blinked, and it was gone.

The sheriff frowned. "You saw that too, didn't you?"

"Maybe."

He kicked the porch rail lightly, frustration in every line of his body. "This is a waste of time."

"Nothing about this is a waste," I said. "They're part of it. I can feel it."

He looked at me the way people look at someone on the edge of a cliff. "You sound just like your father when you say things like that."

199

I met his gaze. "He was wrong about a lot of things. But not everything."

We waited a few more minutes before I scribbled a note on one of his business cards and slid it under the door. "We'll come back tomorrow."

The sheriff didn't argue. He just stood there for a long moment, staring at the stillness of the house, then turned back toward the truck.

On the way home, dusk bled into night. The sky turned the color of bruises, and I could feel something pressing in from the edges of the world, like the air itself wanted to collapse. Neither of us spoke again until the first lights of Greenridge appeared through the trees.

The church stood at the center of town, its steeple still tall but weary-looking, the gold cross at its peak dulled by soot. The square below it was already half-covered in snow again, as though the earth was trying to hide the past twenty nights.

The sheriff dropped me off at my house. "Get some rest," he said.

"I'll try."

We both knew I wouldn't.

The Twenty-First Candle

By evening, the cold had deepened into something alive. The wind wasn't just cold air anymore; it had intent. It moved through the streets whispering, testing doors, rattling window latches.

When I stepped into the square, only a handful of people were there. They huddled together under lamplight, faces wrapped in scarves, eyes darting. The 21st candle waited in the center of the Advent wreath, surrounded by melted wax from the others that had burned before it. Each stub looked like a gravestone.

The mayor stood at the podium, her voice trembling in the wind. "We light this candle for endurance," she said. "For strength. For… faith." The last word barely made it out.

The sheriff watched from the edge of the crowd, his hand resting on his belt. His face looked carved from stone.

The candle's wick sputtered, caught, and burned. The light looked weak against the night, but still, people clapped politely, as if afraid not to.

I lingered as they began to drift away. The square emptied quickly now, no one daring to linger long after the flame was lit. They acted like the ceremony itself was protection, like leaving too soon might anger whatever force had its grip on Greenridge.

The sheriff joined me. "Every night it gets smaller," he said quietly.

"The crowd?"

"The faith."

A sharp gust swept through, making the flame dance. "You think it matters?" I asked.

He didn't answer. His gaze had turned to the church. "Do you smell that?"

The wind shifted, carrying the faintest trace of something acrid— burnt oil, maybe. Or kerosene.

And then came the scream.

We ran.

The sound led us to the church steps. The mailbox near the door was engulfed, the fire roaring upward in a clean, blue flame. For a second, it didn't even look like a mailbox anymore but a cross, burning in perfect symmetry. The air shimmered around it.

People rushed from nearby houses, some barefoot in slippers, others holding coats half-on. The light from the fire reflected in their eyes, wide and fearful. Someone began to pray.

The sheriff pushed through, shouting for everyone to stay back. He grabbed a snow shovel from the rectory wall and began to throw snow over the flames. I followed, scooping handfuls until my gloves were soaked and steaming. The fire hissed, resisted, then finally died, leaving behind a twisted frame of black metal.

Beneath the ash, a message had been painted across the mailbox before it burned. The letters were warped, but still legible: YOU CANNOT OUTRUN JUDGMENT.

The crowd murmured, the sound thick and horrified.

A man whispered, "It's a sign."

Someone else said, "It's her. She's still here."

I looked at the sheriff, expecting him to say something, anything to calm them. But he didn't move. His eyes were fixed on the cross-shaped ruin, face pale and glistening with sweat despite the cold.

He looked smaller in that moment, like a man realizing his prayers had gone unanswered for too long.

"Go home," he told the crowd finally. "All of you."

No one moved until he shouted it again, louder, his voice cracking. One by one they turned away, some glancing over their shoulders as if the fire might reignite just to spite them.

I stayed where I was, my breath visible in the dark. The wind had died completely. The square was silent except for the faint ticking of cooling metal.

The sheriff rubbed his face. "This isn't just vengeance anymore," he said quietly. "It's a sermon."

"Then what's the message?"

He met my eyes. "That none of us are clean."

I looked back at the ashes, the words barely visible now under the frost. "Something big is coming," I said.

The church bell rang once, sharp and hollow.

The sheriff glanced toward the steeple. "What makes you so sure?"

"Because we're running out of candles."

CHAPTER 22

The House at the End of the Street

It had been two days since the twentieth candle. One night since the last fire, small but still enough to remind the town that peace was only ever borrowed. The last scream had barely faded, yet Greenridge already pretended it hadn't happened.

I barely slept. Every time I closed my eyes, I saw the church mailbox burning, the letters warping into smoke. I could still hear the sheriff's voice saying that none of us were clean.

When he pulled up outside my house that morning, I was already waiting by the door. The truck idled, a faint plume of white curling from the exhaust. He gave me a tired nod as I climbed in.

"You sure about this?" he asked.

"Yes."

He adjusted the heat, rubbed his gloved hands together. "It's a long drive for maybe nothing."

"It's not nothing," I said. "If she's the one, they'll have answers."

He didn't argue. He just drove.

The landscape passed in silence. Bare trees lined the road like ribs, the sky the color of smoke. My reflection in the window looked like someone else entirely—pale, hollow-eyed, mouth drawn tight. The sheriff glanced at me once or twice but didn't speak. I could tell he wanted to, but words had started to feel dangerous between us.

When we turned into the cul-de-sac, I felt it again—that wrongness that comes before a revelation. The house was the same pale blue as before, but this time the chimney was breathing, thin smoke rising straight up into the frozen air. The curtains were open. The world looked normal.

Normal always scared me more than the fires.

The sheriff parked. "You ready?"

I nodded, though my hands were shaking in my gloves.

The woman who opened the door looked like she'd stepped out of a postcard. Her sweater was soft cream; her cheeks flushed with warmth. Behind her came the faint scent of cinnamon, something baking in the oven. A small gold cross hung around her neck, and for a split second I wanted to believe that this house existed in a different world—one where bad things didn't happen.

"Oh, my," she said, smiling when she saw the sheriff's badge. "I hope there's no trouble."

"Not at all, ma'am," he said. "We just wanted to ask you a few questions about your daughter."

Her husband appeared behind her, tall and mild-eyed, holding a mug of tea. He wore slippers and looked like a man who hadn't raised his voice in years.

The woman nodded, opening the door wider. "Of course. Come in. It's freezing."

Inside, the warmth wrapped around me like a blanket I didn't deserve. The smell of cinnamon mingled with pine from a Christmas tree in the corner. Photos lined the mantel and the hallway—holidays, birthdays, a family frozen in time. The same two faces over and over, but always with someone new between them. Children of different ages, years apart. But one girl appeared more than any other.

Amy.

The sheriff and I took seats on the couch. The woman sat across from us, her hands folded neatly in her lap.

"You adopted Amy, correct?" I asked.

Her expression softened. "Yes. She was our only one who stayed long enough to call us family."

"What was she like?"

The husband spoke this time, his voice gentle but heavy. "Smart. Gifted, really. She had this way of seeing the world—darker than most kids her age, but not cruel. Just... wounded."

His wife nodded. "She was bright, but she carried that fire with her. You could see it in her eyes. She'd wake up at night screaming about smoke, about children she couldn't save. She talked about the orphanage constantly. We tried to help her let go, but it became an obsession. The nightmares got worse when she turned seventeen."

"What kind of nightmares?" I asked quietly.

"She'd dream about the fire, over and over," the woman said. "Sometimes she'd wake up and draw the building. Every single window. Every door. And then she'd tear the paper into pieces and burn it in the sink. Said she had to finish what was started."

The sheriff exchanged a glance with me. "How long did she stay?"

"She left at nineteen," the husband said. "Said she wanted to go to college, but she never enrolled. We tried to find her, but she'd changed her name. The agency wouldn't give us any information."

The woman's voice cracked slightly. "We loved her. We really did. But she was never ours, not completely. Part of her was still trapped in that fire."

I swallowed hard, eyes scanning the room. The decorations were simple but careful. A wreath on the door. A knitted blanket over the couch. The kind of life built by people who believed goodness could keep the world steady.

And yet, there was a faint chill under all that warmth. Something quiet but uneasy.

The sheriff stood. "Thank you for your time," he said. "We won't take up more of your morning."

The woman smiled faintly, though her eyes shone with a hint of guilt, as if she felt she hadn't done enough for the girl she'd once called her daughter.

"Could I use your bathroom before we go?" I asked.

"Of course, dear," she said. "Down the hall, first door on the right."

I walked slowly, the floorboards creaking under my boots. The hallway smelled faintly of lemon polish and old books. As I passed the end, I noticed another door, slightly open, the faintest sliver of light escaping from within.

A strange pull tightened in my stomach.

I hesitated, then glanced back toward the living room. The sheriff's low voice mixed with theirs—small talk about the snow, the drive, anything that would keep them occupied.

I pushed the door open.

The room was small, neatly kept. The air smelled faintly of lavender and dust. The bedspread was faded pink, worn soft with time. On the nightstand lay a single glass snow globe, the kind children used to collect. Inside it, a church stood in miniature, surrounded by fake glittering snow. My stomach knotted.

There were drawings pinned to the wall—charcoal sketches of a building, rough and obsessive. The orphanage. The same crooked windows. The same bell tower. The same fire drawn in the background again and again.

I knelt beside the bed. Something caught my eye: a corner of a cardboard box barely sticking out from underneath. My pulse quickened.

I pulled it free, dust rising in the air like breath. Inside were fragments of a life—half-burned toys, a melted crayon box, bits of paper that had once been children's drawings. Beneath them, a folded photograph.

I lifted it gently.

On one side was a small girl, no older than six, standing in front of a Christmas tree. Her hair was tied into uneven braids, her smile crooked but sincere. The edges were scorched. On the back, glued unevenly, was another photo—a young woman.

The same face, but older. Her smile gone. Hair cropped short, glasses missing, expression sharp enough to cut. A face no longer pleading with the world but challenging it.

My heart stopped.

It was her.

I didn't know how I'd missed it before. She'd changed just enough. The hair, the posture, the way she looked at people through lowered lashes instead of over them. It was enough to hide her in plain sight.

My hands trembled as I held the photo. The edges dug into my palms like accusation.

And then I heard it—footsteps.

They were light, moving down the hallway. The woman's voice called softly, "You all right, dear?"

Panic shot through me. I shoved the photograph inside my coat and slid the box back beneath the bed, my fingers fumbling. I turned and bolted quietly toward the bathroom, heart hammering. I barely closed the door before the hallway light flicked on.

"Everything okay?" she asked again, just outside.

"Yes," I called out, forcing my voice steady. "Just washing my hands."

The silence that followed was unbearable. Then her footsteps moved away.

I splashed water on my hands just to make the lie sound true. My reflection in the mirror looked foreign—flushed cheeks, wild eyes, guilt painted across my face.

When I walked back, the sheriff and the couple were sitting in the living room again, still mid-conversation.

He stood when he saw me. "Ready?"

I nodded quickly. "Thank you for your time," I told the couple. "You've been very kind."

They smiled, not noticing the tremor in my voice.

Outside, the cold hit like punishment. The sky had turned a pale, bruised color, the sun sinking behind clouds.

The sheriff shoved his hands into his coat pockets as we walked toward the truck. "Nice people," he said quietly.

"Too nice."

He raised a brow. "You think they're hiding something?"

"No," I said after a pause. "I think they're what happens to people who forget."

He didn't ask what I meant. Maybe he understood.

When we got inside, he leaned back against the seat, rubbing his temple. "So what's next?"

I stared at the frost forming on the windshield. "I don't know yet."

He looked at me sideways. "You sure you're all right?"

I hesitated. "I'm fine."

He gave a humorless laugh. "No one in this town is fine."

The drive back was quiet except for the crunch of tires over ice. I kept one hand pressed over my coat pocket, feeling the photograph beneath the fabric. It felt heavier than it should, like it carried the weight of every secret left unspoken.

By the time we reached Greenridge, the sun had vanished entirely. The streetlights flickered to life, dim halos in the cold.

When I got home, I went straight to my room and locked the door.

The photo looked different in the lamplight. The girl's half-burned smile and the woman's unforgiving stare seemed to blend, one feeding into the other until they became something else entirely—something both innocent and monstrous.

I couldn't stop staring.

Amy looked familiar. Too familiar. I knew who she was, but saying it would make it real. And I wasn't ready for that. Not yet.

The Twenty-Second Candle

The twenty-second candle was supposed to bring comfort, but the square felt colder than ever. The crowd that had once filled the space now gathered in a loose, uneasy circle. Their breath hung in the air like ghosts.

The mayor stood at the center, her scarf fluttering in the wind. "Tonight," she said, "we light this candle for protection." Her voice trembled on the last word.

The flame sputtered, caught, and burned weakly against the dark.

People didn't pray this time. They just stared.

The sheriff stayed near the edge, his face unreadable. He didn't join the lighting, didn't speak to anyone. I knew why. The whispers had started already.

When the ceremony ended, the crowd dispersed quickly. The sheriff and I lingered near the steps of the church.

"You feel that?" he asked quietly.

"What?"

"The air. It feels wrong."

I nodded, because he was right. It wasn't just cold—it was charged, heavy, waiting.

Then came the siren.

One shrill, piercing cry that sliced through the night.

We both turned at once. The glow appeared on the horizon first—orange and angry. The sheriff ran. I followed.

When we reached the station, the heat hit first, a wall of it that pushed us back. The building was fully aflame, windows shattering outward, papers burning as they fell into the snow.

People poured into the street, faces lit by the inferno. The sound of crackling wood and screaming metal filled the air.

"Back up!" the sheriff shouted, but no one listened. They were too busy watching.

Someone near me whispered, "It's judgment."

Another voice answered, louder this time. "He's the reason this happened. He was there back then!"

The words spread like wildfire.

"He knew!"

"He covered it up!"

"He was one of them!"

The sheriff froze. The reflection of the flames turned his eyes into mirrors of hell. "That's a lie," he shouted. "You don't know what you're saying!"

But the crowd didn't care. They wanted blood now.

A man stepped forward. "You were supposed to protect us!"

The sheriff took a step back. His voice cracked. "I tried."

The man's wife spat at the ground. "You stood by while they burned!"

"Enough!" I shouted, but my voice was swallowed by the roar of the fire.

The roof collapsed, sending sparks skyward. The flames whooshed outward in a burst of heat that singed my face.

The sheriff dropped to his knees, his expression hollow.

"They're right," he whispered. "I should have stopped it."

I grabbed his arm. "You were a kid back then."

"I was twenty-two. Old enough to speak. Old enough to see."

The flames roared louder, almost as if agreeing.

Firefighters arrived, but it was too late. The station was gone. Only the outer walls remained, black and broken.

As the fire died, the crowd began to scatter. Some in silence, some muttering about curses, about divine wrath. I caught fragments— "sins of the fathers," "cleansing," "no one's innocent."

When they were gone, I turned to the sheriff. He stood by the wreckage, soot streaking his face, eyes glassy.

"This is what she wants," he said quietly. "All of us broken. All of us afraid."

"You're assuming it's her," I said.

He looked at me sharply. "Isn't it?"

I didn't answer. Not because I didn't know, but because I did.

He watched me for a long time. "You're hiding something."

"Not yet," I said.

He frowned, but didn't push.

We both looked toward the center of town. The twenty-second candle still burned faintly, its flame small but steady against the wind.

For a moment, I thought it flickered in the shape of a cross.

Neither of us spoke.

He didn't say her name because he didn't know it.

And I didn't say it because I wasn't ready to believe.

CHAPTER 23

The Quiet Before the Flame

The snow had turned the world the color of bone. It fell in slow sheets that erased the edges of everything, the fences, the rooftops, the streets where no one walked anymore. Greenridge looked like a place that had already died and simply had not realized it yet. The church bell rang once at dawn, then again five minutes later, off-beat and lonely, echoing across the hollow streets like the heartbeat of something sick.

I sat at the kitchen table, buried under papers. The wood was no longer visible; it was smothered in old records and copies of reports that all said the same thing in different words. The edges curled from the damp air. The handwriting on half of them was my father's. His penmanship had always been perfect, each letter deliberate, steady, certain. I used to love it as a child, tracing the loops of his capital G's while he worked on sermons. Now every page felt like a verdict written in blood.

The lamp above the table buzzed faintly, the bulb pulsing like it was afraid of the dark. My tea had gone cold hours ago. I did not even know when I made it, something that kept on happening lately. Somewhere behind me, the old radiator clanked but gave off no heat.

I picked up the adoption file again, smoothing the crease where I had folded it too many times. The photograph inside was grainy and discolored from age. A little girl, light hair, thick glasses, a smile that did not reach her eyes. Her name: Amy K.

I should have put the file away days ago. I should have stopped digging when the pattern started forming in my head, when the connections between the fires and the signatures became too neat, too cruel. But I could not. Each night I told myself I would sleep, and each morning I woke with the same sentence in my mind: find her.

I opened my laptop and pulled up another image, this one newer, bright and modern, printed from a local newspaper's website. A woman surrounded by children, smiling as if the world had never known smoke or guilt. Her hair dark now. No glasses. The calm of someone whose hands had never trembled.

I slid the two photos beside each other. For a while I just stared. The snow outside blurred the light until the faces almost seemed to move. The girl's eyes looked older, the woman's younger. The same bone structure. The same scar, faint but visible, just beneath the right eyebrow.

I felt my pulse in my throat. "No," I said quietly, but my voice did not sound convinced.

I leaned closer, tracing the outline of the younger face with one finger. My hand shook. "It can't be you."

But it was. The more I looked, the less space there was between them. The child who had lost everything in that fire had become the woman who smiled while leading other people's children through the market each morning.

The kettle started rattling on the stove. I had not turned it on. The sound jolted me back, heart hammering. I shut it off just to hear silence again, but even the silence was loud in this house.

My mother's footsteps passed down the hall. She had begun moving softly these days, as if afraid of breaking something invisible. When she appeared in the doorway, her robe was tied too tight, her expression distant.

"You're still at it," she said, not quite a question.

"I'm close," I replied.

"Close to what?" Her voice was almost kind, but there was fear under it.

"Understanding," I said.

She stared at the papers, the cold tea, and then at me. "Your father believed understanding was dangerous. Some things are meant to stay buried."

I met her eyes. "Buried things still rot, Mother. They just take everyone with them."

She winced like I had struck her. For a second I wanted to apologize, but the moment passed. She turned away, moving back toward the living room, humming an old hymn under her breath. The tune wavered off-key, thin as thread.

When she was gone, I sank back into the chair. The house creaked around me, the kind of small noises that start to sound like voices when you have been awake too long. I pressed my palms against my eyes until colors burst behind them.

The fire had started twenty-three years ago. I had been seven. I remembered the heat on my face, the way my father's voice carried over the crowd as he told everyone to pray. He had looked calm then, almost peaceful, watching the flames reach the orphanage roof. People said later he was a pillar of faith. I remembered thinking he looked like a man watching a debt being paid.

He had called it purification. He said fire separated the righteous from the unworthy. That line echoed through every sermon he gave for the rest of his life, and I had believed it because he was my father and because belief was easier than doubt.

Now, looking at his handwriting on the council records, his notes in the margins beside every denied request for safety inspections, I realized how belief had blinded me. He had not saved anyone. He had protected a budget. He had protected his name.

And someone out there was making sure the debt came due.

The town had begun to move differently since the last fire. People no longer met each other's eyes. Windows that used to glow at night stayed dark. The bakery had not reopened. The streets smelled faintly of smoke even when it snowed. The mayor had stopped wearing color.

Every night another candle, another fire. Twenty-two flames so far, each one smaller than the last yet heavier in meaning. Two more remained before Christmas. Two more before whatever waited at the end.

I thought about the girl in the photo again, Amy K., and about the woman I saw every week smiling at the children near the school gates. She was not just surviving here. She was adored. Protected. The town trusted her completely.

If I told anyone what I suspected, they would laugh, or worse, they would turn on me the way they had started to turn on the sheriff. They would call me paranoid, the pastor's broken daughter who could not let go of the past.

I folded the photographs carefully and slipped them into a folder marked "Pending." The label felt ridiculous, like I was working in an office instead of living in a nightmare, but I needed order. If I stopped cataloging, I would unravel.

The kettle began to whistle again, shrill, insistent. I poured hot water over the old tea bag just to feel my hands doing something useful. The smell of cheap black tea filled the room, sharp and metallic.

The snow outside thickened. The world beyond the window looked like it had been erased.

I opened my notebook and wrote down the names one more time, even though I already knew them by heart: Murphy. Thomas. Donahue. Caldwell. The mayor. The sheriff. My father. My family.

One by one, they were being called to answer.

I turned to the last page and added a single new line: Amy K. = ?

The question mark stared back like an accusation.

I closed the book.

The radio on the counter crackled to life by itself, static hissing before settling into the faint echo of a preacher's voice. I recognized the recording. It was one of my father's old sermons, archived years ago and sometimes replayed by the local station around the holidays.

"...and when the fire comes, my brothers and sisters, do not turn away. It is the Lord's hand that purifies. It is through flame that we are made clean."

I reached out and switched it off. The silence that followed felt heavier than the sermon.

For a long time, I sat there staring at the papers. My mind replayed every recent fire in reverse, the gas station, the garden, the library, the store, the houses, and each image folded back into the same burning orphanage. The smoke. The screams. My father's stillness.

The kettle clicked as it cooled. My mother coughed somewhere down the hall. Outside, a snowplow rumbled faintly, its engine muffled by the storm.

I took the printed photos again, laid them flat, and whispered, "It's her. I know it's her."

The sound of my own voice startled me. I looked around the empty kitchen as if someone might have answered. The walls absorbed the words and gave nothing back.

When I finally looked outside again, night was already beginning to fall. The church bell rang once more, its tone warped by distance and wind. Each toll sounded like a countdown.

I shut the lights off and stood by the window. The streetlamps glowed faintly through the snow, their halos soft and weak. The town looked peaceful if you did not know better. If you had not seen what peace cost here.

Behind me, my father's papers fluttered from the draft of the vent, whispering against each other like dry leaves. I turned back to the table and pressed my hand down on them to keep them still, but they kept moving, as if the air itself refused to rest.

I whispered into the half-dark room, "Three more candles."

My reflection in the window mouthed the same words back. For a second I thought it looked like my father.

The Twenty-Third Candle

The square looked different that night, as if the air itself was warning people to stay away. The wind had turned sharp and mean, slicing through coats and scarves, cutting down conversation until all that remained was the sound of boots on frozen ground. Only a handful of people came. I counted twelve, maybe thirteen, each one standing at a careful distance from the next. The ones who had been faithful to the ritual since the first night now kept their hands buried deep in their pockets, their eyes lowered to the snow.

The sky above was the color of bruises. Clouds moved like slow smoke. When the mayor stepped forward, her fur collar fluttered, the movement small but noticeable, like a nervous tic. Her voice was hoarse when she began to speak, a thin thread of sound pulled too tight.

"Tonight," she said, "we light the twenty-third candle."

There was no microphone, no choir, no music. Just that voice, half swallowed by the wind. "A symbol of faith, of hope, of Greenridge standing together." The same words she had said for weeks, but this time they sounded hollow, stripped of conviction.

Someone coughed. No one clapped. The match scraped, the flame caught, and for a second I thought it might die right there, extinguished by the gust that swept through the square. But it held. A small, trembling light in a field of shadows. The crowd exhaled, as if they had been holding their breath since sunset.

I stood farther back, near the alley that led to the churchyard. I did not want to be seen. I watched the flame wobble and recover, watched the faces lit by it, pale and rigid. These people were not praying anymore. They were bargaining. Each candle was supposed to protect them, but now the lighting itself felt like provocation, a dare.

My heart thudded against my ribs. I tried to tell myself this was only ritual, that the fear twisting my stomach was superstition. But then I saw the sheriff. He was off to the side, watching the flame with a look I could not name. It was not disbelief, and not faith. Something between surrender and guilt. The mayor caught his eye once, quickly, then looked away.

The snow picked up, spinning under the weak light of the streetlamps. The candle flame flickered in rhythm with the wind. No one moved to leave, not right away. It was as if we were all waiting for something to happen, for fire, for smoke, for another scream carried by the wind.

But nothing came. Only silence.

Eventually, people began to drift off in pairs, then one by one. They spoke quietly, their voices carrying in the emptiness, words like maybe it is over and thank God and just one more night. I stayed behind until the square emptied, then turned toward home.

The snow crunched under my boots, each step sounding too loud in the stillness. The lamplight shimmered across the drifts, reflecting faint halos that blurred with every breath I took. The houses I passed were dark, their windows black, their roofs heavy with snow. Curtains twitched when I walked by. The town had learned how to watch without being seen.

Halfway home, I noticed it — a faint red glow, weak but steady, reflected in the church's stained-glass windows. I stopped. My first thought was fire, but there was no smoke, no movement. Just that unnatural light spilling across the snow.

The square behind me was empty. No sound. No wind. Only the dull ringing of the bell from somewhere high above, swaying with the storm.

I stepped off the path and crossed the churchyard. My breath came in small white clouds. My fingers were stiff inside my gloves. The closer I got, the stronger the light became, until it illuminated the frost clinging to the church door.

Then I saw it.

Words. Names. Dozens of them. Painted across the stone in uneven red letters that dripped down like open wounds. The paint gleamed under the weak reflection of the candlelight from the square. It was still wet.

At first, I could not read them. The snow and my own trembling blurred everything. I wiped at my eyes, leaned closer, and the letters began to take shape.

Clara. Matthew. Rose. Henry. Abby. Joseph.

Every name I had seen in the orphanage records. Every child who had died that night

The paint ran in rivulets down the wall, frozen in streaks where it met the cold. The letters were not written carefully; they were scrawled, urgent, desperate. Some names were repeated, as if whoever wrote them had needed to be sure they were remembered.

At the very bottom, larger than the rest, one final mark: a question mark, thick and uneven, drawn in the same red.

My throat tightened.

The air smelled faintly of metal.

I reached out, touched the wall with my gloved hand, and the paint smeared instantly, bright against the pale fabric.

Fresh.

Whoever had done this had just left.

A faint sound shivered through the air — laughter. High-pitched, light as a bell. It floated for half a second, then vanished. I froze, breath catching. Maybe it was only the wind scraping through the bell tower. Maybe. But then it came again, faint but real, the sound of children running, giggling, whispering. I turned toward the noise, heart pounding, eyes scanning the dark churchyard. The graves were covered in snow, smooth and unbroken. Still, the laughter seemed to circle me, threading between the tombstones, fading when I moved, growing louder when I stood still.

"Stop," I whispered. "Please."

The wind rose in reply, carrying a sound that could have been a sigh or a sob.

Then, suddenly, a door creaked. Behind me.

I spun around. Light flared across the church's stained glass — flashlights, several of them. The townspeople were coming back. I heard their footsteps crunching on the snow, their voices rising, alarmed and angry. Someone gasped when they saw the wall.

"What in God's name—"

"Oh my Lord, look!"

"It's them. The orphans. The ones who burned!"

The light from their lanterns spilled across the red writing. For a moment, there was only silence as everyone took it in. Then the screaming started.

"It's her!" a man shouted. "She's here again, that Mark girl! She's bringing this on us!"

"Her father did it first!" another yelled. "Now she's doing it again!"

218

"No, listen to me," I said, raising my hands. "I didn't—"

Something hard struck my shoulder. I stumbled back, pain bursting through my arm.

"Liar!" someone screamed.

The sound spread, wild and contagious. Bottles, stones, handfuls of snow mixed with ice — everything they could throw became a weapon. My blood pounded in my ears. The laughter I had heard moments ago twisted into something shriller, like screams, overlapping with the crowd's rage until I could not tell which belonged to the living and which to the dead.

"Stop this!" I cried, but my voice was lost beneath theirs.

The crowd surged forward. The mayor tried to calm them, shouting for peace, but her words were swallowed. The sheriff appeared from the side street, his face pale, eyes sharp. He shoved through the mob, shouting my name.

"Move back!" he ordered. "All of you!"

Someone threw a lantern that shattered near his boots, the fire inside hissing as it met the snow. The heat stung my face.

Then the young pastor appeared — the one who still believed Greenridge could be redeemed. He climbed onto the steps in front of the church, his black coat flaring behind him.

"Enough!" he shouted, his voice cutting through the wind. "Do you hear yourselves? You're acting like the very evil you claim to fear!"

The crowd hesitated, torn between fury and shame.

"She's cursed," an older woman sobbed. "She's brought it back."

The pastor turned to me. "Hannah, come."

The sheriff reached me first. "We're getting you out." His hand gripped my arm, firm and steady. My knees nearly gave out. The town started shouting again as they saw him pulling me away.

"She's the reason our children burn!"

"Witch!"

Another stone hit my side. I cried out. The sheriff blocked the next one with his shoulder, grimacing but not slowing down.

The pastor stayed close, pushing back a man who lunged forward. "You're losing your humanity!" he shouted, voice breaking. "Think of what you're doing!"

They half-dragged me down the side of the church, toward the alley. The sound of breaking glass followed us. Someone had smashed a window. The bell overhead groaned, swinging wildly in the wind.

We turned the corner, snow spraying beneath our boots. My breath came in ragged bursts. The laughter was back — faint, distant, threading through the night like a memory that refused to fade.

I looked over my shoulder. The red letters on the church glowed in the torchlight. For an instant, the dripping paint seemed to move, forming shapes — small hands, faces, the blurred silhouettes of children running across the stone. My vision blurred with tears or snow; I could not tell which.

"Do you hear that?" I whispered.

The sheriff didn't answer. His jaw was tight, his breath heavy.

"They're laughing," I said. "The children. They're laughing."

The pastor looked at me, eyes wide, but he said nothing.

We reached the sheriff's truck, parked crooked at the edge of the square. He opened the door, helped me inside, then slammed it shut as something shattered against the window behind us.

"Stay down," he said.

The pastor climbed into the back seat, out of breath but defiant.

From where I sat, I could still see the church. The crowd was circling it now, a storm of movement and sound. The graffiti blazed red under the torchlight, almost alive.

As the sheriff started the engine, I thought I saw the question mark shimmer, as if someone invisible were still holding the can of paint, waiting to finish what they had started.

The tires spun on the ice before catching. The truck lurched forward, cutting through the blizzard of falling snow and shouted words.

My head pounded. My hands were shaking. My glove, still stained from earlier, looked darker now — almost black.

"Are you all right?" the pastor asked.

220

I nodded, though I wasn't. My body ached from the blows, but it was my mind that hurt more.

"They saw the names," I said softly. "They saw what was written, and it broke them."

The sheriff kept his eyes on the road. "It's not over. Whoever did that wanted chaos, and they got it."

Outside, the town lights faded behind us, swallowed by snow. I pressed my forehead against the cold glass and closed my eyes. Somewhere in the distance, through the roar of the engine and the wind, I swore I heard it again — the echo of tiny footsteps running across the frozen ground, followed by soft, lilting laughter that faded into the night.

Two candles left.

Two nights.

And not a single soul in Greenridge slept that night.

CHAPTER 24

The Final Sermon

Morning came heavy, as if the entire sky were pressing down on Greenridge. The snow had stopped, but the silence that followed felt unnatural. It wasn't peace. It was the kind of quiet that comes after disaster, when even the air seems afraid to move. The town was caught in its own stillness, waiting for something to shatter it.

I stood at the window longer than I meant to, watching my breath fog the glass. The bruise on my cheek had deepened overnight, spreading like ink under my skin. My shoulder throbbed when I moved it. Each ache was a reminder of what last night had become— how quickly neighbors could turn into something else.

When I finally stepped outside, the cold was sharper than it had been all week. The sky was gray and swollen, heavy with clouds that threatened more snow. The streets were nearly empty. A few cars sat abandoned along the curb, their windows frosted from the inside. Someone had scrawled words in the ice on one windshield: Light them or burn.

I didn't stop to read it twice.

The sheriff's office looked smaller in daylight. Its windows were fogged from the heat inside, but the front steps were coated in a thin sheet of ice. I pushed the door open and was met with the bitter smell of burnt coffee and damp wool. The radiator clanged somewhere behind the desk, spitting bursts of steam into the cold room.

The sheriff looked up from a pile of reports as I entered. His tie was crooked, his shirt half untucked. He had dark crescents under his eyes that hadn't been there before. He looked like he hadn't slept, and for a moment, I wondered if any of us still could.

"Morning," he said, his voice rough around the edges.

I nodded, setting my bag down. "Barely."

He studied me for a moment, his eyes softening. "You should've gone to the hospital after last night."

"I've seen worse," I said. My tone surprised even me—flat, matter-of-fact, like someone else was speaking through me. "The children my father failed had it worse."

He didn't argue. Just sighed, rubbing a hand over his face. "You're starting to sound like him."

"I'm nothing like him." The words came out too quickly.

He raised his hands slightly in surrender. "Didn't say you were. Just... you carry the same kind of weight."

I didn't respond. Instead, I opened the folder I'd brought, pulling out the papers I'd been studying for hours—old school rosters, adoption forms, names half-faded but still legible enough to hurt. I set them down, but didn't push them toward him. Not yet.

He leaned forward, expectant. "What did you find?"

For a moment, I couldn't answer. My throat felt dry, my pulse quickening. The truth sat in my mouth like something metallic and heavy. I'd spent days circling it, testing it, convincing myself I must be wrong. But the face, the voice, the timing—it all aligned too cleanly to ignore anymore.

When I finally spoke, it came out low. "It's her," I said. "Amy K."

His brows knit. "Hannah, we already—"

"No," I interrupted. "Not what we thought. I was wrong before. We both were." I stepped closer to his desk. "I know who she is now."

He went still, the tension in his shoulders tightening like wire. "You're sure?"

"I'm sure," I said, my voice trembling. "I wanted to tell you sooner, but I needed to be certain. I went through the photos again, the old adoption records. Her name was changed twice before she resurfaced here. It's her, Collins. She's been right here all along."

His eyes searched mine, trying to read what I wasn't saying. The air between us felt charged, humming. "Hannah, who—?"

I swallowed hard. My hand hovered over the folder, then dropped to my side. "It's—"

The sound cut through me before I could finish.

My phone buzzed violently on the desk. Once. Twice. Then a third time. The vibration filled the silence like a pulse.

Collins frowned. "You want to get that?"

I hesitated, staring at the screen. My mother's name. Relief flickered, stupid and fragile. "It's my mom," I murmured, already reaching for it. "Give me a second."

I pressed the phone to my ear. "Mom?"

But the voice on the other end wasn't hers.

"Hello, Hannah."

The words were soft. Calm. Too calm.

My pulse stuttered.

"You're going to come to your father's special place," the voice said. "Alone. Or she dies."

The tone was steady, almost gentle, but beneath it was something sharp—something that didn't need to shout to make a promise.

"Who is this?" I whispered, though I already knew.

The line went dead.

For a moment, all I could hear was my own heartbeat pounding in my ears.

The sheriff was watching me closely. "What happened?"

I forced my expression into something neutral, though my hands were shaking. "I just… need to check something," I said. "I'll be right back."

"Hannah, wait—"

But I was already out the door.

The cold hit me like a slap. My lungs burned with every breath as I sprinted toward the car. The sky had turned a dull, bruised purple, clouds curling low over the town. My tires slipped on the frozen street before catching, sending a spray of dirty snow behind me as I sped out of town.

The houses on the edge of Greenridge passed in blurs of gray and white. Most windows were dark, though a few glowed faintly from within. Each one felt like an eye watching me go. The deeper I drove, the darker it became.

In the distance, the woods rose like a black tide. The road narrowed, then twisted, leading toward the edge of the world. I knew this route. I had walked it as a child, my father's hand gripping mine too tightly as he led me to Sunday sermons in the chapel that stood alone among the trees.

Now, that chapel waited again.

The last place I ever wanted to see.

I thought about what the voice had said—your father's special place. How easily those words rolled off her tongue, how certain she'd sounded.

My knuckles whitened on the steering wheel. "Don't hurt her," I whispered to no one. "Please don't hurt her."

Snow began to fall again, heavier this time. The flakes caught in the headlights like drifting ash.

Somewhere in town, the twenty-fourth candle would soon be lit. A small flame in the middle of a dying winter. I had a terrible feeling it wouldn't stay small for long.

The road curved through the trees, leading toward a dark shape in the distance—stone walls, broken steeple, the shadow of something once holy.

The chapel.

And whatever waited inside.

The Twenty-Fourth Candle

The chapel sat crooked among the trees, its bones blackened by time and storms. The roof leaned as if it were bowing to something unseen. I parked at the edge of the clearing, hands tight on the wheel, headlights cutting through the snow. The wind was sharp enough to sting my eyes, and for a moment I could not move.

Lantern light shimmered through the broken stained glass. The color of fire. The color of everything I had been dreading.

My phone lay in my lap, the last words from the call still ringing. Come to your father's special place. Alone. Or she dies.

My mother's voice should have been the one on that line. I should have heard her humming the way she hummed when she worried. Instead, I had gotten a calm voice that felt like a held breath. Every word balanced. Every syllable too careful.

I stepped out of the car and the cold bit deep into my skin. The snow was heavy but silent, flattening the world. Only the wind moved, slipping between the trees with a low whistle like a secret passing from branch to branch.

As I walked toward the chapel, my boots crunched over frozen earth. The sound echoed too loud. My heartbeat drowned it anyway.

The door creaked when I pushed it open.

Inside, the air was warm and thick with smoke and old wood. Lanterns hung along the walls, flames flickering over warped pews and splintered crosses. The altar at the far end glowed under their light, and in front of it stood Emily Hill.

She wore white. Not bridal white, not church white. A simple dress, unadorned, spotless in a way that seemed impossible in this ruin. Her hair was pulled back. Her face was smooth. Her eyes shone with an intensity that looked like serenity from a distance and like something far more dangerous up close. For a heartbeat she looked almost angelic. The woman who smiled at children in the schoolyard. The one who baked for every fundraiser. The one the town trusted without ever asking why.

"Emily." My voice cracked on her name.

She turned slowly. A faint smile tugged at her mouth. "You came."

Behind her, near the altar, my mother sat tied to a chair. Her hair hung loose. Her face was swollen and pale, a bruise spreading like a storm across her temple. Her eyes found mine. Terror flashed there, and something else. Relief. She was alive.

"Let her go," I said. My voice shook and I did not care.

Emily tilted her head as if she were working a puzzle. "You came alone, just like I asked. That means there is a part of you that understands."

"Understands what," I said, taking one step forward. "That you are sick. That this is not justice."

"Innocence is an illusion," she said softly. "So is forgiveness."

A small camera blinked red on a tripod beside the altar. In front of it, a single tall candle burned. Wax white as bone. Flame steady.

"You are recording this," I said.

"Not only recording." Her voice deepened, slow and certain. "They are all watching."

I glanced toward the walls where the lantern light jumped. Somewhere far beyond this chapel every screen in Greenridge would be glowing with this same light. Phones on kitchen tables. Televisions in living rooms. People staring at a chapel they had passed a hundred times and never entered.

Emily stepped closer to the lens. Her eyes caught the flame and held it. "They said the fire was God's will," she began. Her voice filled the room. It was soft but it carried like a sermon. "They said the smoke carried the innocent to heaven. But it was not God who locked the doors."

Her words hung in the rafters. The wood seemed to listen.

"Emily," I said, "stop."

She did not look at me. She kept her eyes on the camera. "They preached forgiveness while the children burned. They looked away when the walls cracked. When the lights failed. When the screams began."

Her voice trembled. The calm broke and something raw pushed through. "I remember their faces. I was barely six. I remember the smoke coming in through the cracks under the door. I remember calling for help until my throat tore. I remember my teacher's shoes on the other side, she had heels that clicked and then they did not click anymore. I remember nails screaming out of wood. I remember

227

the heat when the roof began to fall. I remember Lily's hand going limp in mine. I remember everything."

Her breath hitched. "They said God chose who to save."

"Emily," I said, gentle now.

Her gaze flicked from the lens to me and then to the altar. A revolver lay there, metal winking in the candlelight.

She looked at it a long moment and then picked it up. The motion was slow, almost reverent.

"No," I said, and my mouth was dry.

Her hand did not tremble. "Five bullets," she said. "Greed. Neglect. Silence. Obedience. Faith."

"Do not do this."

"Let us see which one your mother carried."

She raised the gun. My mother's breath hitched, sharp and small.

The world narrowed to the size of that barrel.

Click.

No shot. A hollow sound, like the room had exhaled.

For a second we were statues. Then I moved.

I hit Emily with everything I had left. We crashed into the altar. The candle toppled and rolled. The camera went down, still blinking, the image shuddering into firelight and bodies and wood.

We wrestled for the gun. Our hands slid over sweat and wax. Her breath was ragged. Her eyes burned with conviction that looked like fever.

"You do not understand," she shouted. "It has to end like this."

"No," I said. "It does not. You think this is what those children wanted. They wanted to live."

"They wanted to be remembered," she said. Her voice fell to a whisper that sounded like prayer. "That is all. That is all they ever wanted."

The altar cloth breathed flame. The fire ran up the fabric like a creature that had been waiting. Heat pushed against my cheeks. Smoke stung my eyes.

"Emily," I tried again.

She shoved me away. The gun skidded free, rolled toward the base of the altar, kissed the spreading fire, and vanished into it. The flames licked at the metal. It slid out of sight.

We both watched it disappear.

Emily stood. The firelight threw shadows up her face. The white dress was gray at the hem where the smoke curled.

"It is too late," she said. "Too late for all of us."

"Come with us," I said. "We can still walk out."

She looked past me to the camera. Her eyes glistened. "I have walked out of fire before," she said. "I left them behind once. I will not do it again."

Her voice changed then. It grew larger, and at the same time it grew smaller. It was a pulpit voice, and it was a child's voice. She was speaking to me, and she was speaking to the town, and she was speaking to the part of herself that had been six for thirty years.

"You have all told yourselves a story," she said. "A story where the fire was an accident and the dead are at peace and God signed the report. You lit candles and said their names at Christmas and told yourselves that was enough. You smiled at my face when I came back with a new name and a new haircut and a teacher's voice. You said what a blessing. You said what a miracle. You never asked what it cost me to stand in a room full of children and hear the roof falling again in my bones."

She took a step, then another, pacing the line where the altar met the aisle. The camera caught every movement. She wanted it to. She wanted them all to witness it.

"I tried to forgive you," she said. "I tried to live the way the pastor said. I tried to bake for your fairs and knit for your drives and hold your babies and bless your kitchens. I tried to turn my nightmares into good works. Every night I asked God to take the screams from my ears. He did not. He made them louder. Do you know what that feels like? To wake at three every morning because the children will not let you sleep. To press your hands over your ears and still hear them. To sit in the pew and hear a sermon about mercy while you taste ash on your tongue."

She pointed at the lens with the hand that had held the revolver before the fire took it. "You said you did not know. You said you could not have known. You signed the papers. You shut your doors. You called Caldwell hysterical. You told the sheriff to stand down. You told each other that God would sort it out. He did. He sent me."

"Emily," I said, and the plea was in my throat before I could hide it. "You are not God's knife."

"No," she said, and her mouth twisted into something that was not a smile. "I am His memory."

"Memory does not have to burn," I said. "Memory can build. There are children alive now. They need you alive."

She stared at me. A muscle jumped in her cheek. For a second I thought I had reached her.

"I hear them," she said, very quiet. "Right now. I hear them. When the wind moves through these boards I hear them. Tell me how to live with that and I will walk out with you."

I did not have an answer. The truth stood there between us and breathed.

She took the lack of an answer like permission to keep going.

"You want to know why the fires," she said. "You want the steps laid out like a ledger. Fine. I will tell you. The shed by the ruins first. That was the tinder, that was the whisper, that was the town's memory waking from a long nap. Then the messages on your walls because you do not listen unless letters shout. The houses, the cars, the nativity, the bakery, the garage, the gas station. Each one a name that signed. Each one a life that looked away. I sent warnings. I left the files where they needed to be found. I dragged the cabinet onto the steps so you would not miss it. Not erasure. Revelation."

"You could have stood in the square and told them with your face," I said. "You could have said I survived. You could have said your name."

"I did," she said, and laughed once, breathless. "Every night I stood there in front of you with my hair in a bun and a pie in my hands. And you looked at me and said Miss Hill is a saint. Miss Hill is so good with the children. You did not see me. You saw what you wanted to see so you could sleep."

She turned her head toward my mother. "She stood there and watched it all, too weak to stop it, too good at pretending. Your father signed. Others nodded. They balanced a budget on the backs of children who had no one to vote for them. The doors stuck. The alarms failed. The exit jammed. Your town sang."

My mother made a sound, small and broken. "I did not know the exit would jam," she said. "I did not understand the alarms would fail."

"You understood enough to say nothing," Emily said. "You understood enough to go home and sleep under a roof that did not scream."

"Emily," I said, "let me take her out. Then you can say anything you want to me. You can tell me every detail. You can show me every page. But do not make me watch her die."

She studied my face. Her eyes softened for the first time. "You love her," she said.

"Yes," I said.

"I loved them," she said.

We stood in that awful symmetry. Love on both sides. Fire between.

She lifted her chin. "I needed the town to feel what we felt. I needed the air to taste like metal. I needed the snow to turn gray. I needed the candle flames to look like eyes. I wanted them to gather every night and wonder who would be next, the way we wondered which door would open, the way we counted breaths and hoped they would not be our last. I wanted them to stop saying accident and start saying names."

"You have that," I said. "They are saying names. They are saying yours. You can still be the one who tells the truth. You do not have to be the fire."

"The truth needed fire," she said. "Your father taught me that."

"He taught me to fear it," I said.

"He taught me to use it," she answered.

A sound cracked the night. A siren, close. Another, closer. The lantern flames leaned, then straightened. Smoke gathered along the ceiling like a dark sea.

The front door banged open and the sheriff stumbled through it, coughing, gun in hand. "Hannah," he shouted.

"She has my mother," I said.

He moved fast. Knife to rope. Rope to floor. My mother folded into his arms. He dragged her toward the door, eyes never leaving Emily.

"Come with us," I said to her again.

She shook her head. "I am not leaving them a second time."

"Emily," the sheriff said, steady now, voice low. "You do not want to die in a fire again."

"I do not want to live in yours," she said.

The altar cloth gave a sigh and collapsed into a sheet of flame. Heat pushed us back. The camera lay on its side, still blinking. The red light looked strange and small against the orange.

Emily turned to it once more. "You said the children were angels now," she said to the town. "You said they were pure. You said they were better off. You said God had a plan. Here is my plan. You will not forget them. You will carve their names in stone. You will pay for the doors and the alarms and the drills until your hands shake from signing. You will stop asking what it costs. You will stop calling it the past. You will teach your children that candles are not decorations. They are promises. And if you do not keep them, I will come back in every wind that rattles your windows. I will be the match you are afraid of and the matches you cannot find."

The roof groaned. Embers fell like stinging stars.

"Emily," I said, and my throat ached. "Please."

She lifted her face to the rafters. Tears cut clean tracks through the soot. "I hear them," she whispered. "They are calling from the corners and from the stairs and from the space under the door. They are saying my name. They are saying it is time."

"Do not listen," I said. "Listen to me."

"I have listened to your kind my whole life," she said. "To men like your father. To voices that told me to forgive. None of them came when we knocked. Only the fire came. The fire came and it kept its promise."

The sheriff grabbed my arm. "We have to go," he said. The smoke was a wall now. The heat had teeth.

"Emily," I cried, last chance, last word.

She looked at me with an expression I will carry for the rest of my life. It was not triumph. It was not rage. It was love, in a shape I did not understand.

"They will remember," she said. "Every child who screamed and no one came."

Her voice rose. Raw. Wild. "Every prayer you whispered while we burned, every lie you told yourselves, I hear you still. I remember your names."

A great crack answered her. The cross above the altar split. One side dropped and swung and struck her shoulder. She staggered. She did not fall.

"Now you will remember mine," she cried.

The beam broke and came down. A thunderclap filled the room. The sheriff yanked me toward the door, and we stumbled into the snow. Heat blew after us. The windows belched flame. The spire listed and fractured.

Her scream carried once, long and terrible and human. It ran through the trees and down the hill and into the town where screens still glowed. Then it stopped.

The chapel settled. The roof caved. Embers flew up and fell back like a flock of ash birds that did not know where to land.

The red light on the camera went out.

I stood in the snow and shook. The fire ate what had been a building and what had been a life. When the worst of it fell, I could still see the candle inside, burning in the lee of a broken pew. Small. Steady. Impossible. Twenty fourth.

"She had five bullets," I said. "Only one misfired. One against four."

The sheriff did not look away from the flames. I kept my eyes there too.

"Maybe," I whispered, "mercy counted."

No one spoke after that. The wind lifted ash and laid it over the snow until the white turned gray. Somewhere far off a bell rang once, and then the night swallowed the sound.

By the time the engines arrived the flames had chewed through everything that would feed them. Firefighters pulled lines and sprayed and churned the burned wood into muddy paste. There was no body. There was no gun to show a last choice. There was only a melted puddle of wax where the candle had stood, and a scatter of glass that had been a lens.

They set my mother in the back of the ambulance. I climbed in beside her. Her hand was cold. Her pulse was thin but present. She leaned her head against my shoulder and said something too soft to catch. I nodded anyway. Sometimes the nod is the medicine.

The sheriff stood outside with his hat in his hands and his eyes on the ruin. Snow swirled around him. He did not move for a long time.

When the sun began to find the horizon, the smoke turned gold. It made the wreckage look almost clean. It was a lie, and it was also beautiful. That is how mornings work after nights like this.

The twenty fourth candle had burned. The thing that had held this town together had broken. Something else waited in the space that opened. I felt it like a cold hand at the base of my spine and like a small, warm light under my ribs.

My father had always said fire could purify. I had hated that sentence. I had hated what he used it to excuse. Standing there with ash in my hair and my mother breathing next to me and the sheriff staring into what was left, I understood a different version of it.

Fire does not heal. It tests. It reveals.

And somehow, under the smoke, my faith had not died. It had not returned to the shape my father taught me. It had not taken Emily's shape either. It stood up inside me, small and flickering, and it stayed.

CHAPTER 25

Merry Christmas

Dawn crept slowly over Greenridge, pale and fragile, the kind of light that didn't chase away the darkness so much as make peace with it. The air still smelled of smoke—sharp and bitter—but beneath it was something else. Something cleaner. Like the world had been scrubbed raw and left to start again.

Snow had fallen through the night, soft and steady. It blanketed everything—the roads, the roofs, the scorched skeleton of the chapel—muting the scars the fire left behind. Where the steeple once reached for heaven, now only a jagged beam jutted upward, coated in frost and ash. It looked less like a ruin and more like a grave marker.

The town was quiet. No more sirens, no whispers, no prayers murmured out of fear. People walked the streets again, slow and careful, carrying buckets of water and boxes of candles. Someone hammered new boards over the shattered windows of the mayor's office. Another shoveled snow from the steps of the church that had survived the fire. No one spoke much. They didn't need to. The truth had burned through the lies, and silence was all that remained.

I walked beside my mother through the thin layer of snow, her arm looped through mine. She moved slowly, her face still marked by bruises but her eyes steady now. The sun hit her hair, and for the first time in days, I saw a trace of color return to her skin. She didn't say anything, and neither did I. Words felt too small for what had happened.

When we reached the ruins, the sheriff was already there. His coat was buttoned to the throat, hat in hand, breath clouding in the cold.

He looked older than he had yesterday, though maybe we all did. The fire had aged everyone in this town.

He nodded when he saw us, his voice low. "Merry Christmas."

It didn't sound strange coming from him. Just tired. Honest.

We stepped into what was left of the chapel. The snow crunched beneath our boots, mixing with blackened ash. The pews were gone, reduced to splinters and memory. Only the stone altar remained, cracked but still standing. My father's Bible lay nearby, half-burned, its pages curled and blackened but still legible in places. A verse caught my eye through the soot: Blessed are the pure in heart, for they shall see God.

I didn't know whether to laugh or cry.

The sheriff reached into his pocket and took out a candle. It was short and uneven, one of the few that hadn't melted completely the night before. He handed it to me without a word.

My hands shook as I took it. My mother stood beside me, her breath visible in the cold, eyes glistening.

"Let's light it together," I said.

The sheriff struck a match against the stone. The flame wavered in the wind but held. Together, we bent toward it, shielding it with our hands as it touched the wick. The flame caught slowly, a small flicker at first, then steady and bright.

The three of us stood there—just a woman, her mother, and a sheriff surrounded by ruin—watching that little flame fight against the cold.

No prayers. No speeches. Just the sound of the wind moving through the trees and the faint hum of life returning to the town beyond the hill.

The candlelight reflected in my mother's eyes, and for a moment, I saw the same peace I remembered from years ago, before the fires, before the sermons, before the guilt.

"It's beautiful," she whispered.

I nodded. "It's enough."

The sheriff looked out toward the direction town square, where people were probably beginning to gather again, cautious but hopeful. "They'll keep lighting them," he said softly. "Not out of fear this time."

I looked at the candle, the flame steady and alive. "No," I said. "Out of remembrance."

The wind picked up, tugging at my coat, swirling ash into the air. The candle's flame bent but did not break. It burned there in the heart of everything that had been lost—defiant, unyielding, pure.

The twenty-fifth candle. The last one. Not for the town. This one was just for us.

And for the first time, it wasn't about punishment.

It was about peace.

The Twenty-Fifth Candle

Christmas night had never felt so quiet.

The snow had stopped hours ago, leaving behind a world that looked new, untouched, as if even God had decided to start over. The air was still, almost sacred, filled with the faint scent of smoke that clung to everything Greenridge had ever been.

The square was no longer a place of fear. It had become a gathering ground. People came not because they were told to, not because they were afraid of what might burn next, but because something inside them still believed that light could mean more than destruction.

The twenty-fifth candle stood in the center, small and unremarkable, its flame glowing steady against the night. It did not waver, did not shrink. It stood like a promise.

Around it, the people of Greenridge gathered—faces pale in the winter dark, hands gloved, breaths rising in clouds. They stood close, not out of habit, but out of something gentler. Unity.

For the first time in years, I could see them. Not as the guilty, not as the cowards who looked away, but as people. Broken, trembling, and trying to become better than what they had been.

The mayor stepped forward, holding her speech in shaking hands that she never looked down to read. Her voice was rough, stripped of its polished edges. "Tonight," she said, "we light this candle not for penance, but for peace. For the children we failed. For the faith we lost. And for the chance to start again."

No one clapped. They didn't need to.

I stood beside my mother; her arm linked through mine. She looked so small in her coat, her scarf wrapped tight, her eyes glimmering with tears that refused to fall. Her face was turned toward the candle, the flame reflected in her pupils like something holy.

"I think he would have wanted this," she whispered.

My throat ached. "Maybe," I said softly. "But it isn't his anymore."

She looked at me, puzzled, so I continued, voice breaking against the cold. "He built a faith that burned people alive. I won't carry that kind of belief anymore."

Her eyes shimmered. "Then what will you carry?"

I looked at the light. "Grace. The kind that doesn't need permission."

The sheriff stood a few steps away, his hat pressed against his chest. He wasn't the law anymore, not tonight. Just a man among others, stripped bare by truth. When his eyes met mine, there was no pride left there, only exhaustion and peace.

The mayor's voice carried again. "There will be a memorial," she said, looking toward the crowd. "On the orphanage grounds. Their names will be carved in stone. Every child. Every soul."

People murmured, heads nodding. Some stepped closer, offering to help. The same hands that once turned away were now outstretched, trembling with sincerity.

I watched them approach the candle one by one. The old baker with tears frozen on her cheeks. The shopkeeper who once ignored a plea for help. The mayor herself, eyes downcast, fingers brushing her lips in prayer. Each whispered something—small apologies carried upward with the snow.

It wasn't loud. It wasn't grand. It was human.

I felt something warm bloom in my chest, faint at first, then steady. A feeling I had not known since before the fire, before my father's sermons twisted my faith into fear.

He had always spoken of punishment. Of cleansing by flame. But standing here, I finally understood that fire had never been meant to punish—it was meant to reveal.

My father's sins were his own. They did not belong to me. His faith had burned down a house full of children, but it had not destroyed God. It had only hidden Him.

Faith had not died in Greenridge. It had been buried under guilt and ashes, waiting for someone to lift the weight.

The candle burned brighter, as if hearing my thoughts. The light caught on the snow, casting golden reflections across the faces of those who once hid in shadow. The whole town seemed to exhale together, the sound like a prayer answered.

I turned to my mother. "It isn't about forgiveness," I said quietly. "It's about remembering and still choosing love."

She nodded, tears spilling now. "Then maybe we can start again."

"We already have."

A soft wind brushed through the square, but the flame did not move. Not even a flicker.

The mayor stepped down, and people began to gather in small groups, embracing, whispering, holding hands. The air filled with the murmur of apologies and promises, words that meant more than any sermon ever could.

Somewhere above us, a bell rang once—clear, bright, perfect. The sound drifted across the rooftops, echoing through the town that had once been afraid of silence.

I looked at the candle again. "Ashes tell the sinner's name," I whispered, the same words that had haunted me for weeks.

But tonight, they didn't sound like a curse. They sounded like salvation.

My phone buzzed in my pocket. I answered out of instinct. The voice on the line was familiar—the hospital administrator, polite and warm. "Hannah," she said, "we'd love to have you back. The pediatric ward isn't the same without you."

For a moment, I said nothing. I looked around—the town gathering, the sheriff helping the old women light more candles, my mother smiling through tears as she spoke to the mayor.

"I'll think about it," I said softly. "Thank you."

When I hung up, the world felt quiet again, but not empty.

I didn't know if I would go back. Maybe I would. Maybe I wouldn't.

But I knew this: Greenridge needed rebuilding. Not just the buildings, not just the memorial, but the hearts that had forgotten how to trust the light.

And maybe, just maybe, that was where I belonged.

The wind sighed across the square, stirring the snow into a faint swirl around the candle. The flame bent slightly, then rose taller.

It glowed against the night, steady and warm, casting gold across every face that had once been turned away.

The twenty-fifth candle. The final one.

It burned not for revenge. Not for repentance.

But for grace.

And for the first time, I understood what faith truly was.

Faith was not something given.

It was something built—again and again, after every fire.

As the stars shimmered faintly through the clearing sky, I closed my eyes and whispered one last prayer.

"Thank you for staying, even when we didn't."

When I opened them again, the flame was still there—steady, whole, unbroken.

Christmas had come to Greenridge.

And for once, it felt like peace.

Printed in Dunstable, United Kingdom

72271603R00139